SHATTERLORE

Myths of Past and Future

Edited by

Mara Lynn Johnstone

Shatterlore: Myths of Past and Future
Mara Lynn Johnstone, Editor in Chief

Copyright © 2024 Reality Collision Publishing
First Edition: November, 2024

All Rights Reserved.

The characters and events portrayed in this book are fictitious. Any resemblance to actual living or dead people, events, or locales is entirely coincidental. No part of this publication may be reproduced, distributed, or transmitted in any form or by any means including but not limited to photocopy, recording, or other electronic or mechanical methods, without the prior written permission of the author(s), except in brief quotations embodied in critical reviews and certain non-commercial uses permitted by copyright law.

Individual creative pieces are the intellectual property of their respective authors.

Paperback ISBN: 9798227973979
Ebook ISBN: 9798227817204

Cover art and book design by Mara Lynn Johnstone
Published by Reality Collision Publishing

Profits are to be donated to Doctors Without Borders for the first year of publication.

Table of Contents

Foreword..i

Content Warnings..ii

Something to Reflect On...1
    Mara Lynn Johnstone

A Chimera of Three Parts.....................................28
    Craig Rathbone

I Have Come to Lead You to the Other Shore......64
    David M. Simon

The Great Heracles..70
    Darius Bearguard

Intoxication: A Pandora's Box Retelling................83
    Katherine Shaw

Appearing Nightly On the Lido Deck..................105
    David M. Simon

Death's Diary..113
    Imelda Taylor

Agamemnon's Mask..117
    Mark Faraday

The Theft of Thor's Hammer..............................125
    Amanda Shortman

Santilmo...152
    Imelda Taylor

The King Who Would Be Rishi...........................169
    R. A. Cheddi

Mine? Oh, Tar!...206
    Estelle Parcoeur

Minutes After Midnight..237
    Gregory Coley

Seething from Missed Passes................................249
    Estelle Parcoeur

Cy Pearce Deserved to Die....................................271
    Ark Horton

The Beowulf Files..294
    Emily Ansell

The Cyberpunk Tragedy of
Orphy6 and Eury23...321
    Mara Lynn Johnstone

About the Authors...333

About the Editor..338

Foreword

It started with a handful of writer friends who had all written mythological stories, and were undecided about what to do with them. "I wrote mine for an anthology, but there wasn't enough room," said one. "Oh hey, mine too," said another. "I wrote mine because it's an awesome idea," said another. "And I'd love to write more."

The idea of building something out of those humble beginnings swiftly turned into over a dozen writers working together to make an epic collection of mythological tales, featuring multiple pantheons and many alternate worlds. In exploring the possibilities that intrigued us most, we've shattered a stereotypical body of lore into myriad reflections. We couldn't ask for a better home for those stories than this: featured among a fascinating variety of others.

Since the authors themselves come from several different countries with their own writing styles, you'll find both US and UK conventions in terms of spelling and punctuation.

There was no use of generative AI in the creation of this book—it was all done by the authors, with possibly a little help from the gods themselves. But no one's saying for certain.

Content Warnings

If you'd rather avoid spoilers, feel free to skip right over this page. If you'd appreciate a heads-up about disturbing material, topics often considered triggering are listed below.

* Something to Reflect On — *undeath, brief mention of cannibalism/infanticide (Cronus)*
* I Have Come to Lead You to the Other Shore — *death*
* Intoxication: A Pandora's Box Retelling — *arranged marriage*
* Death's Diary — *death, suicide*
* Santilmo — *death, rape*
* Cy Pearce Deserved to Die — *death, domestic abuse*
* The Beowulf Files — *death, dismemberment*
* The Cyberpunk Tragedy of Orphy6 and Eury23 — *death, grief*

SHATTERLORE

Myths of Past and Future

Edited by
Mara Lynn Johnstone

Copyright © 2024
Reality Collision Publishing

Something to Reflect On
Mara Lynn Johnstone

Narcissus was going to be the first vampire with a reflection if it took him all century. He had everything he needed. The time, the laboratory, and the background in human science, if not in supernatural magics. That part he had picked up recently, though "recent" meant something different now that his life was measured in millennia.

He maneuvered a dropper of tea tree oil over the small dish of his own blood, and let precisely three drops fall. Watching through a microscope, he saw … nothing special. He sat back up and blinked his teal-blue eyes into the magical spectrum, just to check, but there were no signs of a reaction there either. Just the usual red glow of vampiric magic in his blood. With a deep sigh, he moved the dish under the scouring dome to dispose of its contents.

Narcissus was proud of that dome, if not of his progress. It was one of his earliest and most useful creations (though of course vampire society at large was unimpressed). No one wanted to see a repeat of the disasters from beforehand, of course: the dump bucket that spawned wild magic or the plumbing system that had to be replaced. Enchanted fire in a scientifically-calibrated glass dome was the way to go.

He fed the fire with a handful of love notes from the basket under the counter, and watched the sample boil away.

All right, he thought as he crossed tea tree oil off the long list of possibilities. *Next up is ... Ugh. Okay.* Flipping the notebook page revealed "garlic, small dose."

Narcissus set down the notepad and pencil as if they had personally offended him, and went to get gloves. Whether this worked or not, it was likely to get messy, and no vampire worth their fangs wanted to risk garlic burns.

Moments later he was back at the counter—made of modern epoxy resin, not the stone that the elder magicians worked with—equipped with latex gloves and industrial goggles. He wore a white lab coat with a flattering cut and a heart embroidered over the pocket. It had been a gift from somebody. His luxurious golden hair bounced free, with no need for a hair net. Because it wasn't quite long enough to get in his eyes, and who had time for that?

He repeated the procedure with extreme caution: fill a dish from the bag he'd drained earlier (getting low; only a couple more experiments today), place it under the microscope, check the focus, then remove the vial of garlic oil from its solitary confinement in a locked case, and transfer a drop with the utmost care.

At the last second, he paused to snatch up a stray sheet of transparent acrylic and wedge it between the microscope and the dish. There was just barely enough space. Awkward, yes, but he didn't want to clean garlic-tainted blood off the lens if it splashed. Or his face, for that matter; the goggles didn't cover everything.

He squeezed a single drop into the dish. Through the microscope, he saw it land and merge with the blood, intermixing and—congealing instantly. He sat up to

Something to Reflect On

confirm: only a dull lump of darkened mess lay at the bottom of the dish.

Well, it's not like I expected anything el—

The blood exploded to splatter against the plastic that he had started to remove. Narcissus froze. Nothing hurt; he hadn't been burned. The sheet had done its job, though barely. Dark red oozed right to the edge.

Rude, Narcissus thought, scowling at the befouled dish. *Into the incinerator with you. And you.* He slid the acrylic sheet out and placed it under the scouring dome along with the dish. It fit, though only just. He set aside the previous dish, stoked the fire, and moved the box of gloves closer.

Cleaning up this mess would take a while. A break from his work afterward sounded nice, with a blood bag or two for a snack. Maybe he'd even go for a walk. It would be nice to get out of the lab for a bit.

Determined, Narcissus threw himself into the cleaning with vampiric speed. It wasn't that much faster subjectively, since he still experienced each swipe of a paper towel, but it *felt* faster, and sometimes that was enough. He would have killed for speed like this in his human undergrad days.

In the end, he hadn't killed, but died instead.

* * *

"Excuse me, madam? Your Majesty? Queen?"

Hera regarded the younger vampire with her most regal look of disapproval. "You're new, aren't you? You and your sisters." As the youngling rushed to explain herself, Hera continued. "You may address me as 'my queen.'"

"Yes, my queen," Echo said with a hasty bow. "Thank you, my queen."

Hera gave her a once-over. The girl's hair was colored an unnatural red by modern chemicals, and her tight-fitting shirt bore the name of something or someone that Hera couldn't be bothered to care about. At least she was wearing a skirt, foolishly-patterned though it was. Cat faces. Honestly, now.

Hera herself wore a purple gown, with her dark hair piled high in an old style that had just come into fashion again. Because Hera had declared it so.

"Why do you disturb me?" Hera asked, pointedly turning her back. She had been inspecting the vast mural for signs of age; fallen tiles just wouldn't do. Not on this wall. Its history should be clear for all to see.

"I actually wanted to ask you about this," Echo said. A glance showed her to be pointing at the wall. "I've been told the story," she rushed to add. "But different versions. ... Was your husband responsible for all of it, or is that giving him too much credit?"

Hera laughed. "Very observant of you," she said. "Of course he takes too much credit. He did lead the fight, I suppose, but that was simply because he was the eldest. And our mother was the one to teach us all the magic we needed to curse our father."

She cast an eye towards Echo, who seemed to be choosing her words carefully. Good. There had been enough younglings fresh from a mortal life who had dared to comment on their king and queen's familial relationship.

They were the ever-living. Quaint restrictions about who one could marry were best left behind with the mayfly creatures of the daylight.

"And is your mother ... still around?" Echo finally said.

"Of course not," Hera told her. "She was mortal."

Echo twisted her fingers together in what was probably nerves. "She wasn't affected by the curse splashback?"

"No, she wasn't a fighter." Hera gazed at the wall, seeing not tiles but memories. "And for all she wanted it to happen, she couldn't bring herself to have a direct hand in the death of the man who had eaten the child they'd had together." Images passed through Hera's mind: her grief-stricken mother, her unrepentant father, the pile of cooked meat that had once been her ailing youngest sibling. The look on her mother's face as that grief turned to anger.

The girl intruded on her thoughts. "Did she know the curses would combine like that?"

"Unlikely," Hera said, blinking away the past. "She was barely able to weave the threads of magic into something that we could live with afterward. She did well for herself, considering." With a judicious look across the rest of the mural—depicting Zeus heroically leading the siblings in throwing curse magic at their villainous father, while their mother mourned in the background—Hera decided that the tiles were all secure enough.

Done with the subject, she swept away to inspect other artwork in the royal halls.

Echo trotted after her. "What happened to your father?" she asked.

"Dead in a pit," Hera said.

"How did the other people in the town or whatever react to all that?"

"About the way you would expect," Hera said. She stopped, and the idiot youth nearly stumbled into her. "Go ask another elder your questions. I have said all I wish on the subject."

"Aw." Echo actually pouted. "I was hoping to learn from you, since you're the most trustworthy source. You were there. And you know so much; you're so wise—"

"Stop." Hera cut the air with her hand, eyes narrowing. "What are you after?"

"Just to learn!" Echo said. "There's so much you have to tell!"

Hera turned away. "Ask someone else first. This is tiresome."

"Wait!" Echo said, daring to catch at her gown. The glare that Hera turned on her only made her raise both hands and start babbling. "Please, I won't ask about your family if you don't want me to, but can you tell me about the early days? There's so much I want to understand about where vampires came from. And is it true that Poseidon rules an island chain with underwater caves? Do we ever go back and forth to visit? I'd love to see all the—"

"Silence," Hera commanded. "Stop talking, and leave my presence."

When she turned again to walk towards her own rooms, and the youngling squeaked out another "Wait," suspicion bloomed.

"Wait for what?" she asked. "What am I not to see?" She cast her hearing forward into the sumptuous hallways and chambers of the royal quarters, and she heard telltale giggles.

When she rounded on Echo like a thunderstorm, the youth quailed in fear. "No, it's not that! I just wanted to—"

"To *distract* me," Hera bellowed. Grasping Echo by the throat, she lifted the traitorous youngling off the floor and squeezed. "Do not speak to me again," she said, then cast her aside.

Hera strode off in a cloud of fury, heading for the chamber that held Echo's sisters and Hera's unfaithful husband. She spared neither a look nor a thought for the miserable form behind her, which lay on the floor with crushed vocal cords.

* * *

Narcissus was out in public, and no other vampire had said a thing to him yet. What a refreshing change of pace. He sat back against the bench under cool blue light, and sighed in contentment. This light garden was a beautiful place. When he'd first been brought into the subterranean complex that local vampires called home, he hadn't honestly expected much. Caves, maybe some lamps and nice rugs. But he hadn't quite made the connection that this underground society had been civilized since the beginning, with every advance that regular humans enjoyed.

Lights, heated floors, and well-circulated air; not a rough stone wall in sight. Even the most humble corridor looked like a high-end subway terminal, with art of all kinds lining the walls. The modern digital works were his favorite.

And this light garden was easily one of the best places around for a quiet snack. Narcissus pulled a blood bag from the pocket of his lab coat, then took a sip and admired the lights.

The whole room was bathed in shifting blue, which flowed like water down walls and past benches. A raised portion of the floor was patterned in the green of mossy river stones. Hidden spotlights threw fiery, fluttering shapes everywhere: flower petals and butterflies. Ghostly images of birds soared across every flat surface, leaving trails of white glittering behind them. Camouflaged speakers provided calm birdsong and the sound of leaves through trees near a babbling brook. Somewhere a vent gushed cool air that was scented with the smells of nature. It was lovely.

Then someone sat down next to him, and Narcissus inwardly groaned.

He had no idea what her name was. She had red hair, modern clothes with cat patterns, and a downcast expression. The lights that played over the bench made it harder to place whether he'd talked to her before. Thankfully she didn't seem much interested in talking now, just giving him an awkward smile and looking jerkily away.

Narcissus nodded and pretended this was fine. He went back to watching the birds, though the peaceful moment was gone. He sipped from the blood bag and hoped that whatshername wouldn't ask to share it. She wouldn't be the first.

A glance showed her staring at him. Narcissus thought longingly of running back to the lab without drawing out the interaction any further, but he held his position. He had to at least try to turn this one down with grace. And he didn't even know who she was. He should really make some kind of list.

The woman reached for the collar of his coat, and it took masterful restraint to keep from jerking away. She was only smoothing it out. Smiling like she was proud of it or something.

A memory clicked into place. "You gave this to me, right?" Narcissus asked. "It's very nice." Her hair had been different before, and she'd run away before he could unwrap the bundle.

She blushed, mouthing something that could have been "You're welcome."

Narcissus was sure she'd talked before. "Is something wrong with your voice?"

When she put a hand to her throat with a wince, he saw a purple area that he'd missed in the shifting shadows. It looked painful.

"Ah." He wasn't sure what to say. "Piss somebody off?"

She nodded ruefully.

That was another thing he'd had to get used to: there weren't really "laws" in vampire society so much as "guidelines on how not to anger the elders." Everyone was responsible for their own problems. On the one hand, it meant no one was going to bother him about lab safety, but also no one was going to prevent him from getting sexually harassed on the regular. Consent wasn't much of a factor here. Though really, with Zeus in charge, what else could he expect?

On that note…

"Was it Hera?" he guessed.

She nodded with tears in her eyes.

"Ah yeah, she can be harsh."

The woman turned those tearful eyes toward him, and apparently read more than polite sympathy in his expression. In a blink, her hands were in his hair and she was moving in for a kiss.

"What? No!" Narcissus shoved her off and jumped to his feet.

She fell, then stumbled into a run, wheezing sobs.

Narcissus stood in a mess of guilt and indignation. *It's not my fault,* he thought desperately. *She shouldn't have jumped at me like that. Why does NOBODY here take no for an answer? And she even looks modern, not like she's been living deep in the tunnels for a century. She should have at least heard of asexuality. Why didn't she SAY anything? Well, I guess with the throat injury ...* He looked down and saw that he'd forgotten about the blood bag in his hand. Red sprays decorated the pristine white coat.

Narcissus waved his free hand about in exasperation, then strode off toward his quarters. Clearly this was going to be a horrible night.

* * *

When Echo's sisters came home, they arrived in a cloud of laughter as they sprawled onto couches, still dressed for debauchery and dancing.

"We should go to that club on purpose sometime," said Harmony.

"Yes," agreed Melody. "For the dancing, not the hiding!"

"Agreed," Summer said. "Echo, you here?"

Something to Reflect On

A loud sniff drifted down the hallway. The sisters moved to the bedroom, and found her draped mournfully across the bed.

"Echo, what's wrong?"

"What happened?"

"Are you okay?"

Echo was not okay, and could barely whisper an explanation. After many questions and few answers—and much shushing of each other—the sisters concluded that Hera had done the bruising, but Narcissus had committed the much worse crime of breaking Echo's heart. She had pined after him for so long. They had advised her many times to make a move, and now that she did, he reacted with a shove?

"How dare he!" Melody declared.

"He doesn't know what he's turning down!" Harmony said.

"He doesn't know *who* he's turning down," Summer corrected darkly. "He's not going to waltz off after this. Not when she made him the coat and everything! Echo, honey, you rest while we take care of this. Echo?"

Echo didn't respond, lying rigid with her hands clasped to her chest and eyes closed. The sisters stared.

"Is she in torpor?" asked Harmony. "Did he hurt her so bad she went into freaking *torpor?*"

"Echo?" Melody said, touching her sister's cheek. "Can you wake up?"

Summer crossed her own arms. "That's it. He's done for."

"How do we wake her?" Melody insisted. "I've never seen torpor, just heard about it."

"You can't," Summer said. "She'll wake on her own. Sometimes it takes a century."

"A century??" Melody and Harmony wailed.

Summer nodded. "Pretty Boy is going down. Let's go find one of those elders who like hurting people."

* * *

This sector of the elder compound was more dark and foreboding than the rest, with swooping archways and leering sculptures lit by LEDs the color of fire. The sisters stood tall and walked with as much confidence as they could muster, but they stood closer together than they had in the more welcoming areas.

"Do you think she's here?" Melody whispered as they approached the heavy iron door.

"They say she's usually here," Summer said. She stepped forward to knock twice.

"Not out doing violent karma?" Harmony asked.

"I mean, yeah, she does that too," Summer said. "But she's fast, and she figured out how to do it with her computer almost before the internet existed."

The door swung inward without a sound. All three sisters clammed up under the judgmental eyes of Nemesis, who was frightening and beautiful in equal measures. The elder was a vision of loveliness that made them all faintly self-conscious: wavy dark hair, good cheekbones and eyelashes, plentiful curves. She wore a white robe that glowed faintly, with details hard to make out. And her posture, presence, and death glare would have cowed more stalwart souls than they. She said nothing.

Summer spoke first. "Sorry to bother you…"

"A thousand pardons!" Harmony put in.

"But someone has done our sister wrong," Summer said. Under that stern gaze, she stumbled over her words to explain the situation, with Harmony and Melody adding details.

Finally Nemesis raised a hand, and they fell silent. "You want vengeance," she said in a voice that echoed into the room behind her.

"Yes," Summer said.

"Karma," Melody and Harmony said together.

Nemesis nodded. "I have heard complaints of heartbreak due to Narcissus before. No one has called on me to intervene until now."

"We're asking," Summer confirmed. "We know your skills are unmatched. Can you make him suffer unrequited love more than anyone ever before?"

"You don't wish him simply hurt?" Nemesis asked, with the hint of a smile.

"We wish a fitting punishment," Summer told her. "Like you said, he's—"

Something made a quiet ding behind her, and Nemesis' robes flared bright enough to make the sisters blink. In that moment she flashed away like a shadow to the far side of the room—which was full of opulent hangings and treasures, with an elaborate gamer chair set up against the wall. Sword-shaped mirror cutouts formed a deadly halo radiating outwards from the seat, which made the room seem larger and more dangerous. The sisters stared.

Nemesis loomed over the computer, wreathed in shadow, and she clicked several things before ghosting back across the room to land in front of them with her robes spreading in winglike, eye-searing white.

"I will confirm your claims, then act," she declared. "Now leave me to my preparations."

The sisters thanked her profusely, only stopping when the door shut silently in front of them.

"Okay, then," Summer said, stepping back. "She'll take care of it."

"I wonder what she'll do," Melody said as they made haste back down the gloomy hallway.

"Maybe she'll make him love Hera," Harmony guessed.

Summer shook her head. "I feel like that would just end with Hera taking him up on it, to make Zeus mad."

"Well, what if he fell for Zeus instead?" Harmony suggested.

Melody whispered, eyeing a cross-corridor, "That guy's into everything including bestiality; do you really think he'd turn down another dude? A hot one?"

"Okay, fair point."

"Anyways, I don't think it'll be them." Melody continued. "It's got to be someone he has NO chance with."

"I hope she knows something I don't," Harmony grumbled. "The jerk is unfairly pretty."

"If there's anyone, she'll find them," Summer said.

* * *

As a single dark shadow among many, Nemesis flitted from room to room, from empty hallway to crowded corridor to open lounge area. She listened. And she

Something to Reflect On

observed. She calibrated her hearing for mentions of her target's name, and she filtered the gossip. It confirmed what she had heard before.

By all accounts, Narcissus was a callous youth, egotistical and scornful of all who looked upon him. He would accept no suitor, for none could match his own beauty. He accepted gifts but spurned advances, leaving a trail of broken hearts in his wake. None had spoken to him about his behavior, nor asked of any reasoning behind it, but that hardly seemed necessary when the motive was clearly ego.

It was a marvel that no one had called for vengeance before this. All that would be rectified soon, though. The spell was not a complicated magic. She simply needed an appropriate target.

Possibly a statue. Or a portrait of someone long-dead.

With her eyes open and thoughts full of calculations, Nemesis shadow-walked between door hinges to make her most crucial observation: of the young man himself.

Narcissus was alone in the lab, scribbling in a notebook with sample jars scattered around him. His coat hung loose on his frame, but it nonetheless managed to look fashionable. His hair shone golden in the light. The fact that its artfully tousled state may have actually been unintentional was something that would have stirred jealousy in many observers.

Slipping from one shadow to another, Nemesis was unmoved. She searched for relevant information about her target.

On the floor was a note sent to him: an anonymous confession of love. It had fallen from a basket of more.

On a small table by the wall was a box with a faint smear of lipstick on it. This held empty syringes. A calendar showed nature scenes, each also with a hastily-wiped-away trace of a kiss. The room was full of love tokens, most with their telltale marks removed, all sent to him with no sign of reciprocation. Not so much as a letter displayed in a place of honor.

What does he value? Nemesis wondered as she inspected the faux-windows that the youth had installed. There were several of them spaced along the walls, between cabinets and equipment, none matching. One appeared to be multiple panes of frosted glass that filtered bright morning sunlight, though the faint buzz of electricity and the lack of any sense of danger gave away the lie. Another was a painting of a deep green forest, complete with window frame and an illusion of shutters opened into the woods.

Another showed a view of a tabby cat sleeping on a window ledge. The next was an underwater seascape full of brightly-colored fish. The last one, which gave her pause, was a framed mirror.

A large mirror, barely fitting between the bookshelf and the door. Was it simply to give the room illusory depth, or was there more to it than that? Had he been mortal, this would be an ideal location to check his appearance before leaving the room. And—she confirmed—he had a clear view of it from his current seat, elbow-deep in paperwork.

Nemesis hung behind him, a dark cloud in the air. Had they been mortal, he would have seen a glimpse of shadow in the reflections on the many bottles that stood before him. But she had no reflection, and neither did he, and what *was* he writing with such focus, anyway?

Something to Reflect On

Oh. Oh, this was perfect.

The child was trying to give himself a reflection. She had been right; he wanted to see himself in that large mirror, undoubtedly so that he could admire the beauty that he lorded over all others. Now that she thought about it, most of the false windows were protected by glass panes that would also reflect, not to mention all the glassware on the various tables. Even the tables themselves shone. One way or another, most of the surfaces in this room were reflective.

Narcissus wanted to gaze at his own face. The ghostly elder lurking behind him smiled deep in her shadows. She would help him. It was ideal for her purposes: the one moment of joy would allow everything to come crashing down.

Now, how close is he to figuring it out? she wondered, reading over his shoulder. This page was of no help. With a flash, she was over in the corner upsetting the pile of empty jars that had been stacked badly, then away before the first one crashed to the floor.

While Narcissus groaned and went to clean up the mess, a countertop full of equipment blocked his view of the shadow turning pages in his notebook. Those pages flipped past in silence, resting exactly where he had left them when he returned, none the wiser.

Up near a ceiling vent, Nemesis gloated inwardly. This really was perfect. The boy had figured out most of the puzzle on his own—impressive, really—to the point of isolating which magical thread would need to be separated from the dense tangle that wove through every vampire. All that remained was a method of loosening the knot, which had become solid and cemented over the centuries, a far cry from the wild mess that had marked their early days.

Nemesis herself hadn't been around for the very beginning, but she'd been brought into the fold early enough to remember efforts at untangling certain other aspects of their peculiar makeup. Like the vulnerability to daylight.

But that was a load-bearing thread, wasn't it? she thought. *The reflections may just work. That's not to say that it's wise, of course—clearly he hasn't considered the value in hunting without one's prey catching sight—such a foolish child. He probably drinks his blood from bottles. No sense for the established wisdom. Well, on his own head be it.*

The wisp of darkness floated back out of the room, and Narcissus never saw it go. He certainly didn't pick up on the vicious smile of an elder whose plan would soon be set in motion.

* * *

When yet another note was slid under his door, Narcissus shook his head and kept working. He had things to do. The acrylic vacuum chamber was ready for this next test: airless exposure to holy water. It was possible, he theorized, that he just needed to find the right combination of factors to damage the magic ever-so-slightly, just enough to loosen it. Holy water normally burned worse than any acid, and it couldn't be diluted reliably. But perhaps air was a factor. Trying to mix blood and holy water within another liquid would have added too many variables. The vacuum chamber was the way to go. Much cleaner.

He set a dish of blood into the chamber, next to a vial of holy water with a remote-controlled grabbing rig that would tip it over when he manipulated the buttons. Then he sealed the lid, turned up the dial, and waited. The motor whirred. Air rushed through the hose with increasing intensity.

Bubbles rose in the water, boiling even though the liquid remained cold. The blood did the same ... with greater intensity than he'd expected.

When the dish foamed over in red froth, coating the floor of the vacuum chamber in boiling vampire blood, Narcissus ran aggravated hands through his hair. Shutting off the vacuum left an inert mess on everything but the dish. He thumbed the controls to pour the holy water anyway, but learned nothing from it. The blood just congealed further.

Narcissus spun on his heel and wrote an angry note in his journal before looking for distractions. He was in no mood to clean that disaster just yet.

Oh, right, he thought with a sigh when he spotted the note by the door. *Might as well.* He allowed himself a bit of a stomp on the way over.

It was a piece of lined paper, folded once. Not a lot of effort put into this one. And the writing inside was a single line.

He blinked and read it twice.

"Crush one daffodil bulb into a pint of your own blood, and sip until you see results."

The rest of the world faded away; only this paper was important. Daffodils? He hadn't tried daffodils. They were toxic when eaten. And used for unproven medicine.

But who sent this? he wondered, flipping the note in search of clues, then dropping to scour the floor for any sign of another note. Swinging the door wide was no use; the hallway was long empty of anyone who could have left it. Why hadn't he checked sooner?

Well, I know why, he admitted as he shut the door again. *But if I'd known—! Who could possibly be helping me with this?*

It occurred to him that the suggestion could just as easily be sabotage. Of the limited number of people who'd shown interest in his work, most had used it simply as an excuse to talk to him, and the others had almost universally told him it was a bad idea.

It's always "Best not to meddle," or "You don't want to affront the elders," or "We've always been this way; it works fine." Narcissus walked in a circle between tables laden with glassware that reflected everything but him. Like he wasn't even there. *Well it's not fine,* he thought. *And I pushed many boundaries while I was human; I'm not about to stop now. Gotta try it.*

In a flash of motivation, Narcissus turned on his heel and sped to the laptop that waited between the cat window and the fish window. Where could he get a daffodil bulb, anyway? Were they even in season? He didn't know. But the internet did.

Moments later, he tossed the lab coat onto a chair and made for the quickest route to the surface, dressed in T-shirt and slacks. Daffodils were in season, there was a gardening store nearby, and the sun wasn't up yet. Perfect.

He raced down the corridor with his best vampiric speed, hair flowing and fangs bared in an excited grin, with no regard for the handful of other vampires he passed on the way. When he reached the corner, he ran up the wall and across the ceiling instead of slowing down. There was the staircase, there was the door into the "abandoned" subway tracks, and there was no one to see him on the other side.

Narcissus dashed out into the nighttime city, a blur that no mortal could track. The garden store was just a few minutes' run away. It was closed at this hour, but no matter. He had no money, no lockpicks, and no moral qualms about smashing in a high window that no human could reach. A bit of parkour, and he was in.

The daffodil bulbs were easy to find. Narcissus acquired a paper bag from behind the register and helped himself to half a dozen. With a cheeky wave at the security camera that couldn't see him—but might soon!—he made a running leap back outside and flashed off the way he had come.

It was an exhilarating run.

He made it back to the lab with his hair a wild mess, and a few more fellow vampires wondering what he was up to. None of that mattered. What mattered was the SCIENCE. He was about to get results.

Okay, right, gotta make notes first, he thought, setting the bag down on a clean span of countertop and spinning in place until he located his notepad. He wrote quickly enough to snap the pencil lead, then peeled back the wood of the pencil instead of finding a sharpener. Ugly notes were fine. *I've got to do a small-scale test first,* he decided. *Gloves, and a tray, and a bucket...*

Gathering supplies was a slapdash affair, but if one or two (or more) things were knocked over, that was hardly significant right now. Once his gloves were tugged into place, he ripped open the paper bag to select the smallest bulb.

Peel, hold, slice ... Slice again for a clean piece, good. Now do I pour the blood over it, or lower this in? Blood first.

The last of his own stored blood went into a tray under the hastily-rigged microscope. With the plastic barrier in place and his eyes blinked into the magical spectrum, he tweezered the sliver of bulb into the blood with the glowing red aura.

The aura wobbled.

Narcissus laughed aloud, moving from the microscope view to his own eyes and back. There it was, clear as anything: threads of interwoven curses that had been diamond-hard, now sliding around like wet spaghetti. It was beautiful.

Okay, okay, let's think this through, Narcissus told himself firmly. *Digestion should be an efficient way of dispersing it; that's worked for many things before. Do I need to worry about side effects, or time frame?*

Removing the tiny piece of daffodil bulb did allow the threads to stabilize to some degree, though remaining juices meant it wasn't an instant change. Side effects were hard to test for, but he did have some guesses about that. Daffodil was toxic, after all.

It's been a long time since I threw up, Narcissus thought grimly, *But I am prepared in the name of science.* He stood. *Time for full-scale! The concept is proven; there's no reason to wait.*

New gloves. Clean bucket. Mortar and pestle for crushing. A new bulb peeled, the largest one this time. Eagerly mashed into paste.

Now all he needed was the pint of blood, but he was all out. Maybe fresh was better anyway.

Narcissus grabbed a blood-drawing bag from the sanitary cabinet, then sliced off the needle and a bit of tube. Just enough to aim the blood stream into the measuring beaker for an accurate pint.

Ow. Let's see if vampire healing works faster or slower with a heart rate that's elevated because of SCIENCE.

Faster. Even with the wide-bore needle to keep the tiny injury open, it tried to seal over twice before the beaker was full. He finally set aside the needle and pressed a thumb to the bend of his elbow for a long few seconds. While he waited, he debated whether or not to drink water or a bag of human blood to replace what he'd lost. Being one pint down might affect the magic. But so might a stomachful of other things. No way to know.

Going without, he decided. *I never did get lightheaded when I donated blood as a mortal; I'll probably be fine.* When he was sure that no blood would be leaking down his arm to contaminate the experiment, he moved to the notebook for more hurried documentation while he finished healing. Then: time to mix.

Pint into the clean bucket, poured carefully. Daffodil paste scooped in with equal care, then stirred with the spatula while gorgeous magical waves bloomed around it.

Narcissus finally set aside the spatula. *Do or die time.* He used the beaker to ladle out a healthy amount, rather than trying to drink out of the bucket. That was a quick route to ruined clothes and a compromised experiment. The beaker would do.

He eyed the unappetizing, chunky liquid. Then, aware of the historical magnitude, he took a sip.

It tasted vile.

Not a surprise, he thought with a wince, forcing himself to drink more. *Until I see results, it said.* He watched his own hand with an eye for the magic tied to it. After a few moments, and a few more revolting mouthfuls, the magic began to waver.

"Ha!" Narcissus said, rushing to trade the beaker for a focusing crystal. It couldn't have come soon enough; the toxins were starting to make his guts twist.

With a stern word to his human memories to keep their opinions to themselves, the vampire held aloft his focusing crystal of choice and prepared to change reality with willpower alone. This "crystal" was the most magical-looking one he'd been able to find, since convincing himself was the first step in convincing reality to change. Palm-sized and vividly colored, this shell had been fossilized with opal instead of a more plain-looking rock. It was sliced in half and polished to a shine.

Narcissus couldn't see his own reflection in it yet, but he would. Oh, he would.

His scientific background rebelled at the simplicity. He told it for the last time to hold its silence, and he pictured in his mind what he wanted to happen. Which thread needed to unravel, where it would re-attach, and what the results would be. Now that it was loosened, it would obey his will.

And, because magic always rhymed in fairytales, he spoke aloud: "Restore reflection, no objection, NOW!" With a shout, he thrust the crystal skyward.

Magic swirled. He could *feel* the threads shifting, which was as unsettling as it was exciting. The queasy stomach could have been nerves as well as poisonous plants.

Something popped into view, wrecking his concentration. Narcissus went through several emotions in rapid succession when he realized it was his reflection on the vacuum chamber walls.

He shouted in jubilation, spreading his arms as if greeting an old friend. "It worked! Wow." He leaned forward, inspecting his grin. *So that's what I look like with fangs. Cool.* As an afterthought, he laughed at the messy hair, then rushed to document his joy.

After a brief detour to throw up in the extra bucket.

His mind was occupied with many things, and he never felt the hex cast from the corner of the room—not when it hit, failed to get purchase even on the weakened magic, and slid off without a trace. He was focused on triumph and scientific delight, not on arousal. When had he ever been? If anyone had ever bothered to ask, he could have given an honest answer about the reason behind his refusals.

Done with vomit and with note-taking, Narcissus darted about the room with childlike eagerness, finding his own face and hands and clothes reflected back from every shiny surface. He didn't notice the frustrated shadow that slipped through a crack in the door to reconsider its strategy.

* * *

It wasn't possible. The exact terms of the agreement couldn't be done if the young fool was immune to love magic. Nemesis was loath to admit it, but this might be a failure. Not ready for defeat just yet, she put away her magic tomes and sought out the trio who had requested her services.

She didn't reach them. There was a lightning storm in the great hall.

Nemesis approached one of the many onlookers just outside, and asked, "What is happening?" Lightning flashed and voices thundered.

"Zeus and Hera," said the middle-generation hanger-on whose name she couldn't be bothered to remember. "This might be the big one."

"What now?" Nemesis asked, thinking back to the detail that the three sisters had glossed over in their tale of grievances. Surely a garden-variety dalliance couldn't be the last straw.

"Reflections," the sycophant said. "Zeus hates the idea, but Hera's in favor. You've heard about that, right?"

"Yyyesss," Nemesis admitted.

"Honestly, he just wants fewer ways to get caught perving," said another onlooker. "And she wants to see how pretty she is without taking someone else's word for it."

"I mean, he has a point about hunting," said the first. "That would make it much harder to sneak up on a mortal without clouding their senses every time."

"Oh, like we even need to do that nowadays," argued the second. "We could order more shipments of blood bags and be just fine never hunting again."

"What? You heathen."

Nemesis edged away from the debate, hoping to get a sense of how severe the fight in the next room was. She heard Zeus shouting about what he would do to whoever had given the young idiot the secret to altering his own composition. There was no way, according to Zeus, that he had figured it out on his own.

Something to Reflect On

Nemesis froze in place, then reverted to shadow form and ghosted away. She had some tracks to cover up.

Zeus and Hera kept fighting, throwing lightning and magic, insults and threats that finally, after all these centuries of putting up with each other, this would be the wedge that drove their empire apart.

Three sisters, listening at a different doorway, made a similar strategic decision and left for their quarters where they could pretend to be waiting out their sister's torpor.

All throughout the complex, vampires spoke of the exciting news. Narcissus had figured out how to restore his reflection, and it was surprisingly easy. Easy enough for anyone to try ... and many did. Factions formed.

None of this hubbub reached Narcissus's lab, where he had returned after spreading the word and sharing his remaining daffodil bulbs. He was happily writing away in his notebook, documenting the historic success and making plans for a new false window. This one would feature a mirror behind a field of flowering daffodils.

On all sides, his reflection joined him in his work. A quiet friend whenever he looked up, ready to share a fanged smile with just as much delight as he felt. The room was much more homey already.

What scientific breakthrough would he tackle next? Whichever route he took, his reflection would be there with him 100%.

A Chimera of Three Parts
Craig Rathbone

Part One: The Creature

"Damn you to hell, you stupid damned soldier bastards!" Wesley yelled after the now distant military truck, muddy water dripping from his uniform and covering his spectacles.

Ginger snorted with laughter a few paces behind him, bent double against a weathered wooden fence. Her umbrella trailed on the patchwork pavement as she fought to catch her breath. "Damn, Wesley, can you go for *five minutes* without some kind of disaster striking you? How do you do it?"

As soaked and irritated as Wesley Lewis was, he couldn't bring himself to take out his anger on his friend. Ginger, or Kerry to adults and sensible people, had come to his defence against a group of bullies in primary school, chasing them off with a Stretch Armstrong doll brandished like a club, and had stayed at his side ever since. For that, he had always been willing to put up with her constant wind-ups and pranks. "Clearly I was built too perfectly. God has got to balance out my karmas or whatever by making me unlucky as hell—hence why I'm stuck with you," he shot back, smiling despite himself.

Ginger, now recovered, placed the canopy of the umbrella back above her head and caught up to him, punching him playfully on the shoulder. "Karma is a completely different thing to God, you moron," she said. "It's, like, Buddhism or something. You should know this, your mum would batter you if she heard you bad-mouthing God."

The walk back home from school on a Friday was always the same. Ginger had been having tea around Wesley's house every Friday for the last four years, which was a boon for her as she loved the Lewis family's traditional Jamaican cooking. Wesley's family was just as studious as he was—his father had taught her a lot about the family's history and how they had moved over to the UK from the Caribbean decades ago. Wesley often joked about how Ginger was more excited to get to his house than he was.

"Don't even! And why the hell is this town full of soldiers, anyway? It's Charlton on Sea, not downtown Baghdad!" Wesley snapped as another two tan-painted trucks rolled past, sour-faced infantrymen staring at them from beneath rolled-up olive tarpaulins. Wesley and Ginger returned their gaze, skipping closer to the fence to avoid another torrent of water thrown up by their tires.

"I know, right?" Ginger replied as they passed a row of run-down-looking shops. "My dad told me that the old airfield outside of town was used in the war or something and that all the soldiers are camping there. Maybe they have some *top-secret mission* going on there, like containing a zombie outbreak, or a Terminator or something."

Wesley laughed loudly at his friend's ridiculous claims. Whatever the military was up to in that overgrown old airbase, he very much doubted that it involved a cyborg Arnold Schwarzenegger.

The two friends continued their back-and-forth until they reached the well-appointed facade of the

A Chimera of Three Parts

Lewis family home, discussing all manner of outlandish things that the army could be hiding up at the old Charlton airforce base including flying sharks, werewolves, and aliens.

* * *

Ginger closed her front door behind her and ran her eyes lovingly over the hall of the tiny terrace she and her father shared. The rooms may have been full of clutter, the furniture much-used and the odd wall suffering dry rot, but to her, it may as well have been Buckingham Palace.

She hated school, hated being known as the scruffy, poor redhead girl who sometimes had to go to school with no lunch. At least at home, she was just plain Kerry Wells. She kicked off her scuffed-up shoes and threw her backpack onto the stairs before passing through the narrow hall and into the dining room or, more accurately, her dad's workshop.

Computer parts littered every surface, many with wiring snaking between them. Mr. Wells sat at the table on a wooden chair, glaring at a huge monitor that probably weighed as much as Ginger did. "Evening, how are Wesley's lot? Hope you behaved yourself?" he asked, distracted by the MS-DOS code flickering across the screen. He always asked the same question, always distracted by his work, but Ginger couldn't find it in herself to be annoyed by him. The man worked long hours to put what food he could on the table and that was good enough for her.

"They're good, Dad. Don't forget to eat, alright?" she said, pecking him on the cheek and receiving a playful shove in return.

"Yeah, yeah, will do Captain, just need to sort this last bit out and I'm all over that can of tomato soup back there," he said with a smile that didn't fit the inherent sadness of what he had just said. Ginger turned to head up to her room but stopped as she reached the doorway.

"Dad, have any of your old army mates told you about what all those soldiers are doing at the airbase?" she asked. "There seems to be tons of them in town at the moment."

Mr. Wells turned to face her at last, a concerned look on his face. "I'm honestly not sure; my friends are all Air Force like me, not the Army," he said, "And Kerry, promise me—*promise me* that you will not go anywhere near that airfield. Whatever it is they're doing they seem to be taking security very, very seriously."

Ginger promised her father that she had no intentions of poking her nose in at the airfield, poured a glass of orange juice, and went up to her bedroom to plan exactly that. With the Spice Girls for company via an ancient radio, she schemed well into the night.

* * *

"No way," snapped Wesley over the hubbub of the school playing field the following morning. "Are you *insane*? We're high school kids, not James bloody Bond! We'd get caught in *seconds*. They'd shoot us and that would be that!"

A Chimera of Three Parts

If her friend's outburst had dampened Ginger's resolve she certainly didn't show it, the wicked grin on her narrow face intensified with every word. "Firstly you can shove James Boring-Old-Bastard-Bond. Secondly, soldiers just don't shoot kids, and thirdly I have meticulously planned this out. I was up until three AM writing out equipment lists and researching fieldcraft *and* my dad used to be a soldier, so I think I know!" she shot back as they wandered slowly toward the science block before the first bell of the day sounded. Wesley shook his head in disbelief as he dodged around some younger kids, sparing them a disapproving glare as they passed.

"Being a soldier isn't in your blood Ginger, your old man didn't pass it down with that red hair and big mouth! We are not, I repeat *not*, going anywhere near the airfield, okay?" he said.

Ginger shook her head in mock resignation, clearly far from giving up on her attempt to recruit her friend. "Fine, not like I can convince the world's youngest grandad to do something interesting for a change. You sit home and play *Streets of Rage* and I'll go and recon the place myself. In and out like a ghost before you even run out of continues, like the amateur you are!"

Wesley stopped so suddenly that a group of girls almost piled into his back, producing a flurry of angry squawks as they manoeuvred around him. "Don't even joke about that. If you go there without my brains you'll get shot for sure and I don't want to be the only black kid at a funeral full of pasty-ass ginger people, you hear?"

Ginger cackled at his response, skipping away from him as the bell finally rang to call them to another day of study and boredom. "Best get yourself fitted for a suit Wes, because I'm going and you can't stop me," she called over her shoulder. "And if you tell any adults, I'll be the pasty ginger kid sticking out at *your* funeral! And I won't even cry!"

* * *

The military airfield was beyond the fields on Charlton On Sea's outskirts and surrounded by dense woodland. The night was pitch black without the glow of the moon, and fog curled around the roots of the trees as two figures carefully made their way through the undergrowth, the lead figure holding a red-tinted torch.

"I can't believe I let you talk me into this, you know? I could be nice and warm at home right now, not wandering around the damned woods following a dumbass with a shitty red torch!" Wesley complained to Ginger's back, a woolly hat pulled low over his head. Both had dressed mostly in black, though Ginger's only suitable footwear for the mission was a pair of pink wellingtons, which ruined the look somewhat.

"I told you, dickhead, the red torch is what they use in the SAS. It's *just* light enough for us to see, but the guards totally won't see us coming. We could get close enough to slit their throats and they wouldn't know a thing!" Ginger replied, somewhat too enthusiastically for Wesley's liking when it came to the throat-slitting part. He shuddered at the thought of getting close enough to the airfield to be spotted, wishing once again that he'd tried harder to talk his best friend out of this endeavour.

The plan was at least a simple one, if a little too dangerous for one of the duo's tastes. At the edge of the woodland stood a hill, mostly covered by the trees. From its dense foliage, dug in among the leaves, they made their base of operations. Ginger believed that this reconnaissance mission would unveil some shady reason for the army's presence in town, the theories of exactly what could be stored within the airbase enough to fill a whole school day's worth of conversation.

Wesley suspected it was something more mundane. Manoeuvres, training, or even fixing up the old Second World War airfield for whatever reason. He shared this opinion with Ginger once again as they began to ascend the wooded hill, his friend cursing as she tripped over yet another tree root. "That's your problem, Wesley Sharp; no imagination," she said as she got back to her feet, "I don't think they need half an army to fix up some overgrown runway. I'm really getting Roswell vibes here. They're definitely hiding a UFO in that hangar, or some freaky burned-up alien corpses!"

"You always did have an overactive imagination, Ginger. Let's just stay a little while, then head back, okay? My parents will *freak* if I'm not back by ten."

The next hour passed slowly. The wind made the tree branches creak and sway ominously, and the undergrowth was cold under the woollen blanket Wesley had brought along. The notepad that Wesley had supplied to record troop movements was now full of Ginger's doodling and Wesley was feeling rather fed up as he looked down into the airfield through his binoculars for what felt like the thousandth time. He expected to see what had become the usual, a few patrolling soldiers here and there and nothing more, but this time something different was unfolding.

"Ginger, something's happening! We have trucks rolling out!" he called to her in a harsh whisper, resulting in her scuttling over to him with a wild look in her eyes and lying prone next to him, notepad and pencil in hand.

"Awesome, now we'll find out what shady shit these guys are up to! Tell me what you see, I'm going to record *everything*! Guns, uniforms, tanks, moustaches even!" she said, positioning the red filtered torch so it shone upon the page. Whatever lack of interest Wesley had shown before was rapidly fading away as several trucks hared along the edge of the runway, clusters of red lights flickering into life along its concrete apron.

"Damn, that's cool. Look at it all coming back to life after all those years," he breathed as the air traffic control building flickered into life, illuminated against the dark night like a strange Christmas tree. "I bet those lights haven't been used in years—decades!"

"Oi, stop drooling over those old lights and tell me what those soldiers at the end of the bloody runway are doing!" Ginger snapped, pushing the binoculars toward the end of the apron where a large number of armed men were pouring out of the trucks.

Wesley mentioned something about his lack of drool as he trained the binoculars on where Ginger was pointing and let out a whistle from between his teeth. "Okay, I'm seeing a load of soldiers over there, they don't look like the others though. They're dressed all in black, body armour and helmets, nothing like the others. They all have rifles too, not just pistols. There's something written on the side of the trucks," he said slowly, allowing Ginger time to scribble down her notes.

"What does it say, genius?" she asked after a few seconds of silence, the binoculars never leaving the activity below.

"Sorry, I was just trying to identify the equipment but I don't have a clue what it all is. Trucks have *Bellerophon* written on the side. What the hell does that mean?"

"How am I supposed to know? It sounds, like, Russian or something, like something from *Rambo*? Hey, what are those things moving out from the hangar?" Ginger asked, waiting for her co-conspirator to retrain his sights on the huge hangar at the far end of the runway near the control building. Its doors were opening and, though the lights were on inside, she couldn't make out anything due to the distance. Two large shapes were trundling out of it onto the apron, spotlights mounted on their hulls.

"It's those tractor things they have at, well, airports. The ones that tow the planes around once they land. I guess they're expecting a plane? Also yes, I reckon *Bellerophon* must be something Russian—it does sound that way," Wesley said excitedly. While he watched the tractors Ginger kept an eye on the tiny distant soldiers, who were now fanning out across the end of the runway setting up their mysterious equipment that, from so far away, looked like video cameras on tripods. Ginger was about to demand that Wesley take a closer look when a distant humming filled the air, like a bumblebee but more intense.

"Hey, listen, you hear that? Sounds like their plane might be coming in!" Ginger hissed, pushing the binoculars down from Wesley's eyes. Her friend met her excited expression with one of his own as the sound became louder. It sounded different from the airliners that criss-crossed the sky every day, much more bassy.

"That's got to be a military plane," grinned Wesley, "They're propeller engines, not jets! Ginger, you were right, we're about to witness some bonafide *shady shit* go down in this boring-ass town!"

The self-congratulation continued as the plane came into sight against the moonlit sky, a red light winking against the void as it slowly approached the airfield. The soldiers at the runway finally stopped rushing around and took up their positions, rifles at the ready. Whatever the plane was bringing in was clearly enough to make the soldiers cautious. Wesley grudgingly admitted that it *may* even be aliens, as per Ginger's favourite theory. The duo watched as the plane came closer still, its heavy-looking fuselage coming into view, the red light perched atop the fin of its tail. Wesley trained his binoculars on the machine. "That's an impressive looking machine—hey, it's on the tail too, *Bellerophon*. What the fuck is going on here?"

Ginger got to her feet carefully, too excited to sit anymore. "Maybe it's what the secret alien research team is called? You know, like, named after some Russian myth or—"

Her words were cut off mid-sentence as a fireball suddenly engulfed the plane, causing Ginger to squeak in horrified surprise. The sound came a couple of seconds later, a boom that made Wesley drop his binoculars. "Oh shit! What the fuck?" he cried as the plane began to veer off-course, a comet trail of flames following as it angled itself straight toward the hill Ginger and Wesley stood on. They froze for a few seconds, mouths open in disbelief until the reality of the situation hit home.

"Oh fucking hell, *run!*" screamed Ginger, grabbing Wesley's wrist and taking off back down the hill. He didn't need telling twice and they both ran through the trees, blindly dodging roots and tree trunks as the sound of labouring aircraft engines grew ever louder. Ginger's breaths came out in great sobbing gasps as the sound became unbearable and Wesley was convinced he could feel the heat of the flames gaining on him. They both dived into the leaf mulch as the plane roared overhead, the undercarriage barely brushing the treeline. They buried their faces in the dirt and braced for the end as it passed, feeling a couple seconds of intense heat as it did so. They stayed down as an almighty *bang* filled the forest, shaking the ground beneath them. It seemed to go on for an eternity and Ginger found herself regretting every poor or rash decision she had ever made. Fighting with the kids that teased her, shoplifting from the off-license owned by that nice Pakistani couple—not saying goodbye to her mum before she died.

"Ginger! Ginger? *Kerry!*"

Slowly, in disbelief that she could still be alive, she lifted her head to meet Wesley's terrified eyes. The forest was flickering with a deep orange light, small fires littering the ground around them. For once lost for words, she scrabbled onto her knees and embraced her friend with skinny arms, her head buried in the fur of his collar where she wept.

Wesley had only seen Ginger cry twice; once when her cat died and again after a beating from a bunch of kids she'd been trying to defend him from. This was different; this was pure terror. "It's okay Ginger, it's okay. We're alive. All arms and legs attached, see?" he said, gently pushing her back to arm's length so she could confirm his words.

"I want to go home Wesley, I want to get away from here!" she sniffed, her eyes red from crying. He could feel her shaking like a leaf in his hands.

"Good idea, let's get out of here!"

Ginger nodded her reply and, together, they started to move away from the trail of fire, the once terrifying darkness of the forest now welcoming. They hadn't moved ten paces when they stopped once more, curiosity cutting through their fear. "What the hell is that?" breathed Ginger in awe. Tilted at an angle before them, balanced atop two crushed trees, was a huge metal vault. It sat atop skids and had a steel door at the front, once held in place by a massive lock controlled by a panel. That door was now slightly ajar, its edge melted out of shape.

"I don't know, but I think maybe we should just leave it be," Wesley replied in a slow and deliberate voice, gently taking Ginger by the arm to lead her away.

But she didn't move to follow, instead letting out a low moan as something reached around the side of the door and began to push it open. Wesley's breath caught in his throat. It looked like a giant cat's paw, as big as a manhole cover. Had Ginger been right all along? Were they about to be killed by aliens?

The door suddenly swung out, hitting the frame of the mobile vault with a hollow thud as the creature inside slowly loped out of the darkness, the friends rooted to the spot with terror.

It looked like a huge lion, the size of Ginger's dad's Transit van, and had bright blue glowing eyes filled with malice, glaring right at them. Growing out of the creature's back was what seemed to be a goat's head, its eyes equally as blue and menacing. A great, scaled tail flicked out from behind it, tipped with a boxy, reptilian head filled with huge teeth. Six mismatched eyes zeroed in on them and none looked friendly. Alien, monster, or whatever it was, this thing wanted them dead.

"Ginger—*RUN!*"

She needed no encouragement and they once again charged into the darkness, now wishing that the military had found them after all. The creature followed as they ran desperately through the brush, with brambles and branches whipping at their hair and clothes and roots threatening to trip them at any moment. Still, the beast followed; Wesley could hear it growling only paces behind him until, without warning, the ground changed under his feet and he pitched forward onto the pitted concrete of a car park, just managing to get his arms out in front of him before his face hit the unyielding surface. Ginger had clearly done the same just ahead of him and was now scrambling back to her feet, reaching back for him.

But it was too late. The beast exploded out of the tree line behind them like a demon from the gates of hell, sliding to a halt on outstretched claws as long as steak knives. Ginger fell to her knees, shielding her best and only friend with her body in a futile attempt to save his life, a look of impotent rage on her face.

"Fine, fuck you then," she screamed at the monster. "Fucking eat me! I'll give you such awful indigestion that you won't be fucking far behind me, you ugly lion-goat-snake thing *fuck!*"

Part Two: The Myth

Ginger glared up at the monster, her heartbeat roaring in her chest as time seemed to slow almost to a halt. She no longer felt any fear of staring death in the face, only an all-consuming rage that she hadn't felt since her mother's funeral, standing before the casket with balled fists and clenched jaw. At least she would be seeing her again shortly and would finally be able to ask her why she had to go and leave her and her father alone in the world.

The creature's tail rose up over its shoulders, the goat head ducking slightly to let it pass. The serpent head at the end of the tail leered in close, teeth the size of Ginger's forearm inches in front of her face. The thing's breath reeked of eggs and sulphur, and thick saliva drooled from its grey-green lips. "Get on with it, prick," she growled, staring it right in one swivelling, reptilian eye.

"No," snapped the lion, causing the serpent to flinch, "not these ones. They are young, defenceless. They are not agents of Bellerophon."

The goat brayed at the lion's words, "Why not these ones? Can we not enjoy fresh meat before they cast us back to Tartarus?" it complained, its voice female, slightly higher than that of the lion. The serpent drew back on the end of the beast's tail, glaring resentfully down at Ginger and Wesley as the latter tried to pull her out of reach. She shook his grip off her wrist angrily, looking up at the goat with naked disdain.

"Listen to your lion head you arsehole goat, we're nothing to do with those Bellerophon people! Look at us, do we look like soldiers to you? I get battered at every fight I end up in and he's such a wimp the thought of confrontation makes him sick. Seems kind of lame to me, big monster like you killing two kids," she shouted as if scolding a badly behaving dog.

To Wesley's astonishment, the thing stepped back. The serpent looked angry, the goat cocked her head curiously and the lion showed them an impressively toothy grin. "I concede, you do not look very much like warriors even if you have the necessary courage," the lion said, pacing around the edge of the clearing, ears twitching at the sound of distant helicopter blades. "And I am no monster, merely a creature from a bygone era. Please accept my apology for frightening you; this is something of a stressful night and I may have acted rather shamefully toward you."

Wesley was surprised to hear such gentle words come from the creature. He had been sure that it was about to tear them to shreds and instead it stood before them humbled, apologetic. "That's okay, I mean they did trap you in that big metal box thing, after all. You must be pretty fed up with humans by now," he replied, aiming for cool and confident but coming across as hysterical and desperate. The creature cocked all three of its heads as the helicopter engines came closer, their bright searchlights backlighting the smoke-filled air as they approached.

"You have *no idea*. Now, begone from here; it is time to face the eternal battle again. Maybe next time the odds will be more in my favour," the creature growled as it turned its back to them, the wicked-looking serpent tail flashing them a withering glare as the creature geared up to combat the incoming soldiers. Wesley stepped back, preparing to take its advice and bolt for home. He reckoned he could run all three miles to his front door at that moment, asthma be damned. But Ginger wasn't following him to safety; she was in fact going after the monster, striding up to its scaled hindquarters without care of whether the serpent's head would attack or not.

"Seems kind of stupid, going up against an army with helicopters and machine guns. Why not just run away from them? I could list, like, five places we could hide even a big, three-headed thing like you!" she shouted as it slowly prowled back into the trees, no doubt working out the best angle from which to launch its futile assault. Ginger wasn't expecting the thing to stop; it wasn't like anybody over the age of fifteen really listened to her at the best of times.

But to her amazement the creature did stop, the goat looking back at her thoughtfully. "We tried to outrun Bellerophon a few times," she bleated, "But he always catches up to us eventually. This is our fate. Better to just face him head-on and awaken back on the ash-covered mountains of Tartarus. Run along now, you won't be getting another chance!"

"Well you didn't have Ginger and Wesley with you last time, did you? I'm sure you're super-tough in a fight, but I bet you can't hide for shit. We can show you how until the soldiers leave!" Ginger persisted, sidestepping a half-hearted snap from the serpent as Wesley did something he would never understand until his dying day and ran to catch up to them.

"Come on, she's right. You don't *need* to fight these wankers! Surely there's somewhere you can live in peace? I mean, the world is *massive*! We'll help you find some mountain top or super deep forest in—in Transylvania or somewhere, nobody will ever find you!" he shouted as the first helicopter emerged, blowing the black smoke cloud above into a maelstrom, the searchlight narrowly missing their location by a few metres.

"Yeah, see? Even he agrees, and he's a total fanny! Just come with us!" Ginger added in a voice cracking with fear and desperation.

The creature didn't take its sapphire eyes off the helicopter until it roared overhead and out of sight over the treetops on the opposite side of the car park, only turning its six eyes onto them when the threat had passed. "There is a place that I have been trying to reach for a very long time, though finding a way into it might be difficult," it said slowly, exploring a thought that it hadn't visited for a long time. "Very well, humankind, I accept your offer of allegiance. Let us get away from here and I will explain everything to you."

"You heard the mythical creature, Wesley. Let's get the *fuck out of here*!" Ginger grinned triumphantly.

* * *

Rain cascaded down through a hole in the roof of the derelict warehouse, the puddles it created casting a reflection of the great Chimera sprawled at the centre of the open space. Wesley and Ginger sat on an old crate, illuminated by dim torchlight and looking exhausted beyond words. It wasn't every night a military aeroplane crashed right next to you and you met a mythical creature, after all. They had said little since showing Chimera into the belly of the dilapidated structure, listening instead to the distant sound of helicopters over the burning forest.

"That was so crazy," Ginger said after a while, her voice tiny in the expanse of the warehouse. "How the hell did we get away from those soldiers? I bet they'll be looking for you all over town now, probably roll in the tanks and all sorts yet, mark my words."

Wesley knew she was right; there had been at least three helicopters patrolling the skies around the plane wreck and he was pretty certain they hadn't been looking for survivors or scattered military equipment. He sighed, putting down the notebook he'd been scribbling in. "You're probably right, there aren't many folks like Chimera here around these days. The closest thing I heard was my uncle Lionel's story about seeing a panther on the Norfolk Broads once, only that turned out to be a really big cat. How did they capture you anyway, and where from?" he asked the great creature.

The goat raised her head, fixing them with her slot-eyed gaze. "Lycia, I always awaken in Lycia, though it has changed much throughout the eras. I remember acres of wildland, then olive trees arranged in neat rows. Now your kind has ruined the once verdant fields, replaced with great illuminated settlements and roads of fused stone. I always tried to seek shelter in the wilderness, but Bellerophon's will manifested, in one form or another, and was on my trail right away. This was the first time they attempted my capture instead of killing me outright. Very interesting how things have changed over time," she said, eyes unfocused as the creature was lost in memories.

Ginger stood up from the crate and splashed through the puddles to stand closer to Chimera, carried forward by overriding curiosity. "I've never even heard of Lycia before. This is Charlton On Sea, in England, probably a really long way away from those olive trees or whatever," she said. "And those soldiers, Bellerophon you called them, they're just regular human dudes like us; how can they have hunted you from the, you know, olive tree times?"

"Bellerophon, the *original* Bellerophon, was a human warrior much like them; indeed they are each possessed by a sliver of his consciousness, allowing his spirit to control them. Essentially they are mortal humankind like yourselves, though their will is bewitched by that damned hero of antiquity. He was famed across your civilisation for his martial prowess, the meaning of the word *hero*. He had many great deeds to his name. One is ending my life. Not that he did that alone; he had Pegasus to help him. That fool always was too eager to serve humankind if you ask me," the goat complained petulantly, before being interrupted by the lion, yawning hugely.

"*Anyway*, following my death I was banished to the darkest corner of Tartarus, forced to wait for a chance to escape, to return to the world of man and make an escape for good. Only each time I do escape that labyrinthine hole in the ground and return here, the gods bring the spirit of dear, dead Bellerophon back again, to hunt me down and send me right back. I have died in two hundred and seventy-four different ways and am no closer to peace."

Wesley was on his feet now too, pacing back and forth with excitement, earning a glare from both Ginger and Chimera's serpentine head. "Wait, this all rings a bell actually, this was on *Encarta!* The Chimera myth, all that other Greek mythology—I totally forgot about it! The Chimera was born of a monster called Echidna—"

"Echidna? Like Knuckles from *Sonic 3?*" Ginger interrupted, unable to help herself.

"Don't be a dumbass Ginger, this is serious! Echidna gave birth to Chimera, and Chimera caused mayhem all over Ancient Greece, so a hero had to go and kill her with Pegasus, just like this Chimera, the *actual fucking Chimera*, told us," he said, unable to control his excitement at this revelation. "And where she keeps going back to, Tartarus, that's the Ancient Greek version of *hell* Ginger, literally hell! We can't let her go back there again, we have to help!"

The goat watched the exchange with interest before intervening. "My mother was indeed Echidna, though I would argue the term *monster*, young humankind, and yes I did cause some trouble for your kind in Lycia, I confess you do taste rather nice, lovely texture and marbling. But that was a long, long time ago. Even I can learn some restraint after thousands of years of imprisonment and the occasional bloody death. All I need to do is find a surface that will bear my perfect reflection, and I can be well on my way to the golden fields of Elysium."

Ginger found herself becoming more and more confused. "How does *that* work? You look in the mirror and *poof* you turn invisible? Or maybe, like, go *into* the mirror and live in a weird, backwards world? Because that wouldn't work, surely there would be backwards Bellerophon soldiers there too?" she asked, her imagination working overtime as she tried to work out Chimera's plan. For once Wesley was unable to talk sense into her—he was just as clueless as she was. Chimera cackled at their confused expressions, all three heads snickering in unison.

"An opposite world in a mirror, how nice to see that you humankind still have a strong imagination! The actual plan is a little more *straightforward*, however. Since her demise, my mother has stood vigil upon the great, golden fields of Elysium—"

"Heaven," Wesley muttered to Ginger, who nodded along, enraptured.

The goat fixed him with a withering glare for his interruption before continuing, "As I was saying, my mother awaits me in Elysium, where I will finally be free from my curse and back among the other creatures of my time and many other good perished souls. She will use her skills in witching to open a gate, but it can only manifest on a large, perfectly reflective surface."

Wesley was pacing more than ever now, splashing back and forth across the warehouse floor. "So all you need is a big reflective surface? We just need to find one then and—oh, get you there without anybody noticing under the nose of the army, who are out looking for you with more guns and helicopters than all of the *Rambo* movies put together. Damn it!" he growled, attempting to kick a small stone and missing spectacularly. Ginger peered up through the broken tin roof, her narrow face lit eerily by the moon.

"It's still dark out there. If we're careful, then we can do this. We just need to stick to the shadows, like two ninjas and—a giant, three-headed animal ninja. It'll be a piece of piss, we just need to think of the best mirror we can!" she said, arms thrown wide as she tried to buoy up the little team. Chimera stood up, stretching her huge, muscular body from lion's nose to serpent's nose and fixed her with an intense expression, seemingly cheered on by Ginger's newfound confidence.

"Yes, female humankind, you may be right. If you believe we can find a place suitable for an Elysium gate, then I can certainly get us there," the lion's head growled, only to be interrupted by the serpent's head, "But we would need to know *where* we are going first, don't you think?"

Wesley returned to his pacing, even more furiously than before. "*Obviously*, we just need to work that bit out. What about in town? The banks all have big windows we could use, maybe the front of Tesco's if we go a little out of town? If we think about it, there are loads of big windows, right Ginger?" But his friend was shaking her head impatiently at his ideas.

"Don't be thick, Wes, those army pricks will be watching anywhere like that. And besides, town will still be full of people drinking and shit. I think Chimera here might stand out just a little, right?"

Wesley smacked his forehead with a palm in frustration, knocking his spectacles slightly out of place as he did so. "Of course, I forgot about all of that. Where then? Where's quiet enough for this to work and also has a fuck-off big window to open this portal thing?" he mused. Chimera's six eyes following their conversation back and forth. And then it hit him.

"Ginger, let's take her to school!"

"I don't think she needs GCSEs Wes, what the fuck are you on about?" Ginger snapped in an impatient reply.

"No, that's not what I mean," Wesley explained as patiently as he could. "The drama studio, one whole wall is literally a huge bloody mirror!" Ginger leapt with excitement at the idea and, without thinking, wrapped her arms around Chimera's lion's head before instantly letting go.

"Sorry, not sure if you're into hugs or whatever, but Wesley is a super-genius as usual and has come up with the perfect plan, right? We're taking you home, you big furry, scaly, three-headed *beauty*!" she babbled, but whatever she said next was drowned by the unmistakable sound of helicopter engines above. All three of the derelict warehouse's residents flinched in surprise as a spotlight pierced in through the broken roof and before anyone could move away from it, bathed Chimera in its light.

"Bellerophon is here! It is too late!" the serpent's head hissed with rage and fear, the great beast tensing as if she intended to pounce at the helicopter straight through the roof.

"Too late? Balls to that, you Greek defeatist, let's get the fuck out of here!" Ginger snapped back, dragging a terrified-looking Wesley over to the Chimera. "Lean down a little, let us onboard would you? Oh, and no eating anyone or anything, okay? I don't want to see any bits of soldiers or anything like that, my dad can't afford counselling for me!"

Part Three: The Legend

Wesley and Ginger hung onto Chimera's thick fur as she pounded across the overgrown loading bay of the warehouse, the wind in their faces forcing them to squint. They had barely cleared the rusted perimeter fence when the first Bellerophon trucks rolled in behind them, soldiers debussing and fanning out across the open tarmac with rifles at their shoulders. Ginger was almost strangling the goat with her grip as she craned back to watch the soldiers. Even through the rain, she could see they were already raising rifles to their shoulders, barrel-mounted flashlights illuminating the night.

"Loosen your grip, humankind!" the goat bleated, her mad-looking eyes almost bursting from her head until Ginger did as she was told. Slightly ahead of her lay Wesley, his body across Chimera's shoulder blades with his hands full of mane. The serpent's head looked back from the end of the tail, keeping tabs should anything follow them. "Are you sure that your plan will work? Will this giant mirror definitely be accessible?" asked Chimera's lion's head between laboured breaths as they pounded over a stone wall and into a field, "I have no intention of placing you any further in danger!"

Wesley tried to catch his breath as they cleared a particularly large ditch, Chimera's muscles flexing beneath him upon landing. "It's going to work, trust me!" he replied, trying to sound as brave as he could. Ginger thought she could hear helicopter blades somewhere behind them, unable to shake the very real fear that they were about to be shot to pieces along with Chimera, the merciless loop of the creature's destiny taking them down with it in a hail of machine gun fire. Spotlights swept the open fields behind them as Chimera galloped toward the lights on the edge of town, but she managed to keep ahead of the soldiers until, with a leap that made Ginger's stomach flip, Chimera cleared the high concrete wall that ran alongside the used car garage and landed with a skid on the tarmac.

"Which way, my friends?" the serpent's head hissed from behind them, its eyes urgently scanning the open skies for the Bellerophon helicopters closing in fast. They had lived in Charlton on Sea their whole lives but suddenly found themselves struggling to remember the route to their school, the pressure of the situation bringing them to the edge of panic.

"Right, head right! We need to get onto Townfield Avenue and head down the hill. Move it, Threeheads!" Ginger ordered after a moment that felt something like an eternity, her sense coming back to her just as the first helicopter cleared the roof of the supermarket.

She shielded her eyes as Chimera took off once again, shouldering a pickup truck aside as if it were made of cardboard as she bounded out of the way of the spotlight. A sudden burst of sound made them scream out in terror as the helicopter's machine gun opened fire, the dealership's cheap concrete exploding to one side of them as if Bugs Bunny were about to burst from the ground. Wesley found himself bracing for more gunfire but it never came, though the machine remained glued to them as Chimera bounded out from the exit lane and onto the main road through the town.

It was thankfully quiet at this time of the evening, though the odd car was forced to swerve aside to avoid a giant lion, goat, and serpent amalgamation as it thundered past them. The helicopter was soon joined by another and Ginger, looking over her shoulder, could see more and more headlights multiplying behind them, most likely more Bellerophon soldiers in trucks joining the chase. "Where next? We are running out of time!" the goat's head asked urgently, its ears flapping in the crosswind.

"Okay, okay let me *think*," Wesley screamed in response, frantically running through the route in his head and wishing there was some kind of convenient computer that could do it for him. "I know! Once you get to the seafront turn *left* and then, as we go past the big park, you need to hang another left and head into the housing estate. Our school is just past there!"

Chimera reached the seafront, taking the corner so sharply that the trucks were forced to slam on their brakes to safely follow them, although Ginger was sure she spotted one of them slam broadside into the safety railings along the promenade as the helicopters were forced to flare out over the open water. The horrified faces of late-night pedestrians flashed by as Chimera sped along, reaching the narrower roads of the estate just ahead of the trucks, two of which ran into one another at a narrow junction and forced the whole convoy to fall behind.

"Fuck yeah, we're kicking their arses here!" Ginger whooped, Wesley continuing to give directions ahead of her. Chimera, Wesley, and Ginger carried on with just the streetlights as a guide for a while longer. The soldiers struggled to keep up, until, at Wesley's behest, Chimera vaulted the high wire fence of their school and landed with perfect poise on the tennis court beyond, feline and reptile claws digging an ugly groove into the astroturf.

The creature's six eyes scanned the area as Wesley and Ginger disembarked from her back and ran across the access road to the locked front doors of the school, the paint long-worn by years of students. As they had suspected, the door was locked and didn't budge an inch despite them hammering against it. "We're going to need your strength here!" Wesley called back over his shoulder.

"I rather think it will be needed more here!" the goat's head bleated, her voice urgent over the screeching of tires. Headlights blinded Wesley and Ginger as they turned into the glare of truck headlights, the big vehicles smashing the wire fence into the concrete and swinging ponderously around to box Chimera against the side of the school. They backed into the door as black-uniformed soldiers poured out from the vehicles, rifles at the ready and pointing at Chimera. The mythical beast moved toward the doors also, covering her friends with her sizable body should the soldiers open fire.

"What the hell are you doing? They're going to *kill* you, get out of here!" shouted Wesley, tensing for the inevitable hail of automatic fire. It was a shame, he thought, he'd rather die an old man surrounded by video games. No doubt Ginger would call him a nerd for that, but it certainly beat being carved to pieces by assault rifles in the shadow of their school.

While Wesley contemplated the nature of his doom with eyes screwed shut, Ginger was granted no such indulgence. Instead, she found herself peering around Chimera's scaled hindquarters into the line of soldiers. One stepped up onto the bumper of the centremost truck and lifted a loudhailer to his silhouetted face, "You two kids, get the fuck out of here! I'm giving you ten seconds and then we open fire!" he snapped, his voice clearly used to giving orders. Chimera roared a reply and, to everybody's surprise, fired a stream of intensely green fire above the heads of the military team. The flames seemed to travel a long way, covering at least half of the tennis court behind them before it petered out. It also brushed the canopy of the truck on which the officer stood, forcing him to dive for cover and setting the thick canvas aflame.

"Run ahead, secure the mirror chamber! My mother will see how close we are and open the gate!" snapped Chimera's serpent's head as the soldiers dived into cover, the lion's head continuing to spray the area with unearthly fire. Wesley barely had a chance to move aside as it flicked out on the end of the creature's tail and sunk teeth as long as his forearm into the thick wooden double door. With an almighty heave, it tore the heavy construction right out of the brickwork, flicking it over the horns of the goat's head and into the front of one of the trucks, rocking it back sharply on its suspension.

Ginger hesitated. If Wesley and she stayed, then perhaps they would be too afraid of injuring them to risk opening fire?

"Ginger come on, you heard her! We need to get to the studio, she'll be right behind us, damn it!" Wesley pleaded, tugging at her coat sleeve with all his might, but she shook him off, trying to move around the Chimera's flank in order to stand between her and a surefire end. The great lion's head let out an almighty roar at the scattered soldiers, a further jet of green flame washing over the cheap tarmac, keeping them in cover behind their beleaguered vehicles.

The serpent spotted what Ginger was trying to accomplish and whipped around to face her, slavering jaws just inches from her face, "You should listen to your betters, fool! *Go!*" it hissed and, with no finesse whatsoever, shoved her hard with its snout back into Wesley's waiting arms as some of soldiers finally gathered their wits and began to fire back at Chimera, bullets smacking into the old brickwork of the school above their heads.

"You're going to *die!*" she wailed at the beast over the staccato of fire.

"It's okay Ginger, she's going to make it this time, because this time she isn't alone, right?" Wesley said soothingly.

She got it then. Wesley was right. All of the stories Chimera had told them, all of her lives ended in terrible death—she had always been *alone*. Even the original Bellerophon had been able to rely on Pegasus and subsequent embodiments had always been ever-expanding teams of people. This time she wasn't alone. She had Wesley Lewis and Ginger Wells and they were going to break the cycle of death for good. "Don't you fucking die, you hear me?" she shouted as she turned and led the way into the main hall at a sprint, Wesley at her heels.

The four years that Wesley had spent at Upper Charlton high school had seemed like forever, and he reckoned that he knew every room and corridor inside out at that point. Yet at that moment, chasing his best friend through the dilapidated labyrinth, it seemed like the very maze in which the Minotaur had stalked Theseus. He barely heard anything over his breathing but fancied he could just make out the distant, muffled sound of helicopters as the damned things circled the building above them. Together they passed the science labs and the maths block, and sprinted across the open courtyard where the school library stood until, at long last, they crashed through the battered doors to the drama and dance studio.

Before them, covering the longest wall was the mirror. Wesley had always tried to avoid his own gaze in it. Ginger had scraped her scruffy hair back into a ponytail in it a million times. It was just a mirror and always had been. Until that moment. The mirror writhed with impossible colours in the moonlight, great ripples of green and blue cascading over one another like the surface of a lake in a downpour, phosphorescence dancing in each trough and rise. "Holy shit!" Wesley panted, the drama of their situation momentarily forgotten at the beautiful sight.

Ginger stepped closer as if to reach out for it. "It's *beautiful*, like a star got mixed in with some tie-dye or something," she breathed in agreement, stopping just short of touching the strangely transformed surface as she spotted new movement on the *other side* of the glass. At first, she thought it was her reflection, fighting to be noticed among the kaleidoscope of colour, except it didn't quite move in time with her. Nor did it look exactly like her. The figure was taller, the hair cut into a bob, though Wesley could see that the face was alarmingly similar to his friend's.

Ginger let out a startled gasp, falling to her knees in supplication before the phantom on the other side of the mirror. "Mum? Is that you?" she whispered, reaching for her mother's translucent hand as it ventured out beyond the glass and intertwined its frail-looking fingers with her own. Wesley hardly dared breathe as he watched this ethereal reunion. Even the sound of concentrated gunfire from the front of the building couldn't tear his eyes from the heartbreaking scene before him. "I'm sorry Mum, I'm so sorry. I should have been there when you—when you went away. I should have *said something*. But I was too scared of seeing you like that. I ran away—I'm *sorry*," Ginger cried, tears running down her gaunt cheeks as she stared up into her late mother's gentle face.

A Chimera of Three Parts

Ginger's mother smiled then, brushing her daughter's tears aside with a gentle thumb. "Don't cry, love. There was nothing you could have done. I would never want you to remember me that way," she said, her voice as faint as a gentle breeze. "Elysium is very peaceful and I want for nothing. Now step back honey, I believe it is time for your new friend to join us at last."

Ginger stood slowly, never taking her wide eyes off her mother's form as she backed away to stand at Wesley's side. The floor was shaking under their feet as Chimera ploughed through the corridors toward them, no doubt with the soldiers at her heels.

"And Kerry," Ginger's mother called to her as the approaching battle bore down on them, "take care of your father for me. He's more delicate than he likes to admit."

Chimera exploded into the room a second later, the door frame and plasterboard blasting inwards as if hit by a missile as the great beast skidded into view, varnished floorboards splintering under her claws as she spun back to face the door. "Get back!" her lion's head roared and, as Wesley and Ginger dived for cover, Chimera gouted another jet of emerald fire through the ravaged doorway to keep the soldiers out of the way. Wesley was pretty sure that Chimera was keeping to her promise and not killing the bewitched soldiers, but their screams of terror and frantically shouted orders still worried him.

Then the sounds stopped. All of them. The crackling of magical flames, the chatter of the soldiers and the distant bass thud of the helicopters outside all just *faded away*. Wesley got back to his feet and helped Ginger up. She couldn't take her eyes off her mother's spectral figure beyond the plate glass of the mirror. Yet, her mother was seemingly occupied, leaning slightly out from the pulsing surface to catch Chimera's attention. "Come quickly, we cannot hold the moment in place for long, time will begin to move again!" Her breezy voice filled the silent, still space. "And I would like my daughter and Wesley to be free from here before things return to normal."

Chimera nodded her great lion's head in assent and, with trepidation, approached the portal. Just before she stepped through, however, she turned to face the two humans, all three heads bowing with deference to them. "Thank you, my friends. I have seen courage before, but never with as much respect and selflessness as yours. It only took me a couple of millennia to encounter that, and it was in you two young mortals, not some great warrior or Spartan demigod. See you, as you say, on the slip side," the lion said, blue eyes shining brightly.

"It's the *flip* side, you three-headed nerd. Now get the hell out of here!" Ginger said, her voice coming out somewhere between a cackle and a sob.

"And look after Mrs. Wells; she's pretty cool for a grown-up," Wesley added warmly, earning a gentle smile from the spirit leaning out from the mirror. Chimera bowed deeply to them and prowled through the mirror as if it were nothing more than mist, the rippling colours swallowing her up until only the scaly head at the end of her tail remained.

"Don't get yourselves killed, you little fools. Get away from here!" it snapped, before disappearing from view.

"Love you too, you charming lizard-headed fucker!" Ginger shouted, a smile cracking her face for the first time in a while. Not even the ghost of her mother could

A Chimera of Three Parts

wipe the smile away when she told her off for using foul language. The absurdity of it even made Wesley laugh.

"You two have been incredibly brave. I'm very proud of you both, even if your language is terrible, Kerry," Mrs. Wells said to them, taking their hands in her own. "Now you must leave; I can't hold time in place much longer and this portal is about to close. Make your way outside before all of these confused soldiers unfreeze, okay?"

Wesley nodded his agreement and moved toward the door, noticing that the green flames in the corridor beyond were as still as if they were a scene paused on a VHS. But Ginger wasn't following, unable to leave her mother's side. "I'm not running away from you again! I'll —I want to go with you, into that mirror world place," she begged, her voice filled with sorrow at the thought of losing her mother again.

Mrs. Wells extricated her hand from her daughter's grip and gently cupped her face, her spectral nose inches from her daughter's. "You will do no such thing, honey, and I'll tell you why."

Epilogue

Wesley sighed as the ballpoint pen bounced off his forehead. "Ginger, I'm trying to do my homework here," he grumbled as he readjusted his spectacles. "Just because you're willing to throw away your education doesn't mean I am. And would you please turn that awful music off?" He used to insist that they catch up on homework at his house, but today Ginger was unwilling to leave her dad after she opened up to him about how she was not over her mother's passing. While Wesley understood, he did miss his solid desk and lack of distractions.

Ginger smirked as she leaned over and switched off the radio, banishing 2Unlimited into silence. She picked up her errant pen while she was at it. "Dude, you're such an old woman. Dance music is going to conquer the world, just you see. How can you even concentrate on that dull shit anyway? We rescued a *mythical creature*, man! And Mr. Bell's face when he told us all that the army had been looking for *terrorists* that trashed the school, that was *brilliant!*" she laughed, throwing her maths exercise book onto her unmade bed.

Wesley waved his hands urgently, in the universal signal for *keep it down*. "You want everyone to know? People are saying all sorts of things about that night! Katie Knowles said her dad saw a giant dog run through town and Miss O'Reilly said she nearly crashed into a lion on the main road—we need to keep our heads down. Thank goodness all the soldiers freaked out once Chimera left; I reckon Bellerophon left when she did, you know?" he said in a low voice.

"Who even cares? I'm just glad they were all too busy wandering about and being sick to see us slip out; that's one detention I wouldn't fancy being in. And Chimera got to go to heaven because my mum helped to open the gate. I got to see her again. That was so fucking cool, nothing will ever beat that moment for me as long as I live!" Ginger replied, getting up from her tatty chair to look out of the window upon a rainy town. She wiped her eyes, and Wesley saw her blinking back tears.

Despite the sudden atmosphere, he couldn't help but ask a question that had been on his mind since the previous night, "What did she say to you? Your mum, I mean?"

Ginger stood at the window a while longer before turning to face him, tears now running down her cheeks. "She said that she misses me and that I have to be honest about—well, you know, my emotions and shit. She also said Chimera's mum is pretty cool, that she'd been waiting *centuries* to see the three-headed idiot again. At least my mum won't have to wait that long for me, I guess."

Wesley tried to hide the sudden tightness in his chest and had to look down at his homework to hide his own tears at his friend's words. Ginger had spent a long time swerving around any serious conversation, it was very relieving to hear her talk so openly. It was also a massive relief that Chimera was back with her mother. He reminded himself to tell his mum he loved her when he got home.

"Oh," Ginger said suddenly, her face serious, "she did tell me one more thing, it was about you, and it was really important!"

Wesley stood up, his heart in his mouth at the anticipation of what advice or sagely wisdom Mrs. Wells could have passed on to him, "What was it? What did she say?"

Ginger leaned forward, placing a hand on his shoulder. "That you, Wesley Lewis, are a *massive fucking nerd*, and thank goodness you've got me to make you look cool!"

She sprung lithely aside, cackling like a witch as Wesley made a grab at her, the strange atmosphere immediately broken as they ran from the room, the boy swearing revenge at his antagonist and best friend. From

Ginger's dirty, fingerprint stained mirror, peering between several half-peeled stickers, six mismatched, sapphire eyes watched them go.

I Have Come to Lead You to the Other Shore
David M. Simon

In the ruins of a temple open to the sun-scalded sky,
on a cliff high above a sun-blasted dry sea bed
studded with the sun-bleached bones of fish and men,
an old woman's life is slipping away.
Hermes watches,
from the dizzying heights of Mount Olympus
and from so close he can feel
her shallow breaths on his cheek,
hear each of those breaths
like the fluttering of broken wings
against her ribcage.

In other places, on other planes,
other gods watch and wait.

A shimmer in the air above the ruins,
Thanatos descends and furls his wings.
As he unsheaths his sword, bends a knee
and takes a lock of her sparse grey hair,
the old woman shivers.
She accepts one last breath that she does not return.
Thanatos shakes his head sadly, resheaths his sword,
smooths her hair with a golden hand,
and vaults into the sky.
A sorrowful hush falls across the many realms.

The old woman's shade sits up.
She looks down at the body she still partly occupies,
eyes opening wide in slow comprehension.

Hermes offers his hands and she takes them,
climbs to her feet.
"So that's it, then?"
It is.
"Am I the last?"
You, Elena Pantazis, are the very last.
"I'm glad it finally happened. I've been lonely
for so long."
No more. I have come to lead you to the other shore.
The old woman nods, and they walk hand in hand
out of the temple, into the heat of the day.
She squints up at the blazing sky and says,
"No angels? I expected angels."
Hermes smiles and tilts his face to the unforgiving sun.
Your belief in the old ways was so strong
that you called me down rather than them.
The angels are up there, skulking among the clouds,
refusing to be seen
because they don't get to escort the last human to paradise.
"Well, then, I'm glad it's you. My ancestors
would be proud."

Subdued conversations from behind the temple.
Hermes leads Elena around the corner
to where a crowd has gathered.
"Who are they? I thought I was the last."
These are the gods of other people, other beliefs.
They wish to pay their respects.

A line forms, and Elena receives them all.
Osiris, crook and flail in hand,
verdigris skin glowing softly,
Anubis beside him, jackal eyes despondent.

I Have Come to Lead You to the Other Shore

Odin and Freyja, clad head to toe in gleaming gold.
Kali, her visage so fearsome that Elena shies away,
but Kali cups her face with many tender hands.
The Shinigami bow deeply, reverently.
Maman Brigitte offers Elena a jug of pepper-laced rum.
She drinks until the warmth spreads
through her spectral body.
Sedna offers her a gentle kiss,
and her lips taste of the sea.

The procession continues,
death deities in all their varied forms—
human, animal, fabulous hybrids,
gods as solid as bedrock,
as ethereal as a ray of moonlight.
Some were prayed to by millions,
some rapturously worshiped by a single tribe,
but they all have manifested for this occasion.
At the end of the line, two gods huddle together,
refuse to meet Elena's gaze.
"Who are they?"
Ah Puch and Mictlantecuhtli.
They've never been fond of humans,
but they still felt compelled to see you off.
Elena waves to them shyly, and they skitter away.

When the last goodbye has been said,
when tears have been shed that turn to diamonds
where they splash the ground, the gods decamp—
in swirls of gold dust and spouts of blood,
riding bolts of lightning and horses of air.
Some simply dissipate,
casting longing looks at Elena as they vanish.

"So many gods. What will you all do now?"
In truth, none of us know.
"I thought gods know everything."
Hermes smiles sadly.
It turns out we do not know much at all.
But now it's time. Are you ready?
"I am. I'll miss what this place used to be,
but not the hellscape it's become."
Take my hand.

Down, then, through layers of antiquity they journey—
shale and sandstone, marble and slate,
basalt and granite.
They travel through sinuous veins
of copper, gold, and silver,
past glittering diamonds and rubies,
sapphires and emeralds, tanzanite and tourmaline.
Elena reaches out to stroke the fossilized bones of
monolithic sea creatures embedded in the rock
as they continue their descent.

Soft as feathers wafting on the breeze,
Hermes and Elena drop into an endless cavern,
a towering cathedral of rocky columns,
curtains, and spires,
stone flowing like liquid in folds and waves
down the cavern walls
from the murky gloom high above.
They land on the bank
of the wide, tranquil River Acheron,
the water black as spilled ink, light and shadow
swirling beneath the surface like dancing revenants.
Hard by the shore, a rough-hewn wooden dock,

I Have Come to Lead You to the Other Shore

tall posts at the corners
carved with the screaming faces of lost souls.
A skiff sits low in the water, moored with woven hemp.
It bobs gently,
each time it rubs against the wood of the dock
sounding like a crying child.

Standing in the bow, one hand curled around his pole,
Charon the ferryman waits.
His other hand is held out, palm up.

Elena realizes what it means
and tears trickle down her cheeks.
"I don't have any coins. I won't be able to cross."
We cannot have the last human soul wandering the riverbank.
Hermes pulls an ancient gold coin from his tunic
and folds it into Elena's hands. She wipes her eyes.
"Thank you. I didn't think ghosts could cry."
You are still you. You can still feel sorrow,
but you can feel joy as well.
"Where do you think I'll go?"
That is not for me to decide.
But I believe you will not be judged harshly.
If it were up to me, you would find yourself in the Elysium Fields.
She hugs Hermes,
and it is like holding sunlight in her arms.

Elena places the coin in Charon's hand
and steps down into the boat.
He unties and pushes off from the dock.
"What are you going to do now?" she calls to Hermes.
For now, I'm going to sit here by the river for a while.
Good luck, Elena Pantazis.

David M. Simon

Elena looks back as they cross,
and Hermes is sitting on the dock,
feet dangling,
sandaled toes stirring slow circles in the water.

The Great Heracles
Darius Bearguard

"You work with Heracles?" the balding merchant at the bar asks of Theripus.

"Yuuuuup," slumped over his drink, he replies, half drunk.

"That must be quite the privilege. I've always wanted to meet him. Is he as amazing as everyone says he is?"

"Nnnnnnope," the shorter man says, playing with the olives in his drink. His leather armour clearly reveals him to be a misthios* of some kind.

"Yes, he is! Oh yes, he is! You are simply jealous, Theripus, and you are a liar!" The balding man insists, scoffing at the most incredulous statement.

Theripus motions behind him with his eyes. "See for yourself."

In the corner of the bar lay half a dozen women, in varying states of undress, strewn about, several jugs of wine, platters of dates and salted boar, and propped up on a mountain of pillows lies a man of incredible height and musculature, a chiselled jaw, with long raven hair, and olive—bordering on red—skin. Some call him the Great One, the Demigod, the Slayer of Monsters, the Divine Hero, the Son of Zeus … But most know him as the one, the only, Heracles. Of course, to hear Theripus

---

*Greek title, literally translated to "hired-hand" but more like "hired muscle."

tell it to anyone who will listen, his title should be 'Pain in the Ass.'

"Oh please!" the merchant cries out incredulously, "A well-deserved rest and revelry! He's probably tired from slaying *another* monster. What did he kill, hm? Is it his fourth or fifth Cyclops?"

"Well, I mean…" Theripus considers the man for a long moment before trying once more to educate the masses. "Technically, he didn't kill the first one."

"Oh really?" The merchant laughs, scoffing at Teripus. Heralds carried the news for months to every square in every city inside and outside Greece. 'Heracles, slayer of Titans' they called him.

"Yeah, Herc was four days deep in a drunken orgy with King Eury's daughters. In the temple, mind you. So, as the cyclops approached, a dust storm kicked up and the oaf tripped over the temple wall and he impaled himself." He clicks his tongue and plops his finger in the middle of his forehead. Theripus leans in grinning conspiratorially, "even as a statue, old Apollo can find the bullseye every time." He chortles. "Anyways, the thing kept thrashing about as it was dying, screaming that it couldn't see, and it was throwing off Sir-humps-a-lot's rhythm. So, they went out and slit its throat."

"See! A wise fighter strikes when opportunity—"

Theripus raises his hand and cuts in. "The *daughters* slit his throat. He was too drunk and uhhh … *backed up*, to even know what was going on outside of his orgy. An hour later people came to see what the commotion was and he just claimed the kill. Telling everyone," he puffs up his chest and pumps his fists up and down with a mocking macho voice. "I tricked the beast into—"

"Why do you do this at every bar we co-o-o-o-me to?" a voice says from behind a table against the wall.

Defensively, Theripus replies, "*Hey!* It's not my fault! Uhh…" Therepus hesitates, motioning to the merchant. "What's your name again?"

"Ceritur!" the merchant answers, offended. "We've been talking for—"

"Yeah, great," Theripus waves his hand dismissively, "He started it!"

"I know he started it." A chubby and unkempt looking man with a bulbous nose sits up from behind the table, scratching his short and well trimmed beard. "The whole damn bar knows he started it. I'm asking why do you keep doing *this?* No one is ever go-o-o-o-o-ing to believe you."

"Hold on," the merchant objects, "you mean to tell me you're on *his* side? And who in Tartarus are you, then?"

"Phestus, and it doesn't matter what side I'm on—"

"The lion!" the merchant cuts in.

"No, no, no, *no!*" Phestus shouts, slamming his small fist onto the table. "No! We are not going to—"

"He slew the great lion; they say you can see the gleam of the pelt a league away," The merchant proclaims proudly, gesturing to the pelt strewn over a pair of buxom maidens.

"So, *Phestus* here made Herc a chicken dinner—" Theripus interrupts.

"Okay, I g—g-g-g-g-uess we are going to—" Phestus says, rolling his eyes.

"—And we're talking, ten or fifteen chickens here. Herc can eat, let me tell you. Anyways, our chef left the carcasses out for soup the next day. Well, shiny fur over there found the heaps of dead birds with some meat still on 'em and ended up choking to death on a leg bone."

The merchant shakes his head. "Doesn't matter if it wasn't in the lion's den, he still laid a trap and killed—"

"*He* didn't kill anything. None of us did. The thing was dead and we didn't even know. We searched eight days in the wrong direction following ol' 'Master of the Hunt' over there."

"We found the thing as we were about to give up," Phestus finishes.

The merchant considers both men, looking at one then the other trying to detect a hint of fabrication. Swallowing hard, he posits "The Hydra?"

Theripus pauses for a moment, furrowing his brow. "What was his ridiculous nephew's name? Lillian? Lyiandra? Lola?"

"Lolaus," Phestus replies excitedly. "The kid with the hair and the—"

"The booze! Yeah!" Theripus says sitting upright and letting out a huge guffaw. "That kid made amazing wine." He smiles, longingly. "Well, the master of beverages over there couldn't handle whatever bathhouse swill the kid brewed up the night before. Turns out all that ... *stuff* mixing in his stomach, and then with whatever was in the swamp, was quite flammable."

"Eurystheus almost lost the who-o-o-o-le kingdom that day," Phestus answers, shaking his head slowly, flashes of the terrible incident seen in his stone gaze. "The flames were green. I'll never forget that smell as the hydra burned alive ... or the sounds of the children..." his voice trails off, cold.

The merchant stares at Phestus for a moment before changing the subject. "Artemis' Hind?"

"She lost it to him in a drinking contest," Theripus answers nonchalantly.

"The stables of—"

"Herc caught King Augeas's kid getting intimate with a satyr," Theripus interjects.

Phestus jumps in with a furrowed brow, "No-o-o-o-o-t that there's—"

"Not that there's anything wrong with that." Theripus nods to his companion, receiving a comforted nod in return. "But still, the prince was so worried we'd say something to the king, he agreed to do Herc a favour. So Herc set up the whole thing with King Augeas' stables, and got the kid to sell the story to his old man."

"The Boar?" the merchant asks, a little less confident.

Theripus' eyes widen, briefly, but he remains silent, unwilling to be the one to tell the story. After a long moment, Phestus answers. "He was trying to have sex with me."

"The boar was trying—"

"Not. The Boar." Theripus interrupts, not making eye contact with either.

"W-what!?" the merchant asks, physically taken aback by the response.

Theripus holds up his hand and shakes his head. "He was drunk. Phestus' screams were … it scared the pig. Scared *the valley*. I don't…"

"We don't usually … I was feeling experimental, and Herc was … well." Phestus smiles the smile of a boy in love. His cheeks flush as he remembers the long months together and the road, and he looks over to Herc, and in that brief glance at his drunken unconscious employer, drool running from the corner of his mouth, he remembers, and shakes his head in revulsion. "I don't really like to talk…"

"It's just better if we don't discuss—"

"But—"

Theripus turns to the balding man, his eyes with a darkness to them, emphasising every word. "Trust. Me."

The merchant looks again from Theripus to Phestus. Many men have tried to call down the deeds of heroes, and many more still tried to claim the great triumphs as their own. But behind both sets of voices there was always an air of desperation. Of bravado. Men full of pomp and bluster. But these two, they look exhausted, worn by the road, and almost ashamed of the tales. After a moment the merchant scoffs, banishing the doubt from his mind. "You must think me a fool if you imagine that I could be tricked by such—"

Theripus continues with a sigh. "He promised Artemis not to tell anyone about drinking her under the table if she made him a Stymphalian roast bird for dinner."

"Oops," Phestus chimes in before waving one of the barmaids over to refill his decanter of wine.

"The Bull!" The merchant pounds his fist on the bar, startling the barkeep and the few concubines milling about. "The Cretan bull! I saw the cursed thing myself when I went to—"

"The half vomit, half swamp water," Theripus replies flatly, finally eating one of the olives he's been playing with.

"I can't believe yo-o-o-o-u kept that stuff." Phestus shivers, disgusted by just talking about it.

"It burned a Hydra—among others—to ash in the space of ten minutes. No way I was going to let …

The Great Heracles

whatever it was, go to waste. However, along with being flammable, it was also noxious. Smell too much of it and you'll pass out. We just threw a jar of it at the damned thing and it fell over after a minute. We tied and bound it, and then waited for it to wake up." Theripus plugs his nose, "Took almost a week."

"The man eating horses of Thrace!"

"Mmmm well, technically that's a misnomer," Theripus offers, tossing an olive into the air and failing to catch it in his mouth. He looks around hoping no one had noticed, then upon seeing both men distracted, grabs the olive from his chest and pops it in his mouth, pumping his fist in celebration.

Phestus scratches his chin as he sniffs a piece of goat cheese and turns his nose up at it. "Technically they never ate anyone, they just bared their teeth a lot."

"Turns out they got a field where they grow nuts and olives pretty close to each other. So the horses ate both and it makes this mushy stuff that gets caught in their teeth and…" Theripus repeatedly rubs his lips over his teeth, imitating the animals.

"So while Herc got drunk, we mashed nuts and oil and then crammed it in the gums of some random horses we found in a field. Then, y'know, the pa-a-a-a-rade."

"What about the belt of Hippolyte?"

"Ah yes, the legendary girdle belonging to the queen of the Amazons," Phestus proclaims with a knowing grin, pouring himself another glass of wine. "Warrior goddesses of legendary beauty and fighting prowess. The daughters of Ares himself, as wise as they are stunning. A Queendom of women, and so beautiful, men fall to their knees in defeat before so much as unsheathing a sword.

Their truce with us hangs by a thread, and only by giving them ships full of men when they come ashore, is the peace maintained."

"Exactly!" the merchant asserts, feeling his point proven.

"Yeah. *Exactly*," Theripus offers with an equally knowing grin..

"What … What do you mean *exactly*?"

"An island of gorgeous women who are raised from the time they can walk to kill, on an island no one has ever seen and lived to tell the tale?" Theripus offers with a grin.

"…Yes?" the merchant offers hesitantly, feeling he's fallen for some sort of trap, though not sure what it is.

"My friend, they're a *fable*. A simultaneous male wet-dream and horror story. No one knows where this island might be, let alone actually seen it? The only proof it exists is a ship of women coming and taking prisoners for breeding?" Phestus offers rhetorically.

"And wouldn't you know it, it's almost always political dissidents or would-be revolutionaries who are taken away!" Theripus says in a patronising tone. "They're a bluff by the Greek kings to keep old men in line, and young men horny. They find a dozen or so strong, capable, and drop dead gorgeous women, put them on a boat, and play out the whole thing, and the Greek kings pay them all handsomely for the service. Phestus figured it out when he recognized one of the 'Amazons' from a drunken night in Sparta, and we bluffed the king right back," Theripus says, laughing.

"King Eurystheus, growing desperate," Phestus continues, sounding proud, "gave him an impossible task, as the end of the labours were drawing near. Herc showed up before the king's court and claimed that a belt he had some seamstress in Thebes make in exchange for 'a ride on the great Greek bull—'"

"Neither of us likes that he calls it that," Theripus says shaking his head. "I just want to make that clear."

"—Belonged to the Queen of the Amazons. It's not like the king could call Herc a liar! How could he? You can't prove a belt that never existed in the first place, worn by mythological women you made up, isn't the girdle in front of you."

"T-t-this..." The merchant stutters, swallowing hard to clear his stomach from his throat, "This is ... This is blasph—"

"Geryon, the three headed ogre, and Herc knew each other back when Herc was still married to Megara," Theripus offers, clearly enjoying himself more and more as they recount each tale. "They were drinking buddies."

Pouring another glass, Phestus offers sadly, "Geryon didn't even kno-o-o-o-w he was on the list."

"Herc, the moment he saw Geryon and his three heads, knew he couldn't kill the only man to ever drink him into unconsciousness. So, Herc resigned himself to taking the loss, and they got drunk on Herc's weird cup/boat thing as a last hoorah."

"Wait!" The merchant interrupts, "What do you mean!? He killed him! I know he did, I've seen the three heads, they're—"

"Oh, we didn't say he didn't die, just that Herc *didn't ki-i-i-i-ill him*," Phestus interrupts.

Theripus purses his lips and shakes his head. "He was huge, and with that much muscle, and that drunk, when he fell out of the boat ... he sank like a stone."

"We dove for a week—"

"*We* dove for a week?" Theripus turns and asks Phestus, clearly offended by the plural.

"I was there!" Phestus shouts back defensively, but Theripus maintains his glare for a long moment, "I was in the cup thing!" Theripus lowers his head an inch, maintaining his scowl. "Fi-i-i-i-ne, *he* dove for a week," Theripus turns back with a self-satisfied nod, "with a saw, before we finally hacked all three heads off."

"The apples of Hesperides?" The merchant asks, a solemn and torn look encroaching on his face, hearing that his hero was not who he claimed to be.

Both men bob their heads back and forth before Theripus replies, "Actually that one's—"

"Yeah, pretty much accurate—"

"Like, right on the drachmae—"

"Atlas is an idiot," Phestus says, shaking his head before taking another drink. "Why even come back with the apples? Just leave the big dumb—"

"I don't remember having to lie to anyone about that," Theripus turns to confirm with Phestus.

"Yeah, me neither." Phestus confirms.

"Aha!" the merchant exclaims, pounding his fist on the table, now causing Heracles and his mountain of concubines to stir. "There you have it! You are damned by your own forked tongues."

"Ugh, here we go," Theripus sighs, motioning for the barkeep to pour him another.

"I told you. I told yo-o-o-o-o-o-u this would—"

The merchant paces, his chest puffed up and his cheeks red. "You would besmirch the good name of mighty Heracles, all for what? To see a great man such as he—"

"Did you hear literally nothing else? It's always some little thing that you guys latch onto, like the rest of it—" Theripus, raising his voice, turns to the merchant.

"You said he wasn't the greatest. That *all* the stories were a lie concocted by—"

"I didn't say they were *all* a lie—"

"When it was you two telling lies *allllll* along!"

"Unbelievable," Theripus says, throwing up his hands.

By this time Heracles, fully undressed, arrives at Phestus' table, fumbling to put on the lion armor. "Telling my tales again, you two?" He lets out a most unbecoming belch and begins to clothe himself, still unsteady on his feet.

Theripus straightens up a bit, and with a forced smile says, "You know us, always spreading the word of your greatness." He clears his throat, grabbing his sword from the bar counter.

"Don't listen to these two, kind sir." Heracles pounds his chest, trying to clear his oesophagus, and finally lets out a second rancid belch. "I'm just trying to serve the people of Greece. Don't call me a hero." He offers a winning smile.

"So humble too," the merchant says meekly, wiping away a tear. "Thank you. Thank you, dear Heracles, for keeping us all safe."

Heracles smiles, raises his hand, and sways a bit, still weak kneed from the orgy. "Your thanks is more than I deserve. Just because I've slain more monsters than any man who came before me, doesn't make me a hero. If not for good men and women like you keeping our economy strong ... Well, I just don't know where I'd be. I swear to you, I'm going to make the Greek kingdoms great again."

"Ahem." The barkeep clears his throat, and holds out an ornate amphora, jingling the drachmae within.

Heracles' eyes flash, and he makes a show of searching his mostly naked person for a coin pouch, being sure not to look at the merchant. "Please, good Heracles, it is on me." He smiles, walking up to the barkeep and splashing a few coins into the pottery.

Heracles smiles a winning smile, and gestures to the merchant in humble praise. The barkeep clears his throat and motions to Theripus and Phestus, and then to the pile of concubines in the corner. "Some for my compatriots as well?" Heracles asks with a sly smile, "I'd be lost without them." He winks.

"Of course." The merchant smiles nervously and digs the last of his coin out of his purse, dropping it into the pot.

Heracles clicks his tongue against the roof of his mouth, looking in awe at the balding merchant, and grabs him by the shoulders. "I will not forget you, Greek. When I stand once again, before the greatest seat of power—" he points up with a nod "—I will tell him of the kindness you've shown me here today." Theripus and Phestus both roll their eyes, but manage not to groan as they finish collecting their things. "Come now compatriots, we have a hound to tame!" Heracles leads them out into the early morning light. Theripus offers a hand out to Phestus who smacks it away, jumping down from the bench on unsteady satyr legs. The merchant looks over at the stretching satyr, nearly spitting out his wine.

The Great Heracles

The pair follow behind Heracles, but Phestus stops at the door and turns. "Thanks for the drinks p-a-a-a-a-l." Then he carries on.

The merchant's hands creep slowly up to his shoulders. All thoughts of the scolding his wife will give him for the sale of their bulls going to pay off a whoring tab disappearing as he says quietly, "He touched me … He actually touched me."

Intoxication:
A Pandora's Box Retelling
Katherine Shaw

Zune stood, straight-backed, hands laced behind him, staring out over the plains. Weak lights winked at him in the darkness, taunting him. Compared to the shimmering luminescence of the tower, they were little more than specks in the murk, but that was irrelevant. The light was *his*, all of it.

'Darling, come away from the balcony. You're only causing yourself stress.'

Zune felt a soft hand settle on the top of his arm, and some of the tension left his heavy shoulders. His eyes remained on the lights, each twinkle a dagger in his heart. 'It isn't right, Hersha. It's an affront to everything we stand for.'

'It's done.' She moved her arms around his waist and pressed her lithe body against his. 'There's nothing you can do, so it's best to forget it.'

Zune closed his eyes, revelling in his wife's touch. For the briefest of moments, the pain and anger left him, and he was at peace, but as soon as his eyes fluttered open again, it crashed over his body like a tidal wave.

Betrayal.

His fingers twitched and he pictured taking the revolver out of its holster, going down to that stinking village himself and showing them who was boss. It wasn't enough, though, and Proto had left the running of Krakos to her stupid sister while she set up that godforsaken network at the next town over.

Treacherous bitch.

Zune took a deep breath to steady himself. Revenge on Proto wouldn't be enough; she'd done too much. Her theft and betrayal had given the plebs an upper hand they didn't deserve, and it was already spreading through their populace like a virus.

A virus.

A devilish grin spread across Zune's face, and he turned to face his wife with blazing eyes.

'That's it!'

* * *

'He's perfect, Festus. Flawless.'

The old scientist flashed a toothy smile at Zune and deep wrinkles pooled around his eyes. Excitement bubbled in Zune's stomach; the man had outdone himself this time. He returned his gaze to the window and watched the young man lifting weights in the training yard. He was the epitome of physical perfection —tall, dark and muscular, with a chiselled jaw and thick chestnut hair. He would be irresistible to men and women alike.

And he's just Epi's type.

'Bring him to the tower this evening. I have a task for him.'

'He'll be an excellent companion for you, sir. I think he's my most successful experiment to date.'

'Oh, he's not for me.' Zune fought to keep the malicious delight out of his voice. 'He's going beyond the walls, to Krakos.'

Festus gasped, sending himself into a coughing fit. Zune waited patiently as the old man finished wheezing and finally stood up straight again. 'What? Sir, with all due respect, he isn't ready for a life in the city, never mind beyond the walls! He's had barely any social training and would be highly susceptible to deception or manipulation.'

Zune placed a hand on Festus's shoulder and allowed a bark of laughter to escape his lips. 'He's perfect. Have him with us by six o'clock. In the meantime, I have another job for you.'

* * *

There was electricity in the air as Zune and his retinue stood in the grand hallway of his tower, awaiting the arrival of Festus and Pando, the young man hand-chosen for this particular task.

In a way, it's a shame. I would have liked to see more of him...

A cough from his left prevented Zune's imagination from drifting any further down that line of thought. Sometimes it was like Hersha could read his mind. That, or she just knew her husband too well by now.

'I don't know what this plan is of yours, love,' Hersha muttered, keeping her eyes expectantly on the large double doors. 'But I certainly hope you know what you're doing. We've built a good life here, a virtual paradise compared to our fathers' and grandfathers'. What does it matter if the lower classes experience a little of that comfort?'

Zune's head whipped around to face her, eyes blazing. 'They are *not* our equals. Power like that which Proto stole—*stole!*—from us and handed over with no thought to the consequences is what separates our civilised society from their rudimentary, inferior way of life. Now they have a taste of it, what will they do next?'

'You really think it so dangerous, Father?' Zune's eyes darted to his son, Herran, casually leaning against the wall with that air of nonchalance he always carried. 'So they have a couple of generators. Let them set up their rickety little network. They're nothing but ants compared to us. Insects.'

Zune took a step towards his youngest child. Herran was a gifted young man—that fact was universally acknowledged throughout Eutympios—but his smart mouth got him into trouble more often than not, and Zune would not stand for his attitude today. 'Have you ever been set upon by a swarm of bees, Herran?'

Herran blinked. 'Well, no, but—'

'A single bee is harmless enough, but an entire swarm can take down the mightiest man. Proto was a dear friend, yet she and her sister are putting everything our family has built since the Annihilation at risk. If we stick our heads in the sand, they could be upon us before we know it.'

'I can't wait to see him. He sounds scrummy.'

Aunt Affy always managed to pull a smile out of Zune, and he barely repressed a chuckle as the older woman licked her ruby red lips. She was older than him by a decent stretch of years, but she still looked as poised and immaculate as she always had, with tight ringlets of golden-brown locks pinned delicately on her head and a flowing, silk gown draped across her perfectly proportioned body. While in the opulent confines of the tower, she looked right at home; one step beyond the walls, she would look like a goddess amongst mortals.

'I think you'd tear him to pieces, Auntie.' Zune threw her a wink, which prompted a musical laugh from his aunt and an audible *tut* from Hersha at his side. Zune's wife was stern and strong, but it was one of the many things he loved about her. Someone had to put him in his place occasionally, and she was the only one with permission to do so.

'Still,' Affy remarked, adjusting her gown so her ample cleavage was more prominent, 'there's nothing wrong with having a look, is there?'

Zune opened his mouth to offer a cheeky retort which would no doubt result in a dressing down from his wife, but was cut short by the chime of the doorbell. Excitement fluttered in Zune's chest as he strode to the door.

It begins. Revenge.

He pressed his hand to a rectangular sensor on the wall, and the large, metal door slid open to reveal Festus and Pando, resplendent in only a pair of loose trousers and sandals. Zune's breath caught in his throat—he had already forgotten how beautiful this man was. It did seem like somewhat of a waste to send him off to Krakos...

No. He's perfect.

Zune shifted his focus to Festus. 'You've excelled yourself, doctor!' He knew formal qualifications had died off with the Annihilation, but the best and brightest of the New World liked to be recognised in some fashion, even if the terms were archaic. 'What does everyone think?'

Pando stood shyly in the doorway as Zune's family stepped forward to examine their visitor. Hersha and Herran didn't get too close, Zune's wife raising an eyebrow at the awkward, semi-naked man before them, while Herran was already grinning with mischief. Aunt Affy, of course, sashayed straight to Pando. His eyes widened as she traced a long, red fingernail down one of his pectoral muscles.

'Oh, I like him, Zuney.' Affy giggled as Pando stared at the ceiling to avoid her close, penetrative gaze. 'Look! He's shy.'

Zune came to Pando's rescue, pulling him to the side and placing an arm around his broad shoulders. 'Yes, he is, so let's not scare him off straight away, hm?' He urged the young man forward a few steps, dodging Affy along the way. 'Pando, meet my beautiful wife and my son, Herran. The rest of the family will be along shortly, I'm sure. Here, make yourself at home.'

Zune left Pando making polite conversation with Hersha, who at least knew how to act with decorum around guests, and took Festus off to one side. 'And what about the ... other project?'

Festus flashed a wide smile full of large, yellow teeth. 'I believe I have finalised the plans. I can have it with you in a week.'

Zune eyed his new house guest, now comfortably engaging Eutympios's best and brightest in conversation over a glass of chilled wine. He would do well.

'Perfect.'

***

Zune was virtually vibrating with excitement as he and Hersha sat down for breakfast on the seventh day since Pando's arrival. Festus had sent a message the previous evening confirming his order was ready, and he'd be there any minute.

'I take it Pando will be leaving us today?' Hersha's bright voice broke Zune's reverie, and he turned his head to see his wife beaming with a joy she didn't even attempt to conceal.

Zune resisted the urge to roll his eyes. Hersha was renowned for her jealousy, and the entire household fawning over Pando had increasingly irked her as the days went on. He himself had managed to keep his eyes off Pando as much as possible, with the exception of the day he stumbled upon his training session with Atha in the courtyard.

One of Zune's eldest—and, although he would never admit it, favourite—children, Atha had insisted on preparing the naive young man for a life beyond the city walls, and Zune had required little persuasion to allow a day's training in basic combat and self-defence. The plains around Krakos and the neighbouring hovels were rife with bandits, wild animals and twisted creatures born from the aftermath of the Annihilation, and she thought it cruel to send him out there without the means to look after himself.

Such a kind and thoughtful woman. She must get that from her mother.

Atha had dedicated much of her youth to athleticism and was a formidable fighter, so it was quite the spectacle to see her putting this impressive youth through his paces. It was a hot and humid day, and Pando's hard muscles gleamed with sweat as the sun beat down on his half-naked body. Zune watched from the doorway, half-hidden in shadow, unable to take his eyes off Pando as he took down Atha with a swift kick to her ankles. He moved with a grace and fluidity that sent prickles running over Zune's skin. It was mesmerising. Of course, Atha recovered quickly, flipping the young man over and pinning him to the ground with ease. She bested him every time, but he was improving.

Pando laughed humbly as Atha helped him back up, taking his defeat in his stride. He truly was a sweet and wholesome creature, blissfully unaware of his role in Zune's plan. Zune had walked away before his thoughts were able to travel any further down that path. Pando was remarkable, but he was a tool, a perfect specimen created by Festus to serve the state and their leaders—nothing more.

'Darling?'

Zune blinked, and he was back at the breakfast table, Hersha waiting expectantly for an answer. He reached into his brain to remember her question, and fresh excitement washed through him. 'Yes, my love! Festus is on his way with a special gift for Pando and Epi, his blushing bride.'

Hersha snorted at that. While Proto was intelligent, thoughtful and reflective, her sister was rash, outspoken and impulsive. 'And you think Epi will accept Pando and this gift without question? She may be bold, Zune, but she isn't stupid. She won't trust you.'

Zune smirked and tapped his nose. 'She won't have to.'

Hersha frowned but had no chance to follow up with more questions as the doorbell chimed and Zune rushed forward to admit Festus, who strolled in holding a heavy wooden crate. His advanced years hadn't diminished his strength, and he carried it easily, hefting it onto the floor in the centre of the hallway. 'Shall I?' He grinned, holding up a crowbar.

Zune clapped his hands together, giddy as a schoolgirl. 'Yes! Let's finally see it.'

Festus shoved the end of the crowbar under the lid and levered it off. It clattered against the hard tiles as Zune rushed forward to look inside. Butterflies came to life in his stomach as his eyes passed over the gleaming metal figure within.

This was it. This would change everything.

'Pando!' he called, his deep voice booming through the building. 'I have something for you!'

* * *

Pando walked slowly down the dirt road leading from the gates of Eutympios, dragging his small trolley behind him, too busy staring around in wonder to listen to Herran's chattering by his side.

Zune had sent his charismatic son to keep Pando company during the long trek to Krakos, and to introduce him to the person he had been told would be the love of his life. While he appreciated having a travelling companion, his long stories about how he had bested his rivals in debates and joke-telling contests were of little interest compared to their new surroundings.

Pando had been told very little about the plains they would be traversing to reach his new home, but his impression had been of a horrific, nightmarish place. True, in comparison to the city, they were simple—fields of dry grass and sparse shrubbery as far as the eye could see—but they were also quiet, peaceful and generally quite pleasant.

He took a deep breath as Herran continued his story. Out here—without the close confines of the tower rooms, without all the machinery and generators piled up inside the city walls, without so many people—the air was fresh and clean. Maybe life in Krakos would be better than Pando expected.

Which reminds me…

'Herran?' he asked, looking back at the chatty young man assigned as his escort. 'What do you know of my bride to be?'

Herran grinned, no doubt aware that Pando hadn't been listening up to this point but not seeming to care. 'She's beautiful, of course. Otherwise my father wouldn't have matched you both.'

Pando frowned. 'Come on, Herran, you've been talking non-stop since we left the tower. You must have more than that!'

Herran's eyes twinkled with mischief. Pando had already seen the curly-haired knave play tricks on many of the members of Zune's household in the short time he had been staying in the tower, and that glint in his eye always suggested he was hiding some trick or other. 'She's passionate and giving, a lover of animals. Strong, willful, but also generous.'

'But that all sounds … well, wonderful?'

Herran laughed. It was a light, whimsical laugh that at once was charming and infuriating. 'Of course! What did you expect?'

Pando shrugged. 'Surely there's a catch? No offence, but this sounds almost too good to be true.'

Herran's smirk didn't budge, and he threw a gangly arm around Pando's shoulder. 'Have you seen yourself, man? I'm sure she'll be thinking the same! You're the real catch.' He gave Pando an affectionate squeeze. 'Anyway, I don't know about you, but I've had enough walking for today. Let's set up camp, and tomorrow you can finally meet your future bride!'

* * *

Pando barely slept a wink that night. He tossed and turned under the canvas of his tent, insides writhing with equal parts nerves and excitement.

This Epi ... she sounded fantastic, but it all seemed a little too ... *easy*. He'd been hand-picked by Zune— leader of the city and father of a multitude of handsome, eligible young men—welcomed into the royal tower and promised the hand of a beautiful young woman. On top of that, Zune had even handed over a wonderful gift to celebrate the union.

Pando's mind wandered to the crate, dragged inside the protection of the tent while the trolley remained outside. He had been stunned when Zune presented him with the bot, cased in gleaming chrome and covered all over in fine, intricate designs which took Pando's breath away. He's seen bots before, of course, but the ones in Festus's laboratory and even the few servicing Zune's tower were nothing in comparison to the splendour of this automaton.

'Just don't try to plug it into the network,' Zune had warned as he handed the figure over to Pando to inspect for himself. Around three feet tall, it was like the most beautiful doll he could imagine. 'There's no programming inside. It's purely decorative. Understand?'

Pando understood and couldn't wait to see it on display in his new home. He was sure Epi would love it.

Pando rolled onto his back, the dawn sunlight already beginning to illuminate the tent. The sound of soft snores drifted in from Herran's tent next to his; he could sleep for hours more. Pando sat upright, eyes fixed on the crate blocking the entrance. It was a wedding gift, meant to be shared with Epi, but surely Zune wouldn't mind if he took one last look before presenting it to his bride?

He shuffled forward on his knees and easily pried the lid off the box, hefting the bot out onto the floor. It was as beautiful as he remembered; nothing back in Eutympios matched it. He sat back and crossed his legs, turning the bot over to examine the detailed patterns etched all over its casing. He ran his hands over them, enjoying the changing texture under his fingertips. They froze as he noticed a sudden change where the casing fell away at the back of the bot's head. A port?

Pando turned the bot over, and his suspicions were confirmed: there, at the very centre of the bot's round head, was a Universal Upload Port—the kind they used all over Eutympios to share data on their hyperspeed network. There were rumours that Krakos had set up a rudimentary network of their own using much of the same technology. Pando frowned as he traced his finger around the edge of the square slot.

But Zune said there was no programming inside.

'Rise and shine, Pando!' He jumped at the sound of Herran's voice, as bright and cheerful as ever. 'How about some breakfast before we finish our journey? You get the trolley packed up while I get a fire going.'

* * *

Sweat beaded on Pando's brow as he stared at the battered, wooden door. There was no doorbell or intercom system, just an old, brass knocker in its centre, which Herran had used to drum against the wood and alert Epi to their presence.

He had been giddy with anticipation when he set out from Eutympios the previous day, but now that they stood on the threshold his stomach was churning with nerves. He had heard great things about the woman he was going to meet, but she didn't know anything about him and could reject him outright. Zune had told Pando she would be thrilled with the surprise, but how could he be so sure?

Herran stood beside him, casually leaning against the doorframe as if he didn't have a care in the world. Being one of Zune's children, he probably didn't, but even now, outside of his father's jurisdiction, he was brimming with confidence and self-assurance. How Pando envied him. Despite Zune's family fawning over his physical appearance, he knew he was nothing compared to them.

Pando's chest tightened as the door finally swung inward to reveal a confused—and *breathtaking*—young woman. Unlike the polished and almost ethereal beauty of Zune and the rest of the upper-class families of Eutympios, Epi looked … *real*. With thick dark hair cut into a shaggy pixie cut, scruffy dungarees rolled up to her knees, and streaks of oil adorning her high cheekbones, she was like no one Pando had ever seen in the city.

'Who are you?' she asked bluntly, looking Pando up and down in a way that made him feel like a breeding bull being sized up by a prospective buyer. Her eyes darted across to Herran, still leaning casually against the doorframe. 'Herran? What on Earth are you doing here?'

Herran pushed off from the doorframe and spoke with a confidence and bravado Pando could only dream of. 'You don't seem very happy to see me, cousin. I come in peace, I assure you!'

Epi raised her eyebrows at him before turning her attention back to Pando. He thought he saw the corner of her mouth start to twitch into a small smirk. 'And him?'

Herran threw an arm around Pando's shoulders and gave him a gentle shake. 'He's for you!' That elicited a bark of bright laughter from Epi, which made Pando's heart race. 'Someone to keep you company, and to show all is well between the two branches of our extended family.'

Epi met Pando's gaze, and her face softened. 'Well, he certainly *is* handsome.' He felt heat rise up into his cheeks, warming his face. Epi laughed again—it was a joyful, natural sound Pando could listen to all day, every day. 'And shy, too! But would an athlete from the city really be happy living in a shack in Krakos? We live simple lives here.'

'Yes ... of course.' Pando stuttered, willing the blush to leave his cheeks. 'That's if ... well, obviously ... if you'll have me.'

Epi's smile broadened. Despite her stern features, it was warm and reassuring, and butterflies erupted in Pando's stomach upon seeing it. She placed a gentle hand on his arm, sending goosebumps racing across his flesh. 'Come on in.'

* * *

Life with Epi was divine simplicity.

Although their home was small and sparse, it had everything Pando could need, including the love of a good woman. He and Epi fell for each other easily, and within days they were lovers. She had a lust for life that bewitched Pando, and every moment with her was a joy. Their days drifted by with a steady routine of chores, Pando carrying out physical work around the house and outside in Epi's smallholding, while Epi worked on the rudimentary computer network she and her sister had set up in the village.

Pando had yet to meet Epi's sister, Proto. Epi seemed reluctant to go into much detail about her, saying she had committed herself to spreading essential technology throughout the deprived towns and villages while Epi improved things at home, but little more. Proto would return once her work was complete, but that could be in weeks, months, or years. Epi missed her, but life had to go on.

Talk of Proto's work on the network inevitably led Pando's thoughts to the bot, still safely stored in the crate in the corner of the dining area, waiting to be opened on their wedding day. The two sisters had built the first basic computer-station, hooked up directly to a generator Proto had brought from the city. It was extremely rudimentary, cobbled together from rusting parts scavenged from in and around the city, but it worked, and Proto's hard work meant Krakos was now connected to much of the known population of the plains. The people could finally communicate with each other, develop new and better ways of working, and bring some prosperity into their lives. Where before there was darkness and isolation, there was now a sparkling community filled with hope.

Occasionally Pando would catch himself staring at the dark screen and trailing cables, imagining hooking up the bot and seeing it come to life before his eyes, but he shook his head and moved on. Zune had been clear: there was nothing in it, even if there was a port built into the back.

Meanwhile, Epi threw herself headfirst into wedding planning. Krakos was a simple place, with very little wealth to go around, but the basic gardens the villagers kept produced beautiful flowers for Epi to wear in her hair, which she accepted with immense gratitude. She wouldn't wear a dress—she had never felt comfortable wearing them—so she made herself an elegant jumpsuit, hand-stitched from a roll of luxurious silk she had brought with her when she and Proto had left the city.

'Why did you leave Eutympios?' Pando asked on the eve of their wedding day, curiosity finally getting the better of him.

Epi took a deep breath and let out a long sigh, never taking her eyes off her hands as she finished stitching the last hem on her wedding suit. 'We were different from the rest of the family, Proto and me. Zune and his side of the family want to live in their bubble of luxury within the city walls, while out here, people struggle.' She looked up at him, eyes shining. 'Proto and I wanted to help them. To make a difference.'

Pando's heart swelled for his bride to be. 'Do you miss the city? Life must have been easier for you both there.'

Epi laughed, and her face brightened. 'Life with Zune's family? Easy? You clearly didn't spend long enough with them.' She rose from her seat at the small wooden table, padded over to Pando and planted a soft kiss on his cheek. 'I would rather be with you in our humble home than anywhere else in the world.'

Pando pulled her onto his lap, and she giggled as she writhed and wriggled and pretended to try to get away. He wrapped his arms around her, drawing her close, and she rested her head on his chest. There, in that moment, Pando couldn't have been happier.

* * *

The wedding passed by in a joyous blur. The people of Krakos welcomed Pando with open arms, celebrating their union with raucous applause. They feasted on a simple wedding breakfast of bread, honey and fruit, shared with the villagers on a long communal table that ran through the square at the centre of their cluster of houses, washed down with locally brewed ale and strawberry wine. As day transitioned into evening, they sang and danced together, Epi leading the chorus with her rich, melodious voice. It was perfect.

Epi slept long into the following morning, quietly snoring in the bed they shared. Having been too excited to drink as much as his new bride, Pando was wide awake, attempting to use the salvaged coffee maker Epi had restored to somewhat working order. It was nothing like the tech Pando was used to in the city—older, a little beaten up and covered in a strange language he couldn't understand. He had no hope of figuring it out.

Exasperated, Pando flopped down onto one of the rickety chairs around their small dining table, and his eyes fell on the crate, forgotten during yesterday's festivities. Epi hadn't even seen the beautiful gift from Zune and his family yet. He crept back to the bedroom and peered through the open doorway. Epi was still unconscious, dead to the world. She probably wouldn't be up for hours yet.

I should get the bot out and have it ready to show her as soon as she wakes up.

Pando strode to the crate and pulled off the lid, still loose. He could take the bot out without waking Epi and display it somewhere as a surprise—it would be much more exciting for her than opening a dusty old crate.

Placing the lid on the table, Pando lifted the bot out and held it up. Even in the stark, yellow light of the naked bulb dangling from the centre of the ceiling, it gleamed. Epi would be thrilled with it. He turned it in his hands, and his stomach fluttered as his eyes fell on the universal port, the dark recess inconspicuous contrasted with the shining chrome case.

But why is it there if there is nothing inside?

It didn't make any sense. Zune had this machine specially made for Pando and Epi, he'd said so himself. So why have a port included if it would never be needed? He had explicitly told Pando not to hook it up to the network, yet made no attempt to disguise or hide the port. It was right there, as clear as day.

Unless he means for me to plug it in and was just teasing me.

That must be it! Zune had most likely installed some sort of surprise message or gift for the couple, knowing Pando would pick up on his hints. That man was tricky, but Pando had figured out his puzzle!

Excitement bubbling in his chest, Pando hefted the bot over his shoulder and strode to the computer-station at the back of the room. Cables of every colour and thickness spread out from the console like a spider's web, connecting the device to every basic device in the small house, along with the central network, which was the lifeline of the community. Epi had shown him how to use it when he first arrived, but not knowing anyone outside of the village, Pando had had very little reason to use it. Until now.

He powered up the station and watched the orange screen spark to life, awaiting his command. The buzz of the generator outside matched the buzz of anticipation within Pando as he sat the bot on a chair by the machine and dug around in the pile of wires for the universal upload cable. This was it: he was going to find out what Zune's wedding gift really was, and then he could surprise Epi with it and make their celebrations complete.

Finally, his fingers closed around the desired wire, and he plunged it into the back of the bot's head.

'Right! Let's see what—'

A loud, grating buzz erupted from the bot, increasing in volume with every second. Pando stepped back, covering his ears with his hands.

'What's going on?' He could barely hear his own voice over the din.

He jumped as two slots opened on what would be the bot's face, revealing two glowing green lights that looked almost like eyes. As suddenly as it began, the noise stopped, and a voice emanated from the bot.

'CONNECTION TO MASTER MAINFRAME COMPLETE. NOSOI VIRUS UPLOAD IMMINENT.'

'Virus? What?' Pando stepped forward to disconnect the bot, but its surface was scalding hot, and he couldn't touch it. 'No!'

The bot's eyes grew brighter. When it spoke again, its voice boomed at an impossible volume, and sparks of electricity sprung from it into the surrounding air. 'NOSOI VIRUS UPLOAD COMMENCED.'

Pando's eyes darted to the computer-station. The screen was red, and row upon row of black text ran up it at such a rate he couldn't make out a single word. The buzzing sound recommenced, louder this time, so loud Pando could feel his teeth shaking in his skull.

'What's happening?' He thought he heard Epi scream from the bedroom, but Pando stood frozen, horror creeping up his throat as each appliance in the room broke down. The coffee machine exploded, the oven screamed and let out sparks. Even the bulb above his head shattered into a million pieces, showering him in glass and filament.

Shouts from outside, barely audible over the din, told Pando the other villagers were being affected too, their homes breaking down as the poison from the bot bled into the network. Pando's eyes bulged as he realised the worst was happening: the entire interconnected network that kept all the towns and villages outside of the city running was being destroyed. Everything Epi and her sister had achieved crumbled as he stood amidst the chaos.

No!

He lunged forward and grabbed the bot, gritting his teeth as searing pain tore through his skin. He tugged at the upload cable, but it was fused into the port, pulsating with energy as the virus pummelled the network with its toxicity.

'UPLOAD NINETY PERCENT COMPLETE.'

NO!

Pando wrapped his legs around the bot, the agony almost unbearable as the heat ravaged his bare flesh. He dug his fingers around the cable and into the port, electricity penetrating his body, ricocheting through his nerves and making his head spin. Closing his eyes, he summoned all of his strength and pulled, tearing the cable out of the casing and wrenching the bot in two.

Silence. Pando collapsed back onto the floor and released the bot to the ground beside him, his chest heaving. A flicker of life flashed in the lights on its face, and Pando prayed he had done enough. Agony wracked his body, and tears stung his eyes, but he worked himself onto his knees and looked up at the screen, desperation shivering through him.

His stomach dropped.

The screen was black, the only colour three large, red words blinking in the centre: TOTAL SYSTEM FAILURE.

Pando sank back onto his heels, numb. His stomach roiled as sorrowful wails and angry shouts drifted through the window from the village outside.

'Pando?' He turned to see his new wife standing in the doorway, tears shining in her eyes. 'What have you done?'

Appearing Nightly on the Lido Deck Main Stage, The Sultry Sounds of the Siren Sisters!
David M. Simon

"Girls, I think we have a live one," Thelma said between furious drags on her Virginia Slim.

The Siren Sisters—Thelma, Aggie, and Paige—were holed up together in their cramped dressing room, taking a break before the last set of the night. Between the costumes of the sisters, the additional outfits hanging from a rack, and feather boas draped over the smudged make-up mirrors and strewn across every other available surface, it looked like a flock of parrots had exploded in the narrow room.

Paige had recently quit smoking, so she was even crankier than usual. The blue haze of cigarette smoke that Thelma was enthusiastically adding to wasn't helping. She served Thelma a heaping helping of side-eye. "Who's the mark this time?" Her voice made it clear she didn't trust Thelma's instincts.

Thelma ignored the judginess, knowing it would put a bug in Paige's feathered bonnet. "Handsome young fella, sitting front and center tonight. Dark, curly hair, nice tan. Greek, I'm sure of it, probably Crete. He's been here every night this week, started at the back of the audience and moved up a little each time. When we're singing he gets that look, like he doesn't know where he is."

"Gods, I love that look," Aggie said with a dreamy smile that momentarily took decades off her round, wrinkled face. She shook off the smile and got down to business. "Money?"

"Absolutely," Thelma said. "I clocked a high-end Patek Philippe watch beneath his expensive Italian linen shirt. Ferragamo crocodile shoes. Fourteen karat gold money clip wrapped around a fat stack. Yeah, he's got money." She stubbed out her cigarette in a ceramic mermaid ashtray and climbed ponderously to her feet. "I want that money clip empty by our next port of call. He's swimming around our bait, now let's set the hook, ladies."

***

The Siren Sisters had been working the cruise ship circuit for years, specializing in a cappella love songs. They did a nice mix of standards and newer material, trading off lead vocals, then coming together in glorious three-part harmony. As Paige liked to say when one of the others groaned about yet another practice session, "Look, we can't rely on our looks any more. Never could, really, let's face it. But on a good night our voices can still draw them in."

"Especially the sailors," Thelma would say with a snicker.

"Not enough sailors anymore," Aggie would add, always with a wistful glance out the porthole.

The Sisters usually hit it hard on the last set of the night, playing for mercy tips, but tonight, with a prospect in the audience, they pulled out all the stops. *When a Man*

Loves a Woman, Thelma's voice a raw, open wound. *Can't Help Falling in Love*, the ache palpable in every word Paige sang. *Take My Breath Away*, because there were Tom Cruise and eighties pop fans in every crowd, and that song ticked both boxes. Then the big finish—*Make You Feel My Love*, *At Last*, and *I Will Always Love You*, flowing one after the other with barely time for applause, soaring from heart-breaking solos to heart-stopping harmonies and back again. When Aggie sang the last note in a hoarse whisper, drawing it out for theatrical effect, even the most jaded cruise junkie shed a tear.

The young man in the front row was openly sobbing. He sat there, trying to pull himself together, eyes red, tanned cheeks wet and shiny. The rest of the crowd shuffled out, heading to the casino, the bar, or their staterooms. Some of the couples walked through the exit hand-in-hand in search of a quiet spot on the deck under the endless stars. The Sisters had been in rare form tonight.

When the theater was deserted, Thelma beckoned the man over with one crooked finger. He came shyly, haltingly, a sheepish smile playing at his lips. "Congratulations," she purred. "We've chosen you as our biggest fan on this cruise. What's your name, sugar?"

"Really? That's amazing! I'm Theo, that's my name. You're right, I am such a fan! Since the first night I came to your show I haven't been able to think about anything else. It's almost like you hypnotized me."

Paige snorted in laughter, but managed to cover it with a cough. "Hypnotized, that's so sweet. We're just three sisters who love to sing, but thank you."

"Girls, we're being rude. We haven't introduced ourselves," Aggie said. "Theo, I'm Aggie, and that's

Paige and Thelma. It's so nice to meet you." Aggie took Theo's hand in both of hers, then walked her fingers up his arm in a way that made Paige roll her eyes.

"I just had a crazy idea!" Thelma said. "What if we invite Theo here up to our stateroom for a drink?"

"Fine by us," Aggie and Paige said in unison.

"What do you say, Theo? Would you like to join us for a drink?"

Theo blushed. "I'd be honored. Thank you!"

***

If the Siren Sisters' dressing room was cramped, their cabin was comically small. Three narrow bunks were wedged into a space built for two. In place of a balcony, two small, round portholes barely hinted at the sea beyond. And like the dressing room, feather boas littered the floor.

Theo did not seem disappointed by the spartan surroundings. "I can see why you love feathers so much. You all sing like songbirds."

"That's very kind. I guess you could say we have a natural affinity with our feathered friends," Paige said.

Aggie busied herself at a small counter tucked into one corner, then distributed four elegant wine glasses filled with a mysterious amber liquid. "This is rakomeo, a special liqueur made from brandy and honey, with cinnamon, cardamom, and other exotic spices." She lowered her voice. "Some say it's an aphrodisiac." Theo took the offered glass, blushing again. "It's made in Crete."

"I'm from Crete!" Theo shouted, nearly spilling his drink.

"What a small world," Thelma said. "What are the chances?" Thelma took a long sip and smacked her lips. "So, tell us about yourself, Theo. What do you do in Crete?"

Theo took his own sip, doing his best to hide a shudder. "My father is an antiquities dealer. I'm learning the business so I can take it over when he retires."

"That's fascinating," Thelma said. "How's business?"

"We're doing well, I guess." He took another sip, and this time it went down easier.

"Splendid! Here, let me top off your glass."

***

By the time the bottle of rakomeo was emptied, Theo was perched on the end of one bed, eyes half-closed, swaying back and forth. His swaying had nothing to do with the movement of the ship.

Aggie popped the cork on a second bottle. It was time to move the conversation along. "Theo, I feel like we've become friends…"

"Absolutely!"

"…So I'm going to be honest with you. As you can see by our humble accommodations, working on a cruise ship has many benefits, but it's not overly lucrative. We do our best to get by. Sometimes wonderful fans such as yourself act as benefactors. So I, we, were wondering—"

Thelma took up the sales pitch. "What my sister is trying to ask you, if she would get to the point—"

"Let me stop you right there, Thelxiepeia." Theo had stopped swaying. His eyes were suddenly clear, his gaze sharp.

"What did you call me?" Thelma wasn't sure she had heard what she thought she heard. She glanced at her sisters but they were oblivious.

"I called you Thelxiepeia. *Thelma*, really?" That got the other sisters' attention. "And if I'm not mistaken, this is Peisinoe and Aglaope."

Something very much like a growl escaped Paige's throat. "Who the fuck are you and what do you want?"

"My name really is Theo, and my father really is an antiquities dealer. But I'm afraid I have no interest in that business. I'm a private detective, hired to find you. It took some doing; I've been searching for you for more than twenty years. And here you are."

Furious, Thelma felt the pin feathers raise along her spine. "That's impossible, you're not that old—wait. You're not human, are you?"

Theo chuckled. "I'm mostly human, a little dryad on my mother's side. My employer has gifted me with a bit of extra time to aid my quest."

"And who might that be?" Paige asked.

"Fucking Calliope, that's who. Dear old mom," Aggie said, her voice dripping venom.

"Yes, your mother would like you all to come home. She misses you. When she couldn't find you with her own formidable resources, she hired me. The cruise ship gig was a smart move, hard to track. I had just about given up when I overheard a couple of drunk American tourists at a bar in Ocho Rios raving about a trio of singing sisters on a Caribbean cruise who blew them away. I took a chance, and here we are."

Paige burst into tears, which, if her sisters thought about it, she had not done in several hundred years. "Please don't tell her you found us!"

"That would be unprofessional of me. I have a job to do."

Thelma didn't cry, just looked miserable. "Look, Theo, you saw our show. More than once. Our powers have vastly diminished over time. If we were to go home, it would be in shame."

"You're the daughters of a river god and a muse. Are you really happy living in this hovel, doing three sets a night, fleecing the occasional lovesick man? It's so … common. You could be living in a golden palace among the clouds."

"I'm offended by that!" Paige said, tears forgotten in her anger. "We don't *just* fleece men. We accept tribute from all types of humans, gender be damned."

"And yes, I'm happy!" Aggie said. "I've never been happier. I love to sing, we all do. Sure, we could be living in a golden palace, but we'd be back under our mother's thumb. I won't do it."

"Please don't make us," Paige said.

The sisters stopped talking then, huddled together with their arms around each other and did their best to look defiant.

Theo began to speak, stopped himself. For several long moments he seemed lost in thought. He stood up and went to a porthole, staring out at the dark sea. "Here's the thing," he finally said. "I've really enjoyed traveling the world on Calliope's dime. I wouldn't mind doing it for a few more years. I'll tell you what. Let's keep this between us. I'll check in with you once in a while, listen to you sing, and we'll share a bottle of rakomeo. How's that sound?"

Theo found himself engulfed then in a group hug, overwhelmed with sobbed *thank yous*, and a flurry of flying feathers.

When he managed to finally extricate himself, Theo headed for the door, but turned back with his hand on the knob and said, "For what it's worth, I really *was* drawn to your songs. If your stage was a rocky island, and I a sailor, I would have shipwrecked. The Sirens haven't lost their touch." Theo left their room.

"Well, that was something," Thelma said.

Aggie poured another round. "It was something, all right." She held up her glass and said, "Yamas!"

"Yamas!"

"So now what?" Paige asked.

"I know just the thing," Thelma said. She stood up and held out her hands. Her sisters took them, and they formed a circle. "Okay girls, *Sea of Love*, from the top. Paige, take the lead."

And the Sirens sang.

Death's Diary
Imelda Taylor

Most of mankind has dreaded my visit through the ages. I am associated with horror, despair, agony and sorrow, which I won't deny is part of what I am. However, as I await a passing, in a brief moment, I get to witness *life*. Let me show you a tesserae of my world as I share some of the moments I witnessed.

***

It was a cold December evening but the room was warm and comfortable. I stood waiting for him. He seemed to have had a good life. A loving wife was stroking his forehead, comforting him.

'You kept your promise.'

'What promise?' she asked, confused.

'Remember the day you agreed to marry me? I asked if you'd still love me when I'm old and wrinkly. It has come, hasn't it?'

She gazed into his eyes and said, 'You're as handsome as the day we met.'

'I'm sorry I can't keep my promise to you,' he said.

'Whatever do you mean, you silly old man?'

'I promised that you'll never be alone. That I'll always be there for you and hold your hands.'

'But you have. You have always been there for me.' She reminisced about their memories with teary eyes. 'Remember the time when I was afraid that we wouldn't be able to do the things that we're used to? I was afraid that we wouldn't be able to dance anymore and have long walks. Do you remember what you said to me then?'

He smiled and said, 'Of course. I said I'll hold you while listening to music when you can't dance. When you get tired after a long walk, we'll sit and admire the view… '

She let out a faint laugh. 'You never made me feel alone. You make growing old beautiful. When you help me out of bed in the morning, count my tablets for me when I can't find my glasses or just even hold my hands when I go to the doctor. '

'We had a laugh too, didn't we?' the husband said. 'We saw many places before they changed. I'm glad we got to see them. Why do they have to build those flats in our park, `ey? I'd love to walk there with you again. We cannot bring it back but its beauty has become a piece of our memory.' They held hands and never let go till the end.

'I will miss you, my love.' Tears fell from her eyes.

'Henry Peterson,' I called.

As he breathed his final breath, she whispered, 'It won't be long, my love. Wait for me.'

***

One autumn evening, I watched a woman who couldn't wait for me to come. 'Any time now, please. I'm ready,' she muttered before going to bed. She had no idea that I was getting ready too. As I looked around the room, I saw photographs of her family. Then I noticed a letter on her bureau. The writing was almost illegible. I looked at her crooked fingers and thought, perhaps it's the arthritis.

Dear Norman,

First of all, I apologise for the state of my writing. I'm writing to ask if there is any chance you can come over to visit. I know you've been busy but I would love to see your family.

I'm sorry about the accident I had in your car. I still feel embarrassed about it. It's undignified. I hope the money I sent to have it cleaned was enough. It's difficult having me around, I know, and I do feel sorry for myself sometimes. Please tell Beth that I didn't mean to shout at her. I know that she was only trying to help.

I wish I could still do more for you instead of you looking after me. Sometimes I look at your pictures and I can't believe that the little baby I held in my arms is now a successful family man.

Lots of love,

Mum

'Her last letter…' I thought. 'Mary Walter, this is the time you've been waiting for.'

***

She was holding a piece of paper. The word "Samaritan" and a phone number were written on it. She dialled the number. I eavesdropped on the conversation.

'Hello … I don't know where to start. I don't know why I called…'

'…I feel like I've overstayed my welcome. I don't see anything on the horizon. I have no children, I'm not married. Old age scares me. I don't want to be alone…'

'…No, I have no terminal illness.'

'…Why now? I need to take control. There will come a time when I'll be weak; I'll lose my independence. When Father died, he had us take care of him. There was always somebody there.'

'But, I have none.'

'…an alternative? The alternative is I keep on living. However, what quality of life will I have? Is it better to live a lonely life and wake up every morning waiting for death to come? It's barely living. That's just existing. Right now I can't see the purpose of my existence. When I'm gone they'll just hire someone else at work to replace me. All my siblings have their own successful lives and families, the world will keep turning…'

'…I've been feeling lonely for years. It has made me realise that perhaps this is a good time.'

'…yes, I have made my decision. I have to be brave…'

'…you will stay with me till the end? You'll do that? Thank you. It means a lot, not dying on your own…'

I watched her open a bottle of spirit and swallow a handful of tablets. She sobbed uncontrollably.

'…yes, I'm still here … I'm scared,' she said. She kept drinking until she passed out.

I was about to call her name when the door opened and in came the paramedics.

'We came just in time, sir. You just saved her,' said one of the paramedics.

'Thank you. I was concerned when I saw her through my window, so I called.'

'What's your name, sir?'

'It's Henry Peterson.'

I had to come another day.

Agamemnon's Mask
Mark Faraday

PROLOGUE

Mount Olympus was rife with animosity. The gods were divided amongst themselves over the Trojan War. On one side Athena, Hera, Thetis, Poseidon, Hermes and Hephaestus sided with the Greeks. They were opposed by Aphrodite, Apollo, Artemis and Ares for the Trojans.

Zeus, the most powerful of all the gods, had promised to remain neutral. However, as the war dragged on into the tenth year, Zeus noticed a new energy in his clever daughter Athena. He ascertained she had stumbled upon an idea that meant a win for the Greeks.

Cassandra, the priestess and seer for the Trojans, foresaw the soon-to-be terror in visions and dreams. She struggled to prevent it.

But Zeus had a revelation himself, and it involved Helen, the wife of the Greek King Menelaus. Helen of Troy had been given in marriage shortly before the war began, in the hope that a marriage would cement an alliance between the Trojans and the Greeks. But the Greeks had launched their "war to end all wars" despite the marriage, and causing nearly a decade of suffering.

Zeus could no longer ignore the pleas and prayers of his most faithful follower, the Trojan leader, King Priam.

ITHACA

"Hera! No!" Penelope cried as she bolted out of sleep, for Hera often came to her in her dreams.

Telemachus ran into his mother's bedroom, not noticing her distress. "Mother, Argos is dead!"

"Oh it was just a bad dream," Penelope told her son. "Not anything to worry about. What are you saying about Argos?"

"My best friend has died," Telemachus whimpered.

"Argos was a good and faithful old dog," Penelope said. "He waited for Odysseus as long as he could, as we all have. I remember just after you were born, Odysseus brought him home as a puppy to keep us company. I remember when Odysseus left for the war, he said, 'Argos, you watch over Telemachus until I get back!'"

"Those were the last words I heard him speak," Penelope said as she stroked her son's hand. "That was ten years ago."

"Is there any news from the war?" Telemachus asked. "Is there anyone who might know, who could tell us something of what is happening and perhaps know something about father?"

"No," said a new voice.

"Mother," Penelope said, "Will you come with us to pick a spot to bury Argos?"

"It won't be long before you'll be looking for a spot for me," the grand dame replied to her daughter. "To more fully answer your question, Telemachus, all the families of soldiers are wondering the same thing." She turned back to her daughter. "I see you have almost finished your tapestry."

"Yes," Penelope acknowledged.

"Has Athena contacted you?"

"She has."

"So what did she say?"

"She showed me a dream as I slept."

"And?"

"It was enough."

ATHENS, the Palace

"Ares, you take down any guards along the corridor on the left," Apollo said. "I will search the rooms on the right and find Helen. Meet me back here."

Ares, with his short sword named "Fear," crept up behind the first guard and lopped off his head, which sent a fountain of blood gushing into the air. He dispatched the next in the same manner, but then there came a group who yelled out for help. More guards came. The god, with blinding speed, sliced through their armor and sent entrails spilling out of bodies, slicing jugulars so that many geysers of blood spouted, like whales at sea, leaving none alive.

"Ares, I have her. Let's go!" Apollo yelled. Holding Helen's hand, he ran out to where their horses were waiting, with the mortal keeping pace eagerly. Ares broke off from the engagement and rushed to follow.

They and their fast mounts set off until at last they lost their pursuers, and made plans to bring Helen back to her family.

TROY, near the Dardanelles

Three women filed in as requested by King Priam: Hecuba, his wife; Andromache, the wife of his son

Hector; and Cassandra the Priestess. They had one additional guest.

"Helen!" King Priam shouted in joy.

"Oh, thank the gods I am freed," Helen said, rushing forward. "I've had no news these past ten years. Is Paris still among the living?"

Paris, standing in the doorway behind her answered, "Yes, darling, I am still here."

It had been ten long war-torn years since they'd seen each other. The two ran into each other's arms and kissed.

"When did you two get to know one another?" Andromache asked.

Helen looked at her. "We grew up together as children."

"Once I remember I made her believe she was riding a pony when really she was riding a donkey," Paris said with a chuckle. "Oh how I laughed for days."

Helen looked at him fondly. "I remember when we went sailing together and a storm suddenly rose up. Lightning was striking the water and you were so scared I had to pilot the boat back to shore."

"I was just testing you to see if you could do it," Paris said.

Just then King Priam's eldest son Hector entered the throne room, interrupting the reunion. "Father, Achilles is standing before our gates. He is alone and appears armed." Hector added sarcastically, "Do you think he wishes to sue for peace?"

His father laughed, then gestured for Hector to lead the way. The elderly king followed his son at a slow pace to a balcony overlooking the main gate, where guards were posted. "Let's see what Achilles has to say," he said.

They were soon joined on the balcony by Paris, Hector's younger brother. The three of them listened while Achilles shouted from below.

"King Priam, I ask for single combat," Achilles said. "Just Hector and I. I'm tired, King Priam. I want to go home. I want to see my family. If I kill Hector or Hector kills me, either way this is the end of the road for me."

Hector murmured to his father, "Losing Achilles would be a great blow to the Greeks. He is their best fighter."

"You, Hector," said King Priam, "are our greatest fighter. Losing you would be a great blow to us, and to me personally."

"Well, King, what is your answer?" Achilles shouted impatiently.

Hector shouted back, "The King accepts your challenge, Achilles. I will be down presently!"

"Oh Zeus!" King Priam said. "Hector, you must give your goodbyes to your mother, wife and son!"

"I will, Father," Hector said. He hugged his father and his brother before departing.

"Father, I have something I remember that I need to do. Excuse me," Paris said as he left in haste.

"Single combat!" Paris huffed. "I'll show Achilles how single combat works!" Paris slung his bow and quiver of arrows over his shoulder. He readied himself on a precipice, took one arrow out, and fired it.

MOUNT OLYMPUS

"Zeus, you are to blame for my son Achilles's death," Thetis said in a vicious snarl reserved for feral dogs.

Zeus, seated on his throne, frowned at her.

"Really, younger brother, you have broken your vow to remain neutral in this war," said Poseidon standing beside Thetis.

"I have no older siblings," Zeus bellowed. "What siblings I have were born of our father Cronos's vomit. I alone was born of a mother. I have not broken my vow. I had nothing to do with Achilles's death."

Thetis looked at her friend the goddess Athena. "Athena, what happened?"

"Our plan was for me to pretend I would help Hector defeat Achilles," Athena replied. "However, Hector never had the chance. Achilles was felled before the fight began."

"It was not Zeus who killed Achilles, but me," Apollo said emphatically. "I guided Paris's arrow that killed him."

"No, Apollo, it is Prometheus who is to blame," Zeus said, pounding his fist on the arm of his throne chair.

"Zeus, you will have no followers in the future," Thetis cried. "I will see to it that no one holds feasts or gatherings in your honor. Zeus, you will be forgotten by mortals in the future." She wiped her tears and turned her back on Zeus.

HELEN'S GAMBIT

"You see, it was all due to Agamemnon's golden mask," Helen told Paris. "I stole it as I was being rescued. When I put on the mask, I could hear the Athenian war council speaking about their plans to use a great wooden horse to get inside our walls."

"If you had not told us the secret of the horse, it would have been a disaster for us all," Paris said, holding Helen's hand.

"There, Hector has lit it on fire!" Helen exclaimed and pointed a finger.

Paris and Helen kissed. They stood on the beach, far enough away from the conflict that they were safe.

***

Inside the horse, Athenian soldiers waited. "I hear them talking, but it's hard to hear in here," one of them said.

"Why have they not started pulling us inside the walls?"

"They will. A prize like this horse, you bet they will pull us inside their walls!" said another.

"Quiet!" their commander Odysseus ordered.

"Smoke!" shouted several voices at once.

"Odysseus, fire!"

"Let's fight and die on the beaches like men!" Odysseus shouted. "May Hera herself welcome us home!" And he led his men in a charge out of the Trojan Horse.

***

Outside, Hector aimed his spear in anticipation. His focus was on the trap door in the belly of the horse, where his Greek adversaries would have to come out. As soon as he saw Odysseus drop down, he threw his spear. Odysseus parried with his gleaming golden shield.

Now all the Trojans surrounding the horse hurled javelins, spears, and arrows at the Greek invaders.

"Form a phalanx!" ordered Odysseus, but his men panicked at the fire that now engulfed the horse and the hail of lethal projectiles coming at them from all directions.

* * *

"Odysseus has failed," King Menelaus said to his commanders. They stood on board the ship that was to follow up a successful breach in the Trojan walls, had Odysseus and his men been successful. "I don't think we can rescue them, either. Even if we could, we would be back to the same problem of breaching the Trojan walls. What do you think, brother?"

"My feeling is that Zeus this night has made it very clear who his favorite was to win the war," Agamemnon said. "Let's go home."

* * *

"Paris, let our father know the Greek fleet is sailing away, the beach is secured, and that he may come down," said Hector. "Also ask Cassandra to come and give us a blessing for the brave warriors who have died this night."

The Theft of Thor's Hammer
Amanda Shortman

There are very few experiences in life worse than waking up with a hangover. The shock of leaving the blissful state of sleep, and gradually becoming aware of far too many symptoms, is enough to put anyone in a bad mood. And so it was that Thor woke with a pounding head, a rolling stomach, a mouth so dry and furry that he could barely swallow, and a sickening realisation that he had no recollection of how he got there.

Hangovers were *not* a part of Thor's world. He hadn't had one since those first few forays into alcohol fuelled adventures in his youth. He was a big guy, even for an Asgardian—six foot three, and stockily built—it took far more than a few drinks to knock him flat these days. Yet here he was, limbs as heavy as lead, and a mind so blank he was surprised he could remember his own name. Just what the hell had he done last night?

He carefully opened his eyes, squinting against the light that pierced holes into his skull, and looked around the room. It was his own bedroom, at least. Whatever had happened, he'd somehow made it home and into his own bed. That was a relief. He hadn't, however, managed to change out of the clothes he'd been wearing, or crawled under the covers. He found himself laying in an undignified heap on top of the bed, clothes creased to high heavens and stinking of stale beer, and was that vomit?

The Theft of Thor's Hammer

Screwing up his nose at the scents now assaulting his nostrils, Thor heaved himself up into a seated position. '*Bad idea*', he thought, '*terrible in fact*', as the room spun and his stomach threatened to rebel. He waited, rather impatiently, for everything to settle enough for him to attempt moving further, and then made his way into the bathroom. He desperately needed a shower. And some water.

The sound of the fan whirring to life battered against his ear drums, as he searched desperately through his cupboard for some painkillers. He rarely needed them, and wasn't sure he even had any. But he didn't want to have to drag himself through the rest of the house looking for some, not if he could help it. There was too much risk that one of his siblings might see him in this state and take advantage of him. Especially Loki. Damn them, they were a menace when they were feeling mischievous. And Thor was in no mood to deal with that today.

Finally he found an old package, with just a couple of tablets left. They were probably out of date by now; who knew how long they'd been sitting at the back of this cupboard, behind all of his beard balms and pomades. If there was one thing you could say about Thor, it was that he took pride in his appearance. Except for today. Today he looked like shit.

He tried to dry swallow the tablets, before remembering his salivary glands seemed to have gone on strike, and almost puked his guts up once more. Sticking his mouth under the faucet, he chugged as much water as he could, and then considered his reflection. Red hair standing on end, dark circles under each eye, and a deathly grey hue to his skin made him feel like he was looking at a stranger. He needed to fix this. Right now.

He took off his clothes and threw them on the floor to deal with later. A cool shower was calling his name. Stepping into the cold spray was somewhat of a shock and tore his breath away momentarily. But then he adjusted to his usual morning ritual, and things began to feel more normal. He just needed to clean up, get some food in his belly, and then he'd be able to face the day.

He reached for his shower gel, a fancy blend of bergamot, lemongrass, and clove, which foamed spectacularly and made him feel more alive. Just the scent of it soothed his mind, and he began to relax as he scrubbed his body from head to toe. And then he noticed it. The missing chain. *Fuck*.

He frantically patted himself down and checked the shower to see if it had fallen in there. When that failed, he got out of the shower, suds still dripping down his torso and legs, and grabbed the pile of clothes he had thrown on the floor. Desperately searching through them, he felt his heart racing at the thought he had lost the USB stick nestled inside the hammer shaped pendant he always wore around his neck. He couldn't have. He just couldn't.

When the clothes revealed no missing hammer, he raced into his bedroom, slipping on the wet and soapy floor he'd left in his wake. '*Damn it,*' he growled, as he slammed into the door jamb, barely staying upright. He'd knocked himself in just the right place to cause a dead arm, just what he needed. '*Shit, shit, shit!*'

Thor dragged all the covers off his bed, even though he knew he hadn't slept under them. The hammer had to be here somewhere. It had to be. The alternative wasn't an option. The USB held the wallet with the Bitcoin he'd persuaded the family to invest in. It was a safer, modern approach to investments, he'd told them. Nobody could access the wallet without the USB stick, and he held that around his neck. Who would take on a man like him, whose size alone was enough to put most people off approaching him. Nothing could be safer. Or so he had thought.

Sinking to the ground, head still pounding from his hangover, and his heart threatening to beat out of his chest, Thor hid his face in his hands and let out a garbled cry. This couldn't be happening. What was he going to do? He tried desperately to remember what had happened last night. Where had he been and who had been with him? But his mind was a blank. '*Somebody must have planned this,*' he thought, '*this can't be a coincidence.*' And then he realised who it must be. '*Loki.*'

***

Loki was drinking coffee with Freya and debating the best way to brew it when Thor thundered into the kitchen.

'Where is it?' he snarled.

'Where's what? Gods, what happened to you, you look awful.'

'You know damn well what happened to me! Where did you put it?'

'I have no idea what you're talking about. Go have whatever this little strop is elsewhere, you're ruining my vibe.'

Thor grabbed the front of Loki's shirt and dragged them to their feet, shaking his fist for punctuation. 'Don't mess with me, Loki, I know you did it.'

'Get the hell off me,' Loki spat, as they tried to dislodge Thor's grip to no avail. They were much smaller, with far less strength in their lithe body, than their older brother. 'I'm telling you I don't know what you're talking about.'

'Hey!' Freya yelled, reminding them that she was here too. 'This is getting you nowhere. Thor, let Loki go, and tell us what's wrong.' When Thor grumbled, she put her hands on her hips and glared at him. 'Use your words, Thor.'

Thor closed his eyes and took a deep breath, trying to compose himself. He knew Freya was right; this wasn't getting him anywhere. Loki was a wily devil and they could continue this for hours. Reluctantly he let them go and stepped back.

Loki brushed their hands down the front of their shirt, smoothing the wrinkles, and scowled at him. 'What's your problem, man?'

'My problem,' he growled, 'is that you got me so drunk last night I didn't realise when you stole my hammer.'

'Someone stole your hammer?' Loki asked, suddenly serious. 'For fuck's sake, Thor, you said it would be safe!'

'It was! Nobody knew what it held except us, so why would anyone steal it? It had to be you, stop playing games and *give it back*.'

'Oh yeah, blame Loki, that's what you always do,' Loki said, rolling their eyes. 'It couldn't possibly be the mighty Thor's mistake, could it?'

The Theft of Thor's Hammer

'You mean you haven't got it?' Thor refused to believe this possibility. It couldn't be true. The alternative wasn't acceptable.

'No. How many times do I have to tell you, it wasn't me? I left you at the bar at 8:00 last night, and you still had it around your neck the last time I saw you.'

'They came dancing with me and the girls,' Freya put in. 'We didn't get home until gone 2:00, and you were already snoring in your room. Thought you were gonna bring the house down it was so loud. Just how much did you drink last night?' She squinted at him, as if she could somehow tell what had happened by his appearance alone. He knew he still looked an absolute mess.

'I don't know. I don't remember.'

'Well you were only a couple of drinks in when I left you, and it takes a lot to bring you down, so what the hell happened?' Loki asked.

'I told you I don't remember,' he said through gritted teeth. His anger was rising again, both at the interrogation and his own lack of memory. He had never felt so lost, and he did not like it.

'You didn't do anything stupid and drink with Thrym, did you? I saw him and his cronies at the bar last night too.'

Thrym? He was there? Thor tried really hard to remember, well, anything about last night. But it was all just a blur. And thinking too hard made his head spin. Ugh, he really needed to get rid of this hangover, and fast.

"You know he'd love to get ahead of you," Loki said. "And he's probably the only person who could outdrink you, too.'

Thor nodded. He knew Loki was right. Thor might be a big guy, but Thrym was positively a giant. He was almost a foot taller than Thor, at seven foot two. And he was solidly built as well. He towered over everyone, and had a voracious appetite. Add in the fact their families had been business rivals for generations, and it all began to make sense.

'Shit.' Thor rubbed his hands over his face and grimaced. 'What am I going to do? The family's going to kill me.'

'Yeah, dude, you fucked up big time!'

'This isn't funny, Loki. Wipe that stupid smile off your face.'

'Hey, I'm just glad it wasn't me for once.' Loki shrugged their shoulders and pulled a sort of *'sorry, not sorry'* face at him.

'Look,' Freya said, stepping into the conversation again. She knew not to get involved when the pair of them were hashing it out. But she also knew when they were just going to stumble into a deadlock, and she was not losing her Saturday to that. 'You need to find out whether Thrym has the hammer, right? This is all just supposition. If he has it, you can figure out how to get it back. And if he doesn't, you need to start hoping you can remember what happened last night. Because Dad is gonna lose it if he finds out.'

'How the hell am I going to do that?' Thor asked. 'It's not like I can just walk up to his house and ask him.'

'Why not?'

'You know damn well why not.'

'What, because you'd lose face? I think you already did that last night, dear brother.' Freya smiled at him. It was a sickly sweet expression that let him know that this time she had the upper hand.

Gods, he hated his siblings sometimes. She wasn't going to forget this in a hurry, was she?

'I can do it,' Loki said, causing Thor to turn and look at them with suspicion. Loki was well known for 'helping' in rather mischievous ways. What were they up to?

'Don't look at me like that. I mean it. This is important. If Thrym manages to access the funds, that's going to affect all of us, not just you.' Then, just to prove that they weren't entirely removed from their usual antics they added, 'I can't believe you lost it,' and tutted at Thor whilst shaking their head.

Thor was about to retort, when something occurred to him.

'Wait, how are you going to do it? You're not going to break in or anything, are you? Because you know if you get caught and this catches the attention of the cops or the press, we're doomed.'

'Give me some credit,' Loki scoffed.

Thor just raised his eyebrows at them. That really wasn't out of the realm of possibility when it came to Loki.

'I know Thrym. We play cards together.'

'You do what?!' Thor hissed, at the same time as Freya asked, 'When?'

'Last Friday of the month. Thrym hosts a poker game at his house.'

'You play poker? At his house? For money? Are you mad?' Thor was apoplectic.

'It's just cards, Thor. Chill the fuck down, man. We play with a fixed limit, so nobody loses too much. And we never talk shop. That's one of the rules.'

'And who, might I ask, is at these games? Is it just you and Thrym's mates?'

'Not that it's any of your business, but no.'

'It is my business when your cavorting with the enemy might well have given him access to my hammer.'

'Don't you dare try and hang this on me. This is all on you. I told you—we don't talk shop!' Loki glared at him, their eyes burning. 'I'm trying to help, but if you don't want—'

'I do want your help,' Thor said, closing his eyes and taking another deep breath to get his anger under control. He wasn't used to this, asking for help. He was the one people came to for help. He felt so humiliated.

'Okay then. I'll go to Thrym's and see what I can find out. I'll need to borrow your car though, Freya,' Loki said, turning to their sister. 'Mine's in the shop.'

'Why not borrow my car? You're doing this for me.'

'No offence, Thor, but your car is boring. I wouldn't be seen dead in that thing.'

'It's one of the safest cars on the market.' It was why he had bought it.

'Like I said. Boring.'

Thor turned to Freya, hoping she would back him up. But she was just smirking back at him. Of course she'd side with Loki; her car was just as reckless as theirs. A bright orange Ford Mustang convertible, which she'd had custom painted with a wing design along each side. '*It's my falcon*,' she'd said when she first brought it home.

She was just as bad as Loki in that respect, all about the look.

'Fine,' he said, giving in at last. It was no use arguing any more. He'd lost all control over this situation, if he'd even had any to begin with. 'Just do it fast; I need answers.'

'Yes sir.' Loki threw him a mocking salute and took the car keys Freya was holding out to them. Thor sighed. It was going to be a long day.

***

Loki pulled up outside Thrym's house. Unlike Loki and their siblings, who still enjoyed the luxury of the family's mansion, Thrym had moved out on his own. That's not to say his house wasn't fancy—it was a modern build, in a gated community, with exquisite gardens surrounding it. But it seemed so compact to Loki after spending so much time on the family's sprawling estate. Every time they came to poker night they realised that they could put up with Thor's nagging and Freya's insistence on trying to hook them up with yet another one of her friends if it meant they had access to so much space.

'Loki, my man. I thought I might be seeing one of you today.' Thrym opened the door and shouted down the drive at them. He must have been waiting for them to arrive, confirming Loki's suspicion that he was indeed the thief. Loki bristled at the use of the word 'man'. Thrym was always misgendering them.

'So you know why I'm here then?'

'Of course I do,' Thrym grinned at them. 'Though I'm surprised it took you this long. Was Thor so far gone that he didn't even realise his hammer was missing, or were you trying to come up with a plan to steal it back? You're not here to steal it back are you? Because it's not here.'

'Where is it?'

'Now, now, Loki, I'm not going to just tell you that. What would be the point?'

'And what is the point, Thrym? Is this just another one of your games?'

'I thought you liked my games.' Thrym winked at them, for once actually riling them up.

'Games are fine when everyone knows the rules, and enters into them freely. Thor did not. This isn't a game.'

'No, you're right, this isn't a game. The stakes are much higher.'

'What do you want, Thrym?'

Thrym smiled at them, but it wasn't a friendly grin. There was a menace to it that Loki had never seen before.

'I knew that hammer must be important to Thor—he never takes it off. But I had no idea just how important it would turn out to be. My, my, what a careless thing to lose. So much value in such a little thing.'

'He didn't lose it. You stole it.' Loki growled, their voice deepening with anger.

'Potato, potahto,' Thrym replied, waving his hand in the air. 'Who cares about semantics. The fact is, Thor no longer has the hammer, and if he wants it back he's going to have to pay for it.'

'How much do you want?'

'Oh, I don't want money. Do I look like I need it?' He swept his arm wide, gesturing to his house and garden. 'No, I want something more precious than that.'

'What?' Loki spat out, fed up with Thrym toying with them.

'I want a date. With your sister.'

* * *

'He wants *what?*' Freya shrieked. 'No way. Nuh uh. Not gonna happen. The guy's a creep.'

'Oh, come on Freya, it's just a date," said Thor. "You go on those all the time.'

'With people *I* want to go out with. And on my terms, Thor.'

'Well, can't you make an exception this time? It's important.'

'You have zero idea what it's like to be a woman in this world, do you?'

'What's that got to do with this?'

'It has everything to do with it,' Freya insisted. 'You've never had to deal with creeps sliding into your inbox, telling you how much they adore you when they hardly know you, and begging you to give them what they want. A girl has to have boundaries!'

'But it's just a date.' Thor was getting irritated. Why was Freya being so difficult? She knew how important it was to get the hammer back. Her lifestyle depended on protecting the family's assets too.

'No it's not, Thor. You're not listening.' Freya raised her voice, something she rarely did. 'This isn't just a date to Thrym—it's a power play. Why do you think he stole the hammer in the first place? He wants the upper hand. You're scared about what he might do with our money. I'm scared about what he might do to me.'

Shit. Thor hadn't thought about that. He never had to worry about anyone hurting him. Well, he never had until this morning anyway. How had Thrym managed to incapacitate him so much that he'd been able to take the hammer? And what might he do to Freya? He sighed and rubbed his hands over his face in defeat.

'Okay, I get it. I'm sorry. But what are we going to do now to get the hammer back?'

'Excuse my interrupting, but I couldn't help but overhear.' Freya, Thor, and Loki all turned to see Heimdall standing in the doorway to Freya's room.

Oh shit, Thor thought, *just the person I didn't want to know.* Heimdall was the main protector of the family's assets. His knowledge of security measures and investment opportunities was unrivalled. It had taken Thor ages to persuade him to expand the portfolio to include Bitcoin, and now he'd lost the wallet. He'd hoped to keep it a secret from him.

'There seems to be a solution that you're missing.' Heimdall continued.

'And what is that?' Thor asked, worry making his words sharp.

'You should go in Freya's place.'

'Haven't you been listening? Thrym wants a *date* with Freya. Not a meeting with me.'

'I never said you should go as you,' Heimdall replied, a smirk catching the corner of his mouth.

'Just spit it out, Heimdall. What do you mean? I haven't got the patience for riddles today.'

'You should go *as* Freya.'

The Theft of Thor's Hammer

Thor gaped at Heimdall.

'That's not a bad idea,' Freya murmured.

Thor turned to look at her. What was going on? Had everyone forgotten who he was? Could they not see how ridiculous this all sounded?

'How am I,' he began, choosing his words carefully, 'supposed to make Thrym believe I am Freya? Have you seen me?'

'Yes,' Heimdall replied, as if this wasn't the most absurd suggestion ever. 'You and Freya have many similarities in your appearance.'

'Many similarities? What about my beard, my red hair, my stature?' Thor sputtered.

'Oh piffle,' Loki joined in, a gleeful look on their face. 'You can shave the beard, colour your hair, and wear a waist trimmer and prosthetic breasts to change your body shape.'

'Shave my beard? Colour my hair? Prosthetic breasts?' Thor was beside himself.

'Thor, your beard will grow back in a few weeks," Freya pointed out. "And you can cope with being a blond for a while. This is nothing more than us women do all the time to look good.'

'But I'm not a woman!'

'Neither is Loki, but they do it too sometimes.'

'I'm not Loki!' Thor had a sudden thought. 'Why not get them to do it?'

'Because I do not look as much like Freya as you do,' Loki said. 'Besides, Thrym has already seen me dressed as a woman before, he'd see right through it.'

'And he won't see through this?'

'No, because he won't be expecting you to do it. Which is exactly why it will work,' Heimdall said. 'Any suspicion he might have will be brushed away as ridiculous, because we all know the mighty Thor would *never* dress as a woman.'

'It's perfect.' Freya clapped her hands in excitement and rushed to grab her laptop and fire it up. 'We'll book you in with my stylist, and Loki can help you find clothes to wear. It'll be fun.'

'It will not be fun,' Thor growled, knowing he had lost this battle but still refusing to accept it. 'And what about my voice? No amount of accessories will hide that.'

'Oh, I can help you with that. There are ways to make yourself sound more feminine,' Loki said, waving their hand at Thor as if it were a mere trifle. They were standing behind Freya, telling her which websites to go to for supplies.

Thor watched them, wringing his hands together with the sheer helplessness of his situation. How had his day managed to get even worse? Heimdall placed a hand on his shoulder and squeezed.

'If you do this, I will give you a way to get revenge on Thrym.'

'How?'

'There are ways to bring down a person's empire if you know how. Trust me.'

Thor looked at Heimdall and saw a wicked glint in his eye. He never wanted to get on the wrong side of this mysterious member of their family. He knew too much, and said too little. And Thor had no doubt he could do exactly what he said he could.

* * *

The Theft of Thor's Hammer

The following week passed in somewhat of a blur. Loki had messaged Thrym, telling him that 'Freya' had agreed to a date, but she wouldn't be free until the following Sunday. This gave them time to prepare. They'd also stipulated that they, Loki, would accompany Freya on her date. Thrym wasn't pleased, but Loki had managed to persuade him by offering a double date with a mutual friend they knew liked them. Particularly in their more feminine guise. It would be fun, Loki had said. And Thor truly believed that Loki meant this.

Thor had hated every moment of the week's preparations, but Loki had delighted in everything. They'd gone with him and Freya to the salon where a stylist had bleached, toned, and added extensions to Thor's hair, to make it impressively similar to Freya's golden waves. And they'd made Thor try on dozens of outfits across multiple stores, before finally deciding on what they declared to be the perfect look. Thor hated the way the band around his waist constricted his breath, and the prosthetic breasts made his back ache something rotten. But he had to give it to Loki—when put all together, he really did look like Freya.

Trying to sound like Freya was a whole different matter, however. He'd watched the tutorials and practiced the exercises suggested by vocal coaches online, but he struggled to sound natural when speaking. His voice was much lower than Freya's and he couldn't help falling into a falsetto when trying to mimic her. It took most of the week to get anywhere close, and even then he was pushing it.

'Look,' Loki said to him one night when Thor was close to calling the whole thing off. 'Thrym hasn't really spoken to Freya all that much in the past anyway. He's admired her from afar, and we know he's really just in it for her body, the creep.' Loki screwed up their nose in distaste. Thor couldn't disagree. He'd had plenty of time to think about it over the past week, and even he could no longer ignore how disturbing Thrym's demand was. No wonder Freya hadn't wanted to do this. If it wasn't for needing to get the hammer back, he might have stormed over to Thrym's house and told him to keep his dirty little hands off his sister.

'So,' Loki continued, 'just keep things light, pretend you're shy, and I'll do as much of the talking as I can.'

Thor liked that plan. Loki could talk for hours, and it also meant he wouldn't have to deal with making small talk. He hated small talk.

'I can't believe we're doing this,' he sighed.

'Oh, we're doing it alright. And we're going to get the hammer back and make Thrym wish he'd never messed with us. You wait.'

* * *

Sunday rolled around, and Thor found himself preparing for the lunch date at last. They'd decided to keep it casual, with food and drink at a local restaurant famed for its patio overlooking the city. Loki had chosen him a fifties style tea dress, which accentuated the curves created by what he wore underneath, and had a quirky print that suited Freya's style perfectly.

Freya had put his hair in a half up, half down do, *to keep it casual,* she had said. And then she and Loki had gone to work on his makeup. He'd shaved his face that morning, going without a beard for the first time since puberty. That alone made him feel unlike himself. Loki had smeared something over his chin, *to conceal any shadow that might appear throughout the day*, and Freya had given him her signature look of winged eyeliner, nude eyes, and a bold as brass lipstick. It felt weird on his lips, and he was worried about smudging it, but she'd reassured him it would stay put. He'd believe that when he saw it.

Finally it was time for them to leave. Loki was waiting for Thor by their car, a bright red Camaro with the top up.

'What's with the hood?' he asked.

'We don't want to mess up your hair.'

'Oh.' Was this really what women had to think about every day? It was exhausting.

Thor looked Loki over. They were wearing a short sleeved blouse, with a long, pale blue skirt, and had a scarf tied around their neck. It was basically Audrey Hepburn's look from the film *Roman Holiday*, and somehow Loki pulled it off completely. They'd even managed to make their hair look similar to hers. Thor had no idea how they did it, how they could take a look that somebody else had worn and make it entirely their own. But they did. They were like a shape shifter.

'Are you ready to go?' Loki asked, getting into the driver's seat.

'I have to be, don't I?'

'Yep.' Loki grinned at him. They were having the time of their life.

* * *

They arrived at the restaurant a little early, hoping to beat Thrym and Loki's date to the table. But unfortunately they had had the same idea, and were already seated when the waiter showed them to their spot on the patio.

'Freya!' Thrym cried, standing up from his seat and holding his arms open to embrace her. Thor quickly grabbed hold of his arms to prevent him from grabbing him entirely, and leaned forward to blow a kiss by each side of his face. He'd seen Freya greet people like this so many times and never understood why she was so dramatic about it. Suddenly he understood the power of the air kiss.

'And Loki,' Thrym said, reluctantly moving away from Thor and reaching out a hand for Loki to shake. 'I'm glad you could make it. Have a seat.'

Thrym gestured for Loki to sit opposite him, and then pulled out Thor's chair for him, scooping him up into it as he sat down. He'd always thought of it as a polite thing to do, helping a lady into her seat. But the actual reality was more a loss of control, and Thor didn't like it. Not one bit. It left him feeling at a disadvantage before the meal had even begun. *Is this how women feel too?* he wondered. This entire week had been an eye opener, and he was beginning to see why Freya complained about things all the time. He'd always thought she was just being fussy. But he'd only been dressed as a woman for a short while and already he was fed up with all the things he had to think about and the way people treated him.

'Svad, this is my sister Freya,' Loki said, introducing the pair of them to each other. 'Freya, this is Svad. He's

The Theft of Thor's Hammer

Jotunn's nephew. You remember Jotunn, don't you? He worked on the extension to our house.'

Thor looked at Svad and recognised the almost black hair and piercing blue eyes that their builder had also possessed. Although Jotunn's hair had been broken up with a smattering of grey too. He also had the tall, stocky build of his uncle. And, for that matter, Thrym.

'Are you two related?' he asked, pointing between Svad and Thrym.

'We're distant cousins,' Svad replied, throwing a side eyed glance at Thrym. 'We see each other at weddings and funerals, that's about it.'

'And at poker night,' Loki added.

'And at poker night,' Svad agreed, smiling fondly at them.

Wow, Thor thought, *he really does like Loki.*

'Enough of that,' Thrym declared, drawing attention back to himself. 'We're here to eat. So let's order. Do you know what you want?'

'Not yet, Thrym, geez, you and your appetite.' Loki rolled their eyes. 'We haven't even looked at the menus yet.'

'Well I looked before I came. I know exactly what I want.'

'Me too,' Thor said, surprising Thrym.

'Oh, really? A girl after my own heart.'

He smiled at Thor. It was a greasy looking grin, one that made him want to screw up his nose in disgust. But Thor knew he had to win Thrym over, at least until he was satisfied enough to give them back the hammer. So he thought back to all the pointers Freya had given him on how to *look interested, even when you aren't*, and leaned forward, resting his arm on the table and his hand in his chin.

'So what are you having?' he asked Thrym, his voice sickly sweet to his ears. He thought he might have blown it, but Thrym seemed to like it.

'I'm gonna have the steak. Nothing beats a good hunk of meat.'

Thor actually agreed with this. That would have been his meal of choice too, had he not been playing Freya. As it was, he'd still managed to get some meat into his main dish too.

'I'm having the Surf and Turf. Balance out the meat a bit with some fish.'

'Are you sure you'll be able to eat all that? It's a big dish.'

'Whatever I can't manage, you can have,' Thor said, smiling at Thrym with what he hoped looked somewhat appealing. Thankfully Thrym seemed to accept it, as he placed his hand over Thor's and patted it gently.

'Sounds good,' he said. 'Come on you two, hurry up and decide already. I'm hungry.'

* * *

The food arrived and they all tucked in happily. Loki had made an excellent choice when recommending this restaurant. The atmosphere was easy, the service quick, and the food delicious. Thor had worried about what he would talk to Thrym about over the course of the meal, but he needn't have. Thrym himself seemed more than happy to dominate the conversation. When he wasn't boasting about yet another one of his achievements, he was trying to make some moves on Thor. *No wonder Freya didn't want to come on a date with him,* Thor thought, as Thrym made yet another comment about his appearance.

'That dress is quite something, Freya. It really accentuates your curves.'

Thor had to work hard not to roll his eyes. Did he sound like this when he was trying to chat someone up, or was Thrym just extra sleazy?

'Thank you,' he said, trying to act as if he was flattered by the comment. 'Loki and I went shopping and as soon as I saw it I had to have it.'

'I can see why.' Thrym moved his foot under the table to rub it against Thor's. Thor moved his foot away, but Thrym simply stretched his leg to follow him. *Ugh, can this guy not?* Thor thought, pushing down the urge to stamp on his foot.

'My suit is custom made by a little tailor downtown. I say 'little' but he's really very exclusive. Only has the best clients.'

Thor felt like he was dying, this meal was torturous. How much could one guy talk about himself?

'A man has to have a good tailor, don't you agree Loki?'

'I'm not a man, so I wouldn't know.'

Thor looked at Loki. He'd never fully realised just how much being misgendered hurt his sibling. But spending the week trying to be something he wasn't had felt truly painful at times. He'd gone into this thinking his siblings were getting too much enjoyment out of seeing him so unsettled. Maybe he had been wrong.

'You know what I mean,' Thrym continued, choosing to ignore the correction. 'You wear suits, you must have a tailor.'

'I do. I'm still not a man.'

'Oh, why must you bring this up every time?'

'Because it's true. And you are being an arse.'

Thor could see Loki was getting riled up, and even though he understood why, he knew he needed to bring the conversation back to a good place if they were to gain Thrym's trust.

'My meal is delicious. Would you like to try a bit?' He piled a mouthful onto his fork and held it out to Thrym. The man turned away from Loki and his scowl turned into a grin as he saw what Thor was offering. *I'm just doing it to get through this*, Thor thought to himself. *It doesn't mean anything, just grin and bear it.*

Thrym made a show of tasting the food Thor was offering him. He looked him straight in the eyes as he slowly wrapped his mouth around the fork, and then closed his eyes as he pulled the food off and began to chew.

'Mmmmmm,' he said, in a voice that dripped honey. 'You made a good choice, Freya. Do you know the difference between shrimp and prawn?'

***

And thus the meal continued, with Thrym showing off his 'superior' knowledge about everything, and Thor nodding along, trying to look interested. He ate his food, without thinking, and soon he had emptied his whole plate.

'Wow,' Thrym said, as he noticed the same thing Thor had. 'You've got a very healthy appetite.'

Thor didn't know how to respond. What should he say? He hadn't planned this. Freya had told him not to eat too much or he'd give the game away. She'd told him she always chose a smaller main dish, so that she left room for dessert. '*A girl's gotta have chocolate*,' she'd said to him with a wink. Thankfully Loki came to his aid.

'Oh, Freya's barely eaten a thing all week. She's been so nervous about this date.'

'Really?' Thrym looked at Thor, his eyebrows raised in surprise. 'I didn't realise you cared so much.'

'Oh yes, Freya has been fretting all week about what to wear and how it will go.' Thor looked at Loki. His sibling looked at serious as ever—how were they doing it? Sure, all they said was true, they had been planning this all week. But how they could say all that with a straight face, especially when they loved a good joke, was beyond Thor. No wonder they were so good at fooling them all—they were a master actor.

'You didn't need to be worried, Freya.' Thor turned back to look at Thrym, who was reaching a hand towards his face. Thor sat back in his chair, trying to create as much distance between them. Thrym frowned.

'I'm sorry. I was only going to remove your sunglasses. Let me look at your pretty eyes.'

Thor reached up and took off his sunglasses, folding them up and placing them on the table beside his drink. Then he looked back at Thrym. The man gasped.

'Your eyes are so bloodshot. Are you okay?'

'Oh, Freya has barely slept all week either. She's just tired.'

Once again, Loki had come to Thor's rescue. How did they think of things so quickly? *Well*, Thor thought, *I did barely sleep last night I suppose. That does explain the bloodshot eyes.*

'My Freya.'

Ugh, Thor thought. *I'm not your anything.*

'You needn't worry yourself so much. You know I love you.'

Love? Thor scoffed to himself. *How can you love someone you've barely met. Is this seriously what my sister puts up with?*

'Why don't you plan a second date,' Loki suggested, finally introducing their plan, 'so that you can enjoy spending some more time together?'

'That's an excellent idea, Loki. What do you say, Freya?' Thrym looked at Thor with such eagerness in his eyes that he almost felt sorry for him. Almost.

'Not until you've given me Thor's hammer. You promised to give it back.'

'That I did,' Thrym nodded, standing up slightly so that he could reach into his front pocket more easily. He held out his closed fist to Thor, who opened his own hand, palm upwards, as Thrym dropped the hammer into it.

'It's a small price to pay to spend time with you,' he said.

Small for you, Thor thought. But outwardly he smiled at Thrym, put the hammer in the little clutch bag that Freya had given him, and pulled out his phone. They hadn't spared any details and had bought a flowery cover for it. It was important that Thrym suspect nothing until the deed was done.

'There's an event I'd love to go to next week,' Thor said, using his fingerprint to unlock the screen and opening the Notes app where he had saved the link. 'I've put it in my calendar already, so I can share the link with you and it'll have all the details in—time and place, etc.'

'Sounds good. What is it?' Thrym reached into his jacket pocket and pulled out his own phone.

'A vintage car rally. You know how I love cars.'

'I do too!' Thrym exclaimed, his eyes bright with excitement. That was exactly what they had been banking on.

'Loki already gave me your number, so I'm sending you the link now.'

There was a quiet moment, until Thrym's phone let out the telltale beep that meant the message had arrived. His thumb moved across his screen and then they all watched as his face moved through several emotions in quick succession. First frustration, then confusion, and finally betrayal. He looked up at Thor, his eyes begging her to tell him it wasn't real.

'Sorry, Thrym. You shouldn't have messed with me,' Thor said, in his normal voice. 'Enjoy fixing this mess.'

'I'm sorry, what's happening?' Svad asked, looking between Thor and Thrym, as the latter's face grew paler by the second.

'Oh, this isn't my sister Freya, it's my brother Thor.'

Svad's eyes bulged as he looked Thor over. It seems he had been fooled just as much as Thrym.

'Thor just sent Thrym a malicious URL that has now infected his phone.' Loki continued, thoroughly enjoying explaining the trick. 'It was Heimdall's idea, you know how smart he is with computers. There was a virus attached to the link, which is now working through all of the connections Thrym has on his phone, accessing his data, and putting everything he's worked towards at risk.'

'Oh shit.' Svad sighed. 'Remind me never to get on your bad side.'

'You never will.'

'Alright love birds, come on.' Thor said, standing from the table. 'We'll give you a ride home, Svad. I doubt Thrym is in any mood to take you himself.'

'Or,' Loki said, wrapping their arm around Svad's waist as they began to walk away from the table, leaving a desperate Thrym phoning someone and asking them what to do. 'You could come home with me...'

Thor just shook his head and rolled his eyes fondly at his sibling.

'The meal's on him,' he said to their waiter, gesturing back at Thrym as they left the restaurant.

Santilmo
Imelda Taylor

Iriss tried to nap on the three-hour journey to the film location. The rest of the crew, laughing, chattering, and singing along to whatever was playing, made it impossible in a cluttered van. Nothing extraordinary for their lot. Outside, it was already dark, and the further they went, the darker it became. Streetlights and houses were further apart.

The music stopped. The driver announced that his phone seemed to have died. The laughter and the chattering faded out. Everybody turned their attention to the surroundings. There was beauty in the darkness. The silhouettes of the trees outlined the view ahead. The shadowy hills and fields, the clear sky above illuminated by the moon, and the sparkling stars were a welcome backdrop as opposed to the towering buildings, street lamps, and bridges of the city they'd come from.

When tendrils of clouds covered the moon, the only source of light was the van's headlights; the vehicle's engine was the only sound they could hear. White lines were painted on the trees to guide visitors to their destination. When Iriss looked at her friends, everybody seemed to be clutching whatever it was they were holding: their bags, their jackets, whatever.

'We have arrived!' announced the driver after a few minutes of navigating the area. Everybody was keen to get out to stretch their legs despite leaving the comfort of the air-conditioned van for the humid summer air. In front of them was an impressive Spanish-period stone house which brought them back to the time when the Spaniards ruled the Philippines. They were welcomed by their host, Neil, who somehow resembled Father Christmas, and his wife.

The crew were greeted by an array of Filipino food spread on a wooden table ornate with carvings. The savoury smell wafted pleasantly around the room and the food was arranged beautifully. Each of the crew took their phones out to take photos.

Over supper, Neil asked about the film they were making. Zash, the director, was eager to talk about her plans for the short film and the locations they were going to shoot.

Soon, the conversation turned to the house. Neil gave a brief of the house's history and pointed out its unique features which were not often seen in modern houses. It was all fascinating, but what drew everybody's attention was the story of the girl who disappeared in the *bodega*, a storage place for the sacks of rice and crops.

'She was a farm girl who used to come and serve my great grandparents during the Japanese occupation. She was very timid, soft-spoken, and popular with the local lads. Then, people heard that her parents sold her to the Japanese to be one of their *comfort women*. When the Japanese came to take her, she ran away and hid in the bodega. That was the last time she was seen. Every year on the anniversary of her disappearance, you can hear howling coming from the *bodega*.'

There was silence for a few seconds. The group loved spooky stories, but what they loved more was debunking them.

'Did she die?' asked Dave, the cameraman and editor.

'Is she haunting this house?' added Marty, one of the actors.

Iriss kept quiet as she took things in. Karen, one of the other actors, did a sign of the cross.

'But who saw her come towards the bodega?' Zash queried and leaned back while crossing her arms.

'Is it even true?' Marty insisted.

'That was the story,' Neil teased. 'I'm not sure if it was true, either, but the girl existed. It's been a talk in the family for generations.'

After they said their goodnights, got washed and changed, the group settled into their sleeping bags on the living room floor. It was soon pitch black. A cacophony of snoring kept Iriss awake. As she was closest to the window, she couldn't help but crack open the *ventanilla*—a small window below the windowsill. Although her eyes adjusted to the dark, there was nothing to be seen outside other than the speckled night sky adorned by the stars and the shadows of the trees swaying to the gentle breeze.

As she gazed into the distance, Iriss noticed something bright floating in midair, something that looked like a ball of fire. She gasped as her heart raced, being careful not to disturb the others' sleep. She squinted but couldn't make out what she was seeing. How could a ball of fire suddenly appear?

'It's not a ghost,' she told herself. 'Maybe it's just somebody walking with a torch.' Iriss tried to convince herself when the ball of fire shot away like lightning into the distance. She quickly shut the window and turned her back on it. She curled up in her sleeping bag and tried hard to fall asleep.

In her sleep, Iriss dreamt of the missing farm girl. It was a stormy night in her dream. She could hear thunder and saw flashes of lightning. She saw the farm girl hiding behind sacks of rice and other grains in her soaked clothes and dripping hair. A Japanese soldier was closing in holding a torch. The light from the torch reminded Iriss of the ball of fire she saw.

Morning broke and the sun shone directly in Iriss's eyes. She was blinded for a few seconds, but when she got up, she realised everybody was getting ready for breakfast. Some were scrambling through their suitcases, looking for their toiletry bags, towels, and clothes. Breakfast was waiting on the table. Traditional pandesal, eggs and a thermos full of fragrant coffee were inviting. Despite being bothered by it, she dare not mention her dream. It was just a dream, after all.

Everybody had their fill of breakfast, equipment was set and packed, and the actors were in costume. Iriss was in charge of make-up and the general running around. Although her job was important, especially in a humid climate, Iriss sometimes wished she was more talented or prettier. She would have loved to be in costumes, say a few lines, and possibly sing or dance on camera. On the other hand, she felt privileged to be included in such a talented group.

Iriss forgot all about her dream. The entire crew focused on their respective tasks. Upon reaching their destination, they still had to cross a muddy rice field to get to a creek to shoot a scene. The actors needed to get out of their costumes once again so they wouldn't get muddy. Iriss had to carry Karen and Marty's costumes along with their picnic.

When they finally reached the exact location, everybody was filthy with mud. They washed themselves in the creek, which put them behind schedule.

The actors got back in their costumes. The equipment was set. Zash was about to say 'action' when the camera froze and wouldn't record. Minutes became an hour before the camera started working.

An hour after shooting, the crew decided it was time for a break. They collectively admired the view and the serenity of their surroundings.

'Are we safe from the wildlife here, by the way?' Karen asked as she realised they were open to nature and were completely vulnerable.

'What are you expecting, wolves?' Marty teased. Karen threw a banana peel at him.

Iriss was taken aback by Karen's behaviour. As she looked around, she realised how much of a mess they created. Iriss started feeling bothered, but she didn't know what was causing such an awkward feeling.

'So where should we go if we need the toilet?' inquired Karen.

'What toilet?' Zash asked sarcastically. 'You have to find a "spot".'

'Where can I find a spot around here?' Karen asked.

Zash spread her arms, pointing at the surroundings.

'It depends how desperate you are,' Marty said. 'I'm going to find one. You can come and "help."' Marty wiggled his eyebrows suggestively. Karen threw an empty water bottle at Marty as he ran away to dodge it.

'Next time, it won't be empty!' Karen shouted back.

Karen asked Iriss if she could come with her. Iriss, barely finished with her sandwich, didn't hesitate. They found a spot behind a huge tree. Karen was in mid-wee when she and Iriss heard a rustling noise. Iriss's heart skipped a beat, and Karen tried to finish quickly. Somehow, Marty's words made her imagine all sorts of things.

'Did you hear that?' asked Karen nervously.

'Yeah, are you done?' Iriss answered.

'Yeah, don't leave me, okay?' Karen nervously rushed towards Iriss.

She held onto Iriss's arms and tried not to look back.

'It could be nothing,' Iriss said.

Something barked, and both Karen and Iriss shrieked.

They dashed and stopped when their legs ceased to cooperate. Looking behind, it seemed like they were safe. Iriss offered Karen a drink from the bottled water she carried with her. In one gulp, Karen handed Iriss an empty bottle.

'What am I going to do with this?' Iriss said.

'Sorry,' Karen replied. 'Come on, let's get back with the others,' she added.

'Which way?' Iriss rhetorically asked, realising she didn't recognise the spot where they stood. She checked her phone to call Zash but there was no signal. Karen started to panic.

'What are we going to do?' Karen turned to Iriss, relying on her for a plan.

'I don't know! Maybe they'll look for us if we're gone for too long.'

Santilmo

'I don't really want to wait till we're gone for too long!' Karen snapped at Iriss. 'Do something!'

Iriss, for a moment, felt she failed Karen but soon realised they were both in the same position, and Karen knew no better than her. In that instance, she felt belittled and thought Karen was acting like a spoiled brat. However, she chose to bite her tongue as it wasn't worth the effort. She just told herself that Karen wasn't thinking straight, therefore acting out of character, although she didn't know Karen that well.

'Do you want to try and find our way back, then?' Iriss asked.

'We're sitting ducks here. What if the wolf gets us?' Karen said, almost sounding like a whining child.

'You seriously don't believe that, do you? There are no wolves in this part of the world. It might just be a stray dog,' Iriss explained.

'That is not any better!' Karen snapped.

'Look, all you have to say is we're better off moving if that's what you wanted,' Iriss argued. She didn't know how long she could keep her cool with Karen. 'Which way do we go then?'

'How should I know!' Karen shouted back.

Iriss walked away following what looked like a path.

'Hey! What the hell! You're leaving me behind? That's just stupid.' Karen called back as she followed behind. Iriss didn't answer back. She didn't want to waste energy although she was worked up and ready to burst. Instead, she told herself that Karen must be afraid. Karen was very superstitious after all.

After what felt like hours of walking, Iriss stopped. In front of her was a tree that looked familiar. It looked like Karen's 'spot'. If it was, it would only mean they had walked in circles. However, it also meant they could trace their way to where the others were. Iriss wanted to tell Karen the good news but she wasn't behind her anymore.

'Karen!' Iriss called. 'Karen, we're probably close. Where are you?' No answer. Iriss panicked and traced the trail she took. Nothing looked the same. Iriss's chest felt tight and her breathing was heavy. Finally, she found Karen sitting on a log.

'Karen! There you are. I was looking for you.'

'I got tired, okay? I wanted to rest.'

'You could have told me!'

'You were ignoring me!'

'All right, never mind. I found the spot where we were. We can probably trace our way back to the others,' Iriss said to Karen, expecting she would be pleased.

'Back to the dog?' Karen snapped back. 'The reason why we ran in the first place, to get away from it and you want us to go back there?'

'It wasn't there anymore. Come on.'

After a few moments, they heard growling again. Iriss grabbed Karen. This time, Karen didn't hesitate to come.

They ran as fast as their legs could carry them. Karen with her long legs, fitter than Iriss, left her behind. She paused when she heard Iriss's scream but carried on running.

* * *

Iriss woke into a nighttime filled with explosions, gunshots and barking. Bewildered by the entire event, she took a while to realise she had no recollection of how she got to where she was. Above her, a dog that looked like a wolf, if not bigger, was barking at her face. As soon as she was conscious, the dog tugged her sleeve so strongly that she heard it rip. Could the dog be helping her? It could have mauled her if it wanted to when she was unconscious, but it didn't.

Iriss tried to get up but fell back on the ground when she heard a blast. The dog started barking at her again as if telling her to hurry up. Crawling on her elbows and knees, she and the dog reached a spot surrounded by tall grass. The dog crouched down on the ground. Soon after Iriss followed its lead, she understood why. Soldiers dressed in Japanese uniforms ran past them with their guns. Iriss couldn't understand yet; there wasn't a moment to stop and figure out what was happening.

The firing and the bombing stopped. By then, Iriss lost the concept of time. Had it been a few minutes, an hour or more? She couldn't tell. Iriss became aware of the damp ground she was lying on and the grass tickling her nose. She was glad she had the dog with her but when she reached out, she couldn't feel it. Panic overcame her. She was alone in a dark field where she could be shot anytime but the same could happen if she didn't move. Her muscles trembled from the cold and fear. However, she managed to support herself with her elbows and get back on her knees, where she was able to see the pitch-dark field. There were no signs of bombing: no smoke, no embers, but the smell of burning lingered.

A ball of light approaching got her attention. Iriss toppled onto her back as it hovered over her. She was mesmerised by its white and soft yellow light crackling like fire. It flew past just quickly enough for her to follow.

The ball of light guided her through the muddy rice field to what looked like an abandoned hut. Only, it wasn't. In the corner of the hut sat a girl with unkempt hair and dirty clothes. Iriss was relieved to find another person. The same could not be said about the other girl.

'What have you brought here!' the girl shouted in a chilling shrill voice. Her face was a picture of terror, with pale and bulging eyes, which looked empty and soulless. Iriss ran back and fell when something heavy jumped at her and pinned her on the ground.

'I have nothing! I brought nothing.' A sob broke out of fear as she shouted back to the girl.

Iriss heard a deep loud bark.

'I wasn't talking to you. Who are you?' asked the girl in a much calmer voice.

'Iriss,' she said, still trembling. Her fear slowly faded as she felt something wet on her cheek. It was the dog!

'Elmo! Stop that!' the girl pushed the dog off Iriss.

'And who are you?' snapped Iriss, annoyed with being pinned down by the heavy beast, yet pleased to feel the weight off her back.

'Anita,' the girl answered.

'Let me guess, this dog is Elmo.' Iriss pointed at the dog with her chin as she stretched and rubbed her back.

'That's not a dog,' said Anita.

'A wolf then?'

'Neither!' Anita growled back, not taking her eyes off the dog.

Iriss asked no further. At first, she thought she was going to get mauled by what could easily be the hound from hell. However, her fear shifted to being in the company of a mad girl. She didn't know where she was or where her friends could be.

Anita and Elmo sat eerily across from each other, not blinking nor moving. Everything seemed to be at a standstill, as if time was frozen. As this happened, Iriss couldn't help but notice what Anita was wearing: a faded floral dress with its hem torn and its collar frayed. What happened to this girl?

Woof!

Iriss snapped out of her daze. Elmo moved but Anita stayed petrified. Before her very eyes, the dog turned into a ball of fire.

'Hey, wait!'

Iriss chased Elmo through the grassland, across the rice fields, jumping dykes. She kept her eyes on the ball of fire until they reached a familiar house. Once they stopped, Elmo turned himself back to a dog.

'You brought me back? Oh thank you, thank you! I'd give you a hug but I'm still slightly afraid of you.'

Iriss crouched down so she was level with the dog. She held out her hand to let Elmo sniff it but Elmo rubbed his head on Iriss and came closer.

Their bonding moment was interrupted by a woman with long hair running past them, soaked. It was only then that Iriss realised it was raining heavily but neither she nor Elmo were wet. Iriss turned to look in the direction where the woman ran to. As she stood up to have a better look, she saw the woman run around the corner of the house. She thought the woman was strangely familiar. It wasn't long till a couple of Japanese soldiers ran past going in the same direction. Elmo followed.

'Wait!'

Iriss wasn't sure why she had to come after Elmo especially when her instinct suggested she hide. However, a small part of her feared for the woman. She watched the soldiers split up. One went straight on, the other in the direction the woman headed, the one Elmo chose to chase. As they turned to the corner, Iriss was engulfed by darkness. Her legs kept moving though it felt as if they were on air. A force pushed her through the darkness as if she was coming out of a thick black curtain. Elmo was behind her this time.

Confused, Iriss found herself standing by the bodega's door. She could hear thunder and the pelting of the rain. After a few moments, the same woman ran towards her ... then through her.

'Am I a ghost?' Iriss whispered to herself.

Iriss watched the woman struggling to open the door with wet hands, her footwear slipping on the muddy ground. At that point, she realised that it was Anita.

The bodega cracked open. 'Come in now, hurry,' whispered a male voice.

Elmo followed and so did Iriss.

'Stay here and don't make a noise,' instructed the male voice. Through the cracks in the door, a light shone across Anita's face.

Iriss realised that this was very similar to her dream. Perhaps she wasn't a ghost, after all; this could only be a dream. She shut her eyes tight and forced herself to wake up. But, when she opened her eyes, she was still in the same place.

There were voices outside. The Japanese soldier commanded the man to open the door. With a rifle pointing at him, he had no choice but to obey orders.

The soldier scanned through the bodega with his torch. Satisfied that the girl was not on the premises, he left.

'You're safe now,' whispered the man as he sat next to Anita. Iriss finally made out what he looked like through the lamp he lit. He was a little fairer and neater than the male household staff she met. His shirt was soaked so he took it off and tossed it on one side.

'You're soaking wet too. Here let me help you out of those,' the man offered.

Anita flinched as the man tried to come closer.

'Don't be shy, I'm just trying to help,' said the man, sounding more frustrated than concerned. 'How about coming inside in the warmth?'

Anita shook her head, not uttering a word.

'All right, stay here; I'll get you something to dry yourself. You're safe here, but don't make a sound. The soldiers might still be around.' The man's warning made Anita shiver even more, not just from the cold but also out of fear.

'I have a bad feeling about this, Elmo.' Iriss turned to Elmo. She crouched down to check on Anita. 'Hey, can you hear me?' Iriss whispered to Anita but Anita couldn't see or hear her. Iriss tried to grab Anita's shoulder but her hand just went through like touching a hologram. 'This is just a dream,' she reminded herself. Elmo barked, alerting the return of the man.

He came back with some blankets. 'Here, take off your wet clothes and wrap this around you, I won't look.' The man turned around to give Anita a chance to get dry.

'You've been serving our family for years. I'm hardly a stranger.' He looked over his shoulder at Anita who was now wrapped up in the blanket. The man moved next to her but Anita looked in the opposite direction.

He tucked Anita's loose hair behind her ear. 'You know, I find you very beautiful. I heard you have many suitors. If only I wasn't married...' He stroked Anita's arm with the back of his hand. 'I'd look after you and you wouldn't have to be a servant ... or a harlot to the Japanese. Would you like that?'

Anita looked away and kept silent.

'Have you ever been kissed?' asked the man, as he moved closer to Anita.

'Stop!' Iriss looked away and faced Elmo. 'Why do I have to see this?' Elmo barked back. Behind her, she could hear Anita's plea. Iriss covered her ears but even the muffled noise was unbearable.

'Be quiet, you'll wake my wife!' the man warned.

Elmo whimpered at Iriss, nudging her with his nose.

Iriss pressed her hands harder on her ears, shut her eyes tighter. 'Stop! Please stop!'

Silence.

A breeze wrapped around Iriss, tickling her cheek with her hair. Calmness finally transpired.

As Iriss released her ears slowly, the wind gently whispered and the cockerel signalled it was morning. She could hear gushing water. Her eyes opened slowly, light emanated. Dawn was breaking.

Grass was the first thing she saw as her eyes adjusted to the light. Elmo was still sitting next to her but his attention was fixed at a distance. He started whimpering. As she looked around, Iriss realised she was on the dam where they were filming. Had she finally awoken from her dream?

Elmo's bark betokened a person emerging from a distance carrying something heavy on his shoulder covered in a sack. A chill overcame Iriss as she realised it was the same man who had violated Anita, and the load on his shoulder was the same size as Anita. As the man threw the body off the dam, Elmo howled and once again turned into a ball of fire so bright it blinded Iriss.

After moments of silence, Iriss heard clacking. In the bright white light, a shadow started to form, a woman? Anita?

How could it be when I just saw her get thrown off the dam?
'Iriss,' a voice called.

From a shadow, the figure became a blur.

'Anita?' Iriss called back.

The figure gradually became clearer as Iriss blinked: long black hair, bright red lips, well sculpted eyebrows and a bandana tied round her forehead. Around her neck, she wore several charms and amulets.

'Hi. Who's Anita?' The unfamiliar woman asked with a grin on her face.

And who are you? Thought Iriss.

Iriss looked around her surroundings without her head moving. She was in someone's bedroom. She could smell candles and herbs. When she was finally able to move her head, she turned toward where the scent of the candle was coming from. On a bedside table next to her, there were several candles lit along with some crystals, a big bowl and some leaves and twigs. On the other side of the bed were her friends.

Dave was, of course, filming.

'Take it slowly. Have some water,' the woman instructed Iriss as she offered her a glass of water. 'I'm Jowee, a spiritual healer. You were found near the woods and you were muttering something. When you're ready, you can tell us what happened. But only if you want to.'

Jowee held a big notebook with scribbles on it but it was nothing legible.

Iriss finally had the strength to sit up. 'What's happening?' she asked.

'It seems like you were possessed—but nothing malevolent,' Jowee explained as she consulted her notes.

Iriss tried processing this information.

'Can you tell us what happened? What did you see?' Jowee continued.

Iriss recounted what she thought was a dream, about Elmo turning into a ball of fire, about her strange encounter with Anita and her being chased by the Japanese, the rape and finally, Anita being thrown off the dam. 'I think Anita was the servant girl who disappeared,' Iriss concluded.

Little did Iriss know, Jowee had known all along. Everyone around her knew, as Jowee ran a commentary as key events unfolded with the use of candle drips and the scribbles on her notebook.

Jowee showed Iriss pieces of wax in the shape of a dog that looked like Elmo.

'I don't understand all this …' Iriss said.

'Anita waited a very long time for a person like you to come and save her,' Jowee revealed.

'But I didn't … I didn't.' Iriss felt she failed, her eyes swelled.

'Nobody can change the past let alone their actions,' Jowee said.

'Why me?'

'Because you're the strongest,' revealed Jowee.

Karen's jaw dropped slightly, and she raised an eyebrow while the rest ignored her gesture.

A tear trickled down Iriss' cheek.

***

Neil felt it was his duty to make right what his ancestor did and offered to call the village priest to perform a ritual to send Anita off.

The group said goodbye in the evening they finished filming. They hopped in their hired van and the driver turned the radio on, knowing the group like music. He asked how the filming went and Zash filled him in. It wasn't long after that everyone drifted off—in silence. They turned their attention to the surroundings: the hills, the fields, the trees under the pillowy clouds under the dark blue sky—and the dam. Each one did a sign of the cross.

'Goodbye, Anita,' Iriss muttered. 'Goodbye, Elmo. Wherever you are now, and thank you.'

Inspired by real events.

In memory of Zash Villareal, Mary Ann Tolentino, Jowee Curiano, Anna Lopez-Tan, and Neil Tonge.

The King Who Would Be Rishi:
The Tale of Vishwamitra
(The Abridged, "Good Parts" Version)
R. A. Cheddi

It has been a hard week for us all, but the gods challenge us in our most trying of times.

It was something I contemplated as I prepared two cups of herbal tea for my wife and son. They were ill with a severe cold and I was lucky enough to not catch it.

I placed the cups on a tray and first went to my wife, Anushka, who was curled up on the couch under a thick blanket. Her Indian soaps played in the background. I placed the mug by the table, covered by mounds of tissues. She turned her head, puffy eyes looking at mine and she smiled in thanks.

Running a hand through her hair, I rose and took the second cup upstairs to my son, Vish's, room. I could hear his hacking coughs from the bottom step. I heard him sit up and turn to the door as I entered his room. "Papa," he said weakly, his brows furrowed. "Being sick sucks."

"I know," I said, chuckling as I placed the cup on his bedside table. "Can't sleep?"

"No," Vish said before breaking into another fit. I suppressed a sigh as I rubbed his back. When his cough subsided, he lay back and looked at me. "Papa, could you tell me a story?" he murmured, his voice scratchy. "I know you're not as good as mom is, but could you?"

The King Who Would Be Rishi

I sat and thought for a moment. His mother usually told him stories to put him to bed, while I tidied up for the night. *What story could I tell him?*

Suddenly, as though the gods had answered my plea, I had an answer. "Vishwamitra," I addressed my son by his full name. "Have I ever told you the origin of your name?"

He looked at me, a spark of wonder apparent in his tired, baggy eyes. "My name ... came from somewhere?"

"Mmm." I nodded. "It's a story from ancient India, when the gods fought against demons, when Shri Ram defeated Ravana to recover his beloved Sita, and when rishi—the sages—were renowned for their mystical powers." I paused. "Would you like to hear this story?"

"Does it have any superheroes?"

I had to will myself not to laugh—all Vish could ever think about were superheroes. "Yes, it does!" I said, before a thought entered my mind. "Well, to a certain extent, that is. It also has fighting, revenge, a wish-granting cow and, at one point, an attempt to create a brand new universe from scratch. Oh, and godly miracles. Can't forget that." I added it as an afterthought.

Despite his exhaustion, Vish looked askance at me when I said those things. "This isn't gonna turn into something about religion, is it?" he asked.

"No, son," I said, shaking my head. At ten and a half, Vish dreaded going to the mandir. For if there was one thing that a child at his age cannot do, it's sit still while an old man lectures about the nature of good and evil in the world. "But if it worries you so, I'll leave whatever philosophies out of this tale. Call it ... the abridged, Good Parts version? So, what do you say?"

My son said nothing for a moment, before slowly taking a pillow and propping it up against his headboard. He then leaned back, drew his comforter close and settled in. I took that as a yes. Smiling, I cleared my throat and began the tale.

"Once upon a time, thousands and thousands of years ago, there was a king..."

* * *

Kaushika was a young and mighty king of a prosperous land who commanded a vast and fearsome army. And he was bored.

'*There are no enemies to fight, no kingdoms nearby worth conquering, and my council have all but secured peace within my realm.*' the king thought listlessly, picking his teeth as he lazed on the rich, silk cushion of his throne. '*While this is very good for me, overall, I still wish something exciting would happen...*'

Suffice to say, King Kaushika soon got his wish. One day, a vassal—whose name is not important, but he sported an impressive moustache and goatee—burst into the chamber and crossed the marble hall leading to the throne. "M-My lord," he said breathlessly as he approached the king.

Kaushika sprang up from his prone position and sat regally. Excitement welled within him and he felt it difficult to maintain his composure. "Out with it, man!" he demanded.

Moustache straightened, caught his breath and said to the king, "My lord, I've-I've heard word of an ashram which holds a wondrous creature. A cow said to grant whatever wishes a man desires."

Kaushika's breath hitched and a grin spread across his lips. "A wish-granting cow, eh?" he implored. "That sounds like something that a kingdom would need, not some silly ashram. Pray tell, vassal, whose ashram is this, anyway?"

The vassal in question went into another stiff bow. "M-Milord, it belongs to the great rishi, Vasishta," he said.

The king felt a chill go through his spine at the mention of the name. He couldn't describe or even understand why the name struck such a chord with him, seeing as it was the first time he ever heard of it. But there was something about the name that brought about a small feeling of dread.

But, he shrugged it off. "Rally a company; we shall head to the ashram of Vasishta," he commanded, pushing himself off of his throne. "By my word as king, this sacred cow shall be ours!"

* * *

"Papa, hold on."

Vish interrupted me mid-story before doubling over in a coughing fit. Once he settled back against the pillow, he stared at me quizzically. "I thought this story was about why I have this silly name? What does this Kaushika guy have to do with it?"

"Everything," I replied, hands spread akimbo. "For you see, Vishwamitra used to go by the name Kaushika. And it's important because the events to come will shape our king into the man you were named after." I folded my arms. "But, perhaps you're not interested, so drink your tea and go back to bed."

Vish looked at me sulkily. "No, I do want you to continue," he whined piteously.

I let out a breath and then shook my head at the boy's indecisiveness. "Then less lip, more zip," I said. "Besides, we're at a pretty good part now."

"King Kaushika and a large company of men then travelled to the ashram of Vasishta…"

* * *

"I was not expecting this."

Kaushika and his entourage gaped at the majesty of Vasishta's ashram. What he'd assumed would be a few mud huts and dirt floors was instead a grandiose, single-level compound made of fine, pale sandstone surrounded by a sea of tall, strong trees. The ashram was bedecked with golden trims and architectural flourishes that reflected the light of the sun, which gave the building a divine, golden aura. There was neither a gate nor walls that surrounded the complex—this fact puzzled the king as it left the ashram open to attack from foreign invaders.

Here's hoping that they give me what I ask for, or else I would feel really bad about laying waste to such a marvellous building, Kaushika thought as he approached the open threshold.

There were no guards, but a single man—a yogi—wearing a bright orange lungi who sat cross-legged at the entrance, his eyes closed in meditation. His long hair was tied up in a bun, his equally long beard was trimmed and neat and he had several dozen bands of prayer beads wrapped around his upper arms and wrists. Though he appeared to be the same age as he was, Kaushika got the feeling that this yogi was wiser than he let on, which led him to believe that the man would be wise to heed the words of a royal.

"Ho there," Kaushika called out to the man.

The yogi did not stir, his hands still clasped within his lap, his body erect, and his eyes and face in the perfect portrait of serenity.

The king's lips parted in awe. "Truly, this is a man of dizzying devotion to the gods," he whispered to himself. "He is so focused on his meditation, he does not hear the calls of those on the mortal plane." Kaushika then cleared his throat and called out again to the meditating yogi, this time, much louder. "Ho there, is this the ashram of the great rishi, Vasishta?"

The yogi did not stir, but instead, slowly raised a hand upwards. "You've interrupted me from a very good nap, so keep your 'Ho, there,'" he said, his deep, tenor voice sounding scratchy. "What do you want?"

He was asleep the whole time? The king didn't know whether he should be insulted by the yogi's tone or shocked at the fact that he wasn't in the throes of tapasya —an intense spiritual meditation. Behind him, he heard his company of men shuffle about, unsure of what to make of the situation. Nevertheless, he collected himself and took charge. "Forgive me," Kaushika said. "But my men and I have journeyed long to visit this place and speak to Vasishta. I've heard tales of his wondrous ashram—"

"And you wanted to see it for yourself, huh?" the yogi cut in as he stood and dusted off his lungi. "Yep, sure, you're not the first ones to say that. Nor are you the last," he muttered that last part to himself. "Please, do come in as our honourable guests. Vasishta will join you shortly."

So, the King and his men entered the ashram, and its inside was just as grand as its facades. There were small homes surrounding a central clearing, each of which was built with the same, fine sandstone. The clearing was a bountiful meadow of long, green grass, a pond filled with crystal clear water and several trees to provide plenty of shade. Set atop the meadow were several rows of sumptuous food—golden brown parathas, rich, vegetarian curries served alongside fluffy rice and the finest of lentils.

There was more than enough for Kaushika, his company and the residents of the ashram, which made the king wonder. *How were they able to procure this much food so quickly? Do the gods truly favour Vasishta and grant him this bounty? Or is this all the work of the cow?*

The yogi led the men to the clearing and sat under the shade of one of the tall, mighty teak trees. "Please, sit and eat," he said, waving to the food on the meadow. "I, Vasishta, welcome your company and your intentions to seek enlightenment within my ashram."

Kaushika did a double-take and his jaw dropped. "YOU are Vasishta?" he exclaimed.

"Indeed, who else were you expecting? Some *other* yogi dressed in orange?" Vasishta inquired, raising an eyebrow. "Now, come, sit and eat. The food's getting cold."

As they feasted, Kaushika inched closer to Vasishta and spoke to him in hushed tones. "How is this all possible?" he asked. "The quality of the stone, the richness of the interior, this beautiful clearing and all this food and comfort … Is it due in part to—"

"—Sabala? Yes," Vasishta finished for him. He then turned to the meadow and whistled through his teeth.

Emerging from a patch of long grass was a peculiar cow with the head and breasts of a woman and the wings of a bird. Her body was covered with velvety soft snow-white fur and her large, brown eyes gazed dolefully at the gathering of soldiers as she approached and knelt by Vasishta's side.

"Sabala is a divine kamadhenu—a goddess capable of materializing anything one desires—"

* * *

"Oh! So she's a living Horn of Plenty," Vish interrupted me mid-sentence.

"A what of what?" I blurted, doing a double-take.

He coughed a bit before explaining himself and smiling. "Yeah, a Horn of Plenty. An object that provides unlimited items. Amit and I heard about it from other kids at school playing a board game or something … I think it was called Dungeons and Dragons? One kid was going on and on about Horn of Plenty and what it does."

"Oh, I see," I said, my lips parting at Vish's rapid-fire explanation. I must have looked silly because Vish started laughing, which then erupted into coughs.

I chuckled. "Well, then, ready to continue?"

At his eager nod, I cleared my throat and continued the story. "Once Kaushika had confirmed what he heard about the cow, he was determined to have her for his own. He begged and pleaded with Vasishta to consider his request but was turned down every time. And then, things got serious…"

* * *

"No."

"But—"

"No," Vasishta countered again as he swept the floors of his ashram with his disciples.

"If you could just hear me out—"

"I said *No*," the rishi said yet again, his face and voice as calm as still water. "Now, I suggest you head to the main chamber and chant some mantras to help ease your mood. One of my sons can help you choose something calming." He then went back to his sweeping and left the king to his own devices.

It had been two days since the great feast and Kaushika was determined to have Sabala for himself. He tried to persuade Vasishta at every opportunity, but the rishi denied him each and every time. His refusals only strengthened the king's resolve to have the cow for himself.

As the sun began to set that day, he'd had enough. Kaushika stormed out of the room he stayed in and crossed over to the meadow where Sabala lay. Taking a bit of rope, he tied it around the cow's neck and began to pull.

Startled out of her stupor, the cow let out a shrill, piteous moo, alerting everyone within the compound. Some of the king's men saw what their ruler was up to and rushed over to help him.

"Hm? What's going on here?" Vasishta said as he emerged from the main chamber to the chaos. "Kaushika? What are you doing?"

"I have had enough of your refusals," the king shouted, grunting as Sabala tried to fight off her aggressors, her wings fluttering furiously. "This cow doesn't belong to a dirty little ashram like this. A creature with powers like hers would be better suited to serving a kingdom and its people."

Sabala looked at Vasishta with tear-stricken eyes as she struggled against the men pulling her. The rishi just stood there and she wondered what she had done to offend him, to cause him not to lend a hand to help her. The sorrow and fear that she felt allowed her the strength to overcome her aggressors. She fled from them towards Vasishta and knelt at his feet.

Vasishta bent over and placed a hand on Sabala's head. He smiled. "Oh, my dear Sabala, who is like a sister to me," he said, in a voice loud enough for Kaushika to hear. "Bring forth men to oppose King Kaushika."

The cow's body glowed as a sharp wind began blowing from the east. It roused the dirt and sand from the ground and began forming it into humanoid shapes, each bearing terrible weapons. In the span of seconds, a great army that outnumbered Kaushika's company had materialized. They pointed their weapons at the angry king.

Gritting his teeth, Kaushika ordered his men to retreat from the ashram to his chariot. Once there, the king drew his bow and shot arrow after arrow in a blind rage. But for every stone soldier that he felled, two more took its place. The inexhaustible force summoned by

Sabala soon routed the royal forces of King Kaushika. The king's anger only rose as he watched his own sons, who joined his entourage at his behest, be cut down in front of him. Disgraced, the ruler was forced to withdraw, with his dead children in tow.

* * *

"That's it?" Vish asked as I took a pause.

"Not quite, my son," I answered. "For Kaushika vowed revenge on Vasishta. He saw his refusal to hand over Sabala and his subsequent retaliation against him as a personal insult. He would now stop at nothing to destroy the rishi, which is why he went to the Himalayas…"

* * *

Sitting cross-legged in a small cave nestled within the tallest mountains of the world, the former King Kaushika chanted mantras devoted to Lord Shiva over and over. Shiva—known as the remover of all obstacles—would be the only deity that could assist him with defeating Vasishta, he decided.

His pride wounded and his children dead, vengeance against the rishi consumed the king's mind. To that end, he'd abdicated the throne and handed it to one of his remaining sons. He then set off to one of the tallest and harshest places known to man to perform intense spiritual prayer so as to satisfy Lord Shiva.

For years, he devoted himself to a single purpose: to gain the favour of the God of Destruction. One day, upon the recital of his one hundred and eight thousandth mantra, he felt a presence.

A voice, which sounded like everything and nothing at the same time, spoke out to him. "I AM PLEASED WITH YOUR DEVOTION, KAUSHIKA. STATE YOUR REASON AS TO WHY YOU ARE PERFORMING SUCH SEVERE TAPASYA?"

"O Lord Shiva, remover of all obstacles," Kaushika said in reverence. "If you are indeed satisfied by my devotion, then please grant your blessing to be master of every and all weapons known to the Devas, the Rishis, the Gandavaras, the Yakshas and the Demons."

There was a pause. "...EVERY WEAPON?" Lord Shiva asked cautiously.

"Every. Weapon." Kaushika answered.

"...ALRIGHT THEN." And as he spoke, Kaushika's mind was filled with the verses required to summon the divine weapons belonging to the Devas, the Rishis, the Gandavaras, the Yakshas and the Demons.

Rising from his spot for the first time in many years, Kaushika's cracked lips split open as he smiled. "Now Vasishta, you *shall* be destroyed," he shouted as he hobbled out of the cave.

* * *

"Oh, for the love of Us, *please* don't tell me you gave that mortal access to *every* divine weapon, Lord Shiva!?" Lord Brahma, God of Creation spoke shrilly, pacing around in his counterpart's abode up in the mountains.

Lord Shiva made no indication to acknowledge Lord Brahma's presence as he sat rigidly in the lotus pose. After a long pause, the god replied, rather cryptically. "Patience, Lord Brahma. Wait and you shall see what happens next…"

* * *

Weeks later, Kaushika, his hair and beard unkempt and wearing nothing more than a tattered robe, approached Vasishta's ashram. Unlike last time, there was no one at the threshold to welcome him. He didn't mind this as he raised his hand skyward and chanted the divine words bequeathed to him by Lord Shiva.

In a flash, the sword Nandaka, the favoured weapon of Lord Vishnu the Protector whose keen, flaming edge incinerated all ignorance, materialized in his hands—

* * *

"Oh, now I get it."

Another interruption. I repressed another sigh. "What do you get, son?"

"I get why the divine weapons sound familiar to me! It's like in cousin Rahul's video game, Final Fantasy XV," Vish rambled. He sipped on his now-cool tea to whet his throat and continued. "The main character was able to make weapons appear out of nowhere! Just like Vishwamitra!"

I had many questions, but the one I vocalized was not the one I expected. "If it's called Final Fantasy, why are there fifteen of them?"

"Nevermind that Papa," Vish brushed the question aside. "Keep going. I want to know what happens next."

"Only if you promise not to interrupt again!" I retorted, crossing my arms. "One more and it'll be time for bed."

"OK, OK, I promise I won't interrupt again," Vish parroted.

I stared at him critically for a few beats before smiling once more. "Very well, let's continue…"

***

With Nandaka in hand, Kaushika swung it at the threshold door. The portal shattered into splinters and then caught fire. People and animals fled in wild panic as the flames began spreading all throughout Vasishta's ashram.

Striding forward through the chaos, Kaushika soon reached the meadow in the middle of the complex. There, Vasishta sat under the shade of the tree. "You again?" he said, standing up, a tinge of annoyance in his voice. "Didn't you learn your lesson?"

"I have!" Kaushika retorted angrily. He planted the blue-hued sword into the ground, whispered another verse and summoned the divine weapon, Sharanga—a mighty bow and arrow decorated with intricate, gilded curves and gemstones. "For your utter disrespect towards me and my request for Sabala, you and this ashram will be burnt to cinders."

Pointing it skyward, Kaushkia pulled on the bowstring and let it loose. From the string, an innumerable volley of arrows materialized, each one racing towards and impaling Vasishta's sons.

Despite the loss of his kin, Vasishta remained impassive. With careful, measured movements befitting his status as a Brahma Rishi, he placed his hand behind the tree in the meadow and clasped a normal, wooden stick that leaned against its trunk. "Well, then," Vasishta said, brandishing the stick. "If you truly wish to direct your anger at a single point, why not come at me? Leave my ashram and its people alone."

Kaushika looked at the simple man holding the stick and laughed long and hard. "Hah, a challenge, is it?" he said mockingly. "Well, I automatically win. There is no *conceivable* way that you can beat me with that puny piece of wood." He dismissed the bow and took up the gem-studded handle of Nandaka once more. Holding it with a two-handed grip, the former king rushed forward and brought the blade down on Vasishta.

With one hand, the rishi brought the stick up to meet the blade and a strange thing occurred. There was a bright flash, followed by the sound of something being sucked up.

When the light faded, Kaushika saw, to his eternal surprise, that Vasishta still stood. Even more shocking was the fact that Nandaka seemed to have vanished from his hands! "W-What's going on here?" the former king demanded as he tried and failed to summon the divine sword. "This is inconceivable! Ah! Fine then, I'll just use another one."

Kaushika then recalled the mighty bow, Sharanga. He aimed and fired a volley of arrows at Vasishta. However, they and the bow itself vanished the moment the first shaft struck the rishi's staff.

"What? Again? Inconceivable," Kaushika yelled as he looked on, utterly confused at what was going on right now. "That's it, you're getting every weapon. That stick of yours has to have *some* weakness."

And so, the former and vengeful king summoned every weapon belonging to the Devas, the Rishis, the Gandavaras, the Yakshas and the Demons. Each and every time they struck Vasishta's staff, they became absorbed into it. And at each moment, Kaushika would bellow "Inconceivable!"

* * *

"OK, really Papa?"

My mouth hung open as Vish cut in once more. I closed my mouth, my lips pressed in a tight line and threw him a pointed look. "What?" I asked.

"Don't act like you don't know," he responded, folding his arms and looking smug. "There's no way this is how the story's told. You're just going off of *The Princess Bride.*"

Nuts. I didn't think he'd pick that up, especially since we didn't watch that movie together yet—

Wait. Hang on a moment.

"Vish, how do *you* know about *The Princess Bride?*" I asked, my eyes narrowing.

"Easy," Vish replied after a cough. "I sat upstairs last week and peeked down while you were watching it with Mama—"

He went silent as he clapped a hand over his mouth.

I glared at him. "It was a school night and you were supposed to be asleep," I said through gritted teeth.

Turning away, I pinched the bridge of my nose and let out a withering breath. "Well, I guess that's it for the story, then," I said, rising off of the bed. "You should probably get some sleep—"

Vish's hand shot out and caught my arm, tugging me back. "No, don't leave yet," he protested. "I-I want you to continue."

I stood in place and let him sweat for a few seconds. "Alright, fine," I conceded. "But one more interruption and that's it. Bedtime for you. Understand?"

Vish nodded vigorously.

I took my place on the edge of his bed. "OK, now where was I…"

* * *

After an hour of trying and failing to kill the rishi, Kaushika was at his wits end. "I didn't want to resort to this, but you left me with no other choice. I will use … the BRAHMASTRA!"

* * *

"The Brahm-what-tra?"

This time, I didn't mind the interruption. "The Brahmastra," I exclaimed, turning to Vish and spreading my hands wide. "The most powerful weapon ever created by the gods. Using it even *once* risks destroying the universe."

"Woah," my son said, his jaw dropping in shock. "The king was *that* desperate to beat Vasishta?"

"Uh-huh, so let's get back to the story," I replied, shifting on the child's bed to get more comfortable. "Now, the mere mention of the Brahmastra caused a dark shadow to be cast over the ruined ashram…"

* * *

Hands to the blackened sky, Kaushika summoned the greatest of weapons, the Brahmastra. It was a weapon so fearsome and incredible, it was impossible to describe or even define what it was. Hefting the improbable ordinance, the king then hurled it at Vasishta. "There's no way you'll survive this," he called, cackling as it soared towards the rishi.

Vasishta merely raised the tip of his stick and touched the Brahmastra. A flash, as bright as the sun, enveloped the rishi. When it faded, he remained standing, his body enveloped in a golden aura. The Brahmastra was nowhere to be found.

"No, that's impossible," Kaushika howled, jumping up and down like a toddler having a tantrum. "That was the strongest weapon! You could not, *should not* have survived! It's inconceiv—"

"You keep saying that word," Vasishta cut in loudly, his body and staff radiating the energy of a star. "Stop saying it. It doesn't mean what you think it means."

Truly and utterly defeated, Kaushika dropped to his knees. "But-But I had *every weapon*," he stuttered in disbelief. "How could I have lost?"

"Sorry to say, you didn't have *every* weapon," Vasishta said as he stepped toward the broken king. The aura around him faded and the sky brightened once more. "The staff I hold in my hand is the holy staff, Brahmadanda, the one weapon that can nullify other divine weapons, including its counterpart—the Brahmastra."

"How did you get this?"

"Hmm ... Lord Brahma himself gave it to me when I became a Brahma Rishi," Vasishta answered in a bored tone as he looked around his destroyed ashram. "Good thing I had it too, considering the current universe is still in its infancy. It's a bit *too* early for it to be destroyed and returned to Lord Shiva."

"Speaking of which, Lord Shiva has indeed fooled me," Kaushika admitted. "He promised me every weapon, but failed to mention that the Brahmadanda was not included in the package." Still in a daze, he stood up and made his way out of the complex. As he crossed the threshold, he turned back to the rishi. "I admit my defeat, Vasishta," Kaushika said forlornly. "I can neither return home nor face my people. I have caused such great suffering. Therefore, I see no further alternatives for my path forward except to become a Brahma Rishi like you." That said, Kaushika left Vasishta to his own devices.

"Alright then," the rishi called to his back as he placed the staff against the tree in the clearing and set about cleaning up. "Have fun attaining rishi-dom, I guess? Oh, and don't come back."

***

Lord Brahma breathed a sigh of relief as he watched the conflict de-escalate from Lord Shiva's mountaintop hermitage. "It's a good thing I gave the Brahmadanda to Vasishta, eh, Lord Shiva?"

Lord Shiva sat as he always did, in deep, controlled meditation. "If I may, Lord Brahma?" he intoned.

"Yes?"

"One of these days, your penchant for granting boons like sweets during Holi will bite us on our divine posteriors," Lord Shiva said. "And when that happens and we have to beg Lord Vishnu to incarnate to the mortal plane to fix it, I will be the first to say that I told you so."

"Oh, come now, Lord Shiva," Lord Brahma said, waving off the other god's concerns. "I doubt it will have to come to that."

"Didn't you *just* grant a boon of near-invincibility to that demon king, Ravana of Lanka?" Lord Shiva asked, barely repressing a tone of annoyance from His voice.

"Well, I'm of the opinion that it was a *sensible* boon," the God of Creation said flippantly. "What's the worst he could do, anyway? Enough of him though, I'm much more interested in what this Kaushika fellow will do next." he stroked His impressively immaculate beard. "Let's see how hard he'll work to earn that title, hm?"

* * *

I stopped and paused to look at the clock on Vish's bedside table. "Alright, it's getting late, Vish," I told the boy. "I think it's time to go to bed. You need more rest. We can continue the story tomorrow."

"Awww, man," Vish exclaimed, startling me for a moment. "I wanna know what happens next, Papa. Can't you *please* keep going?"

I blinked in surprise. Never in a million years did I think that my son, a child who believed so passively in the stories of our faith, would be so enamoured with this tale. Either it's the fact that he and his mother being sick presented the perfect opportunity for him to listen to these legends, or I was a better storyteller than I thought?

I decided it was the latter. Take that, Anu.

Noticing that the boy was waiting for an answer, I smiled ear to ear. "Hmm … I mean, I'm sure your mother wouldn't mind if you stayed up a *bit* longer," I said conspiratorially.

Vish flashed a similar, mischievous grin as he snuggled deeper into his covers and awaited the next part of the story.

"So, having failed to defeat Vasishta, but vowing to become a rishi in equal stature, Kaushika travelled south, set up an ashram of his own and began a most rigorous tapasya," I began. "For years, he stored auspices - yogic power, in other words—"

"Oh, like magic points." Vish cut in again. "It's another thing from Rahul's video game."

Right. Last Story Whatever. "I suppose so," I answered uneasily. "But never mind that now; Kaushika attained enough auspices that Brahma descended and declared him a Raja Rishi, or a king amongst rishis. But Kaushika was not satisfied with being a Raja Rishi; he wanted to attain the title of a Brahma Rishi. Thus, he continued with his intense meditations and attained even greater spiritual power.

However, one person would drain him of all that power, while at the same time teaching the sage a very valuable lesson."

"And who is that person?" Vish asked, cocking his head to the side.

"King Trisanku."

* * *

A loud commotion from the outside stirred Kaushika from his meditation. Rising from the ground, he exited the small mud hut and approached the wooden walls that made the threshold of his ashram. His own complex was a far cry from Vasishta's grand sandstone structures, but it was enough for the Raja rishi and his disciples.

"You-you stinking chandala!" One of the aforementioned disciples roared at a man cowering in the dirt. His skin was darkened heavily from the ash that coated his skin and the rags and iron jewelery he wore were falling off of his withered and malnourished body. Though his cheeks and eyes were sunk in and his face was altogether unsavoury, Kaushika recognized this individual from somewhere.

Sidestepping his followers and approaching the man, the rishi addressed the man. "Aren't you King Trisanku?" he said, startling everyone around him. "But … it appears that you have been cursed to be an untouchable. Who has brought you to this state?"

The man fell to the sage's feet in reverence. "Oh great sage," he cried, recounting his tale. "I have been a devoted and benevolent ruler to my people. I never swayed from the path of righteousness and never committed a sin. My only desire was to take my beautiful body with me to the heavens when I die." Trisanku raised his head and looked into Kaushika's eyes, pleadingly. "I brought this forward to my guru and his sons. I pleaded with them to help. Alas, not only did he desert me and called my desire all but impossible, but his sons also placed this wicked curse upon me. Please, you must help me!"

"And who was your guru?" Kaushika asked, quirking an eyebrow upward.

"Vasishta."

Kaushika's heart had stirred at the pitiful king's words. It then turned fiery with rage at the mere mention of his arch-nemesis. He stood at full height and spoke loudly. "Oh, great king! I have heard your words and today, you will find refuge here. We will prepare a great Yajina—a sacrifice so majestic that, even in that cursed, chandala body, you will reach the heavens. I have spoken." He then turned to his disciples. "Go, spread word to the other rishis and their disciples of this magnificent event. Tell them all to attend in a week's time."

His disciples looked at him with a mix of shock, awe and trepidation. They knew full well of Kaushika's impulsive nature and quick temper and so, they set off to inform the sages of the upcoming Yajina. The sages too knew of Kaushika's mighty anger and so, agreed to attend.

The King Who Would Be Rishi

Only Vasishta and his disciples declined, to which Kaushika uttered foul curses that they be reborn into bodies that feast on dog's flesh—

***

"Ewh, gross," Vish said, making a face.

"Hush," I said, my eyes narrowing crossly. "We're at a good part, so listen well."

***

The day of the Yajina soon arrived. Rishis and their acolytes from all over filed into Kaushika's ashram and sat in front of a great stage. Sitting prominently in the center of the stage was King Trisanku, his cursed body fitted with fine silks befitting one of royalty. Next to him was Kaushika, meticulously preparing the steps necessary to send Trisanku's body to heaven.

Taking a ladleful of ghee, the Raja Rishi called to the audience before him. "Let us begin the Yajina," he bellowed, tossing the ghee into the flames and beginning the mantras to extol the virtues of the cursed king. Reluctantly, the other rishis followed suit.

The sacrifice went on for hours as Kaushika and the others chanted in unison. Finally, they reached the part when they requested the gods descend and accept their offering—that being Trisanku's body. The ashram was quelled into silence as Kaushika uttered the last verse. Seconds turned into minutes, which then turned into an hour. But no gods came.

Inwardly, the rishis who attended began to laugh. *What a fool,* they thought. *What a failure of a sage—a former king who challenged Vasishta and lost disgracefully.* Seeing that the Yajina was over, the group began to rise.

"STAY SEATED," Kaushika bellowed, taking another ladleful of ghee and approaching the flame in the Havan kund. His body began to take on a bluish-white glow. "If the gods will not accept Trisanku into the heavens, then I will use the power I have accumulated, all the auspices that have gathered within me, to send him there myself!!" Dumping the ghee into the flames, he then raised his glowing arms at Trisanku. "Rise, O great King Trisanku! Rise and ascend to heaven!"

The energy shot out of Kaushika and into the king's body. The pent-up force caused Trisanku to propel upwards from the stage like a rocket into the heavens. The onlookers gaped in astonishment at the miracle before them and saw firsthand the fruits of Kaushika's terrible labours to himself.

Trisanku's body flew higher and higher until it penetrated the realm of Svarga—that place where the righteous reside before their next incarnation. This startled Indra, King of the Devas and ruler of Svarga. He rushed to the ascending king in his chariot, his mighty thunderbolt weapon, Vajra, clutched tightly in hand.

Indra soon caught up with Trisanku and grabbed him out of the sky. "You foolish mortal, who has earned the curse from his guru on the mortal plane," he said, his voice booming like the thunder in the sky. "How dare you defile this place with your chandala body. Go down and return to where you belong."

And as he did so often with Vajra to those who have sinned, Indra hurled the cursed king back down to the earth. Despite his cheeks flapping wildly from the wind resistance, Trisanku managed to holler out to Kaushika, "SAVE ME!"

Back on the ground, Kaushika watched with panic as the subject of his great sacrifice fell from heaven. Summoning up every ounce of his power, the rishi raised his hand to the falling man. "Stop there," he yelled.

Miraculously, Trisanku stopped. His body hung between Earth and Heaven. The energy sent from Kaushika caused him to glow brightly like a star in the sky.

Kaushika gritted his teeth. *If the heavens and gods will not accept him … then I shall create a new heaven of my own.* With a great roar, the sage expunged the entirety of his aura and sent it skyward. From there, as if he was Brahma the Creator Himself, Kaushika began constructing a new heaven and new Devas that would accept Trisanku.

As he rapidly neared the completion of a constellation of stars for his new heaven, he was approached by Indra and the rest of the Devas. The king of the Devas himself looked at the sage imploringly. "Kaushika," he said, his normally booming voice reduced to that of a pitying spark. "Please, let us end this here. Let Trisanku stay at his present location with the other stars in the sky. Let them be a symbol of your great and mighty power. Control your anger and let us move forward as friends."

Kaushika stared defiantly at the Deva for a few beats. He then exhaled and lowered his arms, the bluish-white aura surrounding him fading into the ether. "Fine, then," he said with a smile on his face. "Trisanku will stay there, suspended between Heaven and Earth and all will know what I've accomplished."

Indra said nothing but tilted his head downward with respect. Turning around, he and the other Devas returned to Svarga.

As elated as he was at the outcome, inwardly, Kaushika was disappointed with himself. His pity for Trisanku, combined with the anger he felt for both Vasishta and the Devas for defying him had drained him of all the yogic power he had accumulated over many decades. *I suppose I'll have to start over again,* he resolved. *But I have learned something valuable here. Next time, I will not let my emotions dictate my actions, for that is not the way of a Brahma Rishi.*

And so, Kaushika left the ashram he'd built and went west to reclaim the divine power he'd gained through intense meditation then so foolishly spent. Years and years passed and Lord Brahma once again presented himself to the former king.

"You really are committed, aren't you?" he said, hands clasped in front as he stood benevolently in Kaushika's rustic hut. "You have stood apart from other Raja Rishis before you. Therefore, in light of all that you accomplished, I grant you the rank of Rishi. Go, with my blessings." With that, Lord Brahma left.

Again, Kaushika was disappointed. His desire was to become a Brahma Rishi, an equal to Vasishta himself. Steeling himself, the newly minted rishi then performed an even more severe tapasya, which greatly displeased the Devas.

Indra, who still felt humiliated by the rishi's actions, called upon Menaka to distract Kaushika from his quest.

She was a heavenly beauty, borne from the churning of the oceans and desired more than anything a family. With this in mind, Menaka descended and caught the eye of the Rishi. He became instantly infatuated with her appearance and—

* * *

"Romance? Aw man," Vish cut in, pouting. "Only Mama likes that stuff."

I barked out a laugh. "Vish, it's not like that," I said, grinning. "Yes, our rishi did fall in love with Menaka and she with him, eventually. But after ten years, Kaushika learned that the love he felt for her was all a ruse orchestrated by Indra. On making that realization, the desire to become a Brahma Rishi overcame his desire to be with her."

The boy's lips parted. "Really?" he asked curiously. "Things like that happen?"

"Yes," I said, nodding sagely. I sometimes forget that the boy is only ten years old and unaware of some of the complexities of life. I took my time to formulate some sort of response that he would understand.

"Sometimes ... People can't move on with their lives without completing their unfinished business. Kaushika's journey to become a Brahma Rishi may have started purely from spite, but throughout the many years, it became something of a destiny that he had to fulfill. Though he desperately wanted to stay with the love of his life, once he learned the truth, he ultimately knew that he had to finish what he had started all those years ago."

The boy's silence felt permeable as he processed what I said. Turning my head away from him, I let out a heavy, pent-up breath as I thought of the many things that I'd left unfinished and the regrets I had. Some were related to old friends who drifted away, others from missed experiences and opportunities that slipped from my fingers. If I had set off to complete those things that I put behind me, like Vishwamitra did on his path, would I be in the place that I am right now? A son, a wife, a steady job and a house?

"Papa?" Vish's voice cut through my racing thoughts. I must have sat there for several minutes, just thinking of the past. "Are you going to finish the story?"

"Yes, yes I will," I answered, pushing the images of what could have been back into the recesses of my mind. I settled back onto the bed and continued.

* * *

Saddened but determined, Kaushika left Menaka after those ten long years. He did not elicit any curses towards her for breaking his focus, for he knew he was the one to blame for that happening. Leaving behind those happy days, he made for the forests near the Himalayas and spent a thousand years enduring the most severe spiritual meditations so as to gain control of his emotions.

Unbeknownst to him, Menaka, the love he had to abandon, had her wish fulfilled. She bore twins: a daughter and a son. The daughter's life and eventual marriage to a Gandavarian king would be mentioned once more in the Mahabharata, the most epic of Indian legends. But, that is another story for another time.

Meanwhile, Kaushika's efforts over those thousand years would bear fruit, as Lord Brahma descended and appeared to the rishi on the request of the Devas.

"Ahh, the rishi is still at it, hm?" Lord Brahma said, His lips curled into a smile. "You never cease to amaze me with your rigorous tapasaya, my son. Therefore, I bequeath to you the title of Maharishi—a Great Sage."

Unlike before, Kaushika was neither disappointed nor pleased with the title. Instead he spoke to the God of Creation, his hand folded in reverence and adoration. "My Lord, does this title mean that I have indeed conquered myself? My senses and emotions?"

"Not at all," Lord Brahma exclaimed, a twinkle in His eyes. "You must strive to control them further," And upon saying those words, the god departed, leaving the rishi alone in his forest hermitage.

Spurred on by those words. Kaushika then entered another thousand years of brutal tapasaya. This frightened Indra and the other Devas, who implored their leader to do something.

Going with the thought that 'If it ain't broke, don't fix it,' Indra summoned another celestial beauty named Rambha to tempt Kaushika into breaking his concentration. In her wake were the Gods of Love and Spring to enhance her flirtations.

As she set foot on Kaushika's threshold, he opened his eyes for the first time to behold her radiant beauty, which was accented by the scents and sights of springtime. Instead of being enamoured by her, the rishi felt nothing but anger. "Fool me once, shame on you, Indra," he said through gritted teeth. "But you will not fool me a second time with these tricks!"

He then pointed a finger to Rambha. "Temptress, for attempting to break my focus on mastering my anger and desire, you shall be turned to stone for ten thousand years," he yelled.

Rambha could only scream helplessly as her body solidified into pure marble.

The action did nothing but show Kaushika that he was far from his goal of mastering himself. He abandoned the forest home and the stone statue of Rambha and climbed back to the top of the Himalayan mountains. There, as he restricted his breathing and ceased to eat entirely, he sat in a cave for another thousand years.

Now, Indra did not become king of the Devas through his sheer strength alone. He also had a cunning and calculated mind. Realizing that sending women to capture the rishi's heart and break his spirit was a fool's errand, he instead decided to handle this personally.

On the eve of the two-thousandth year of his tapas, Indra approached Kaushika in the guise of a Brahmin—a priest. Approaching him, Indra begged for food, just as the sage was ready to break his many thousand-year fast by eating some rice. The Deva expected him to ignore his pleas and keep the rice for himself, but he was surprised when Kaushika gave him all his food and resumed his meditations.

"I know it's you, Indra," the rishi said, his face as calm and serene as a pool of crystal water. "You will tempt me no further. After many years, I have finally mastered my emotions and senses."

Defeated, Indra cast aside his ruse and left the cave, humbled by the rishi's resolve. Returning to heaven, he sought counsel from Lord Brahma and implored Him to grant Kaushika his ultimate desire.

Sometime later, Lord Brahma materialized in the cave where Kaushika sat. The rishi made no indication that he noticed the God of Creation in his presence.

"Kaushika, you have done well, my son," Lord Brahma said proudly. "After thousands of years, your yogic powers have reached their pinnacle. You have succeeded and I now grant you the title of Brahma Rishi."

"Thank you, Lord Brahma," Kaushika said, finally opening his eyes to the Father of the Universe.

"I have one more gift for you," the God continued. "When you sat, you were but a Kshatriya named Kaushika—a warrior-king of a great nation. When you rise from here, you shall be known throughout as the Brahma Rishi, Vishwamitra—the friend to all. I give you this name for your unlimited well of compassion you show to all who approach you."

"Again, I thank you, my Lord," Vishwamitra said, rising from his spot after breaking his fast. "And now, if you'll excuse me, I have someone I must pay a visit to."

Lord Brahma nodded understandingly. "Then go with my blessing," He said one last time, before disappearing.

With his new title and name in hand, Viswamitra scaled down the mountains and crossed the forests and rivers until he arrived at the place his journey started: the rebuilt ashram of Vasishta. Sitting at the foot of the threshold was the very sage that prompted him to start this long and arduous journey.

Unlike his first encounter, Vasishta was not asleep. Vishwamitra, with his heightened awareness, could tell that he was in true meditation. As he approached the man, he tried to maintain a calm disposition, but inwardly he felt elated and proud. He knew that it was customary for a sage to greet one who was an equal or superior person.

He dimly remembered as well that if that individual was inferior, then the sage would only bless and send them on their way.

Still, Vishwamitra knew that he was at least Vasishta's equal. He, too, was a Brahma Rishi. Vasishta could not deny that. So, he had to greet him properly.

As he stepped onto the base of the entrance to the ashram. Vishwamitra saw that the sage became aware of his presence. Opening his eyes, Vasishta raised a hand towards Vishwamitra, and said two words that crushed his spirit entirely:

"Bless you."

The pride and desire that Vishwamitra felt at becoming a Brahma Rishi had been washed away at the utterance of those words. Strangely, the rishi discovered that he was not disappointed at being blessed—rather, he discovered that he didn't need Vasishta's approval in the first place. With the last vestiges of desire finally stripped away from him, Vishwamitra became a true Brahma Rishi, both in name and in spirit.

Stepping away from the entrance to Vasishta's ashram, Vishwamitra turned to leave. He travelled a few paces when a voice called out to him. "Hey, wait."

Vishwamitra turned slowly to face his caller. It was Vasishta, who stood up from his seated position. He extended a hand towards him. "I was mistaken," he admitted. "I had not realized that I was in the presence of a fellow Brahma Rishi." He then threw a lopsided smile. "You have changed greatly, Vishwamitra. No longer are you the vengeful king out to destroy me."

"Hmm … Speaking of that," Vishwamitra said, scratching the back of his head sheepishly. "Sorry for trying to take your cow, burning down your ashram, trying to kill you and for nearly ending the current universe." He then extended his own hand tentatively towards his equal. "Forgive me?"

Vasishta chuckled as he took Vishwamitra's hand in his own. "Water under the bridge, my brother," he said, guiding him inwards to the ashram. "Now, come, let's sit together and eat. I want to catch up with you. You'll have to tell me all about what happened with King Trisanku?" He flashed a humorous grin at his fellow sage. "Did you *really* almost create a new universe?"

And as Vishwamitra began the tale of how he nearly sent the cursed king to the heavens, the door leading into the ashram closed behind them.

* * *

"And that's the end of that story," I concluded.

To my surprise, Vish frowned as a thought crossed his mind. "So, if I got this straight: The guy I was named after was a sage who used to be a king, but then only became a sage because *another* sage refused to give him his cow of plenty?"

Well, that was succinctly put. "Yep, that's the gist of it," I said.

The boy's lips parted into an ear-to-ear grin. "That's so cool," he said, letting out another cough. "And-and he almost created a new universe and turned someone to stone and lived for thousands and thousands of years!"

"Someone seems to have enjoyed my story," I said smugly.

"Yeah, I did," Vish admitted sheepishly. "And I even learned some things from this. Even if I didn't want to, at first."

My eyebrows shot upward. "You did?" I asked slyly.

Vish nodded, which made my heart swell with pride. If I was being honest with myself, telling a story wasn't as bad as I'd thought it would be. Even though I left most of the storytelling to Anu, it was, in fact, fun. And I found that I wanted to tell him more stories from our faith.

Thinking it over for a moment as we both sat in silence, I came to a decision.

"You know," I began. "Even though this was the end of his origin story, Vishwamitra was still a key figure in several other epics. If you want, I could tell you those stories as well?"

Vish didn't say anything and my pride deflated. Perhaps he doesn't want to hear more, then? Maybe once was truly enough.

I looked at the clock and did a double-take. It was nearly midnight. "And now, truly, it's time for bed, son." I stood up from the bed and took his now-empty teacup and the tray as the child settled properly into his bed.

As I reached the door, a finger hovering over the light switch, Vishwamitra's tired voice called out to me. "Hey, Papa?"

"Mmm?"

"I'd like you to tell me another story tomorrow? Something similar to what you told me about Vishwamitra?"

"By my word as your father, it shall be done," I said with a smile, before shutting off the light and closing his door.

* * *

"It's nearly midnight! Where were you?"

I flinched at Anushka's sharp, hissing tone as I entered our bedroom. The light by her bedside table was on and her tiny frame was wrapped up in a mound of blankets.

"S-Sorry, I was telling Vish a story," I said haltingly. Anu gets touchy when she's sick and I chose my words carefully so as not to set her off.

Anu gave me a questioning look. "Sish, *you* told a story?" she asked as she blew her stuffy nose into another tissue. It soon landed in the nearly overflowing garbage can beside her bed.

"Yep," I nodded, changing into my pajamas before settling into bed beside her. Anu instantly shut off the light and snuggled into my chest. "I told him a favourite of mine from my youth."

"The one about the two sages?"

"The very one."

Even though the room was dark, I recognized the flat look she gave me. "And let me guess, you added a bunch of references to old movies and books that completely flew over his head?"

I looked to the side. "Maybe?" I said, a ghost of a grin forming on my face.

Anu smacked me lightly on my chest. "God, you're such a nerd, Vasishta," she muttered. "This is why I handle storytime."

"I know," I said, my smile widening. "But you still love me, regardless of my cheesy storytelling prowess."

Anu said nothing, but yawned and started to drift off into slumber.

Settling in as well, I closed my eyes and reflected on the story I'd told my son. I was glad he'd learned something from it: that no matter what obstacles lie in the path, one should always forge ahead and meet every challenge head-on. Especially if that challenge is to become a rishi out of pure spite.

I felt myself starting to drift off as I thought of new stories to tell. Perhaps the Ramayana? Or even snippets of the Mahabharata? Maybe Vish would like those?

Hold on, does my throat feel scratchy?

Mine? Oh, Tar!
Estelle Parcoeur

The old man spread his steepled hands wide
as he scanned beyond his porch
then leaned forward in his rocker chair,
gripped the arms, and hoped
to hold the attention of the one whose inquiry
prepared the way for this offering.
He'd coveted the opportunity to regale his own tale.
This is it, he thought as he leaned back and settled in.
"What's the secret to my success, you ask?
Eh. Well, it's a journey."
Framed fame had taken away his voice;
his choice in the stories that were retold.
He'd been bad; he'd been bold.
He was saged, sated with age.
But being renowned had taken away his ownership
of the story. T'was time to dwell and tell.

"Had me at several stops and on significant detours
along the way.
My most known conquest took me through a maze
and back.
I made it 'in' shrouded by laurel and thorn.
As you likely know, I'm an Olympian marred by the
accused use of 'roids."
Memory lane made his voice an echo, a reflection.
The tone somber. The tome solemn.

"Jumbled as the paths may be, I damn well have the decency to show shame at that."
His mind took him back, his heart continued to hold the ache of sacrifice.
"Laid me almost as low as when I was outed by the winding ways of a woman's heart,
bless her soul." The wizened old man looked up from his position of hand-over-heart
with raised-to-heaven gaze to glower at the young lad standing and snickering at him.

"My southern roots won't be denied, young fool.
I know well the power of words and owed kindness.
I've known just as sure I'd arise triumphant,
for I've been in more than one sticky situation.
You see, I kept my cool, in both Atlanta and Cali,
and that's why I just know I'll leave a legacy.
Never you mind the few bastards lining up behind me."

The old man was quick with retorts,
as slow as his answer was in coming.
Infused and defused.
He believed illumination to be only achieved with elaboration.
Tales spun must tell of that rewon.
T'was high time to redeem himself
and the reputation put through the wringer.
Don't wring your hands.
Don't wring his neck.
Keep your cool, old man.
He exerted control he didn't have in his youth.
He'd been too eager to prove.

Mine? Oh, Tar!

The old man took a few centering breaths before continuing on to set the record straight.
"Now, now, they aren't technically bastards; I made honest with the baby mamas.
Only had me two sons, one too many if you ask me, though I had me two hot mamas to match from that family branch."
He muttered. "Shoulda known then that was one too many too."
He spoke loud for the lad, broadcasting bravado.
"Life has been divine, but alas and alack
I'm also a mere mortal."

The old man saw how the boy's eyes darkened at the slight of the second son.
Knew too well himself the feeling of being slighted, slotted.
He almost worked a way to reframe forecast words.
But truth is overcast.
Over-thinking curator of cloudy conditions.
The old man wondered why the young lad would relax so about babes being recast not bastards.
But wonder is indicator of awe, and those awed watched the awesome.
The old man had to shake off the mantle he found discomforting.
Had to play it cool.
The boy had friends loitering along behind him.
They were watching the interaction from afar.
An account must be given to the gathering.

"Pshaw. You know what they say, ain't no thang but a G-thing."

Estelle Parcoeur

The old man tried to bob his head side to side.
To be hip to the hop. Hoping all the while he was not acting out a wile.
He envisioned himself a bobblehead.
Snapped back into an upright posture.
Only to launch himself forward at the reply of his not-so-rapt audience
though they'd all gathered round now, he noted,
pleased with himself.

"G-string! Clean that wax out your ears, boys.
You the ones coming to me 'cuz those years of experience I got on yas.
You not got them ears to hear?
Buck up. There's more to getting a girl than fixin' on what's between her legs.
Er, wrapped around them."
Ugh. They'd caught his proximity to error, his course correction.
"Tend to your own tripping on words.
Go on and walk off with them two twigs y'all be sportin'
Snap, we both know the logs in your eyes are larger than your stride!"

The old man briefly entertained wonder again.
Would these young ones even know what it meant to walk with a big stick?
The whippersnappers moseyed away and the old man once again turned to his thoughts—
constant companions they'd been, haunting him as he aged out of youthful folly.

Too many memories leaked out
as the old man's skin gave off skunk.

Mine? Oh, Tar!

The afternoon's sun bore down hard on him.
He slicked back hair.
Considered himself a greaser.
Considered the traits and tales that made a reputation.
Considered the shadow of that he was most known for—
four score and some years ago he'd bested a beast.
But he'd lived longer in beast mode—
making women his prey along the way,
some would say.
But they were silenced.
Those tales unwritten.
Too many chapters of his live-long life given
short stick—
there was much to be documented still,
much to be accounted for in his personal interactions…

* * *

The setting sun in the old man's eyes was replaced by the shadow of the inquiry returning.
He smiled and squinted against the slanted light.
"You ready to listen? Oh, and you gathered closer a few like-minded friends?
Listen here, lads. Ladies and lovers aren't something you just pick up
to throw in the back of the pickup truck.
There's some courting involved iffin you wants to be continuing the relations.
'Course some gonna have burrs from the last dog that did 'em wrong.
So don't you be just another reason for the finer sex to damn dem men."

He held up hands in surrender.
"I know, I know, how we's get demonized, but I've known our demons too.
Been 'round the block a few times more than you.
Known the dirty south.
Known poverty and luxury.
Known women classy and those acting like cool cats.
Hike them pants up north a bit more, would ya?
You lookin' like a slouch. Naw, don't go grouching, now."

"Oh, you think you real cool?
Wearing all your ice. Psft.
Flashing them pristine and shined up teeth.
Psst, you just frontin'.
Ain't no fine female gonna be fooled by how you present once your lame words come out your lousy mouth."

"You questioning me?
Y'all should know when I was a young buck
I had to endure these six things that really could stress someone out,
I mean, brought some to the brink and sent 'em over.
But a man's gotta prove himself, eh?"

"Sure, sure. Now you want all them details.
Okay. So, first, I stole me the artist's rendering stick.
Then I used someone's methods against them.
Only to need to make some bacon.
Man, all that hard work must be put into it
makes a beefcake want a good, hearty, breakfast.
Like *The Notebook* shows us in that scene

Mine? Oh, Tar!

when the carpenter gets his lady into the space he made for her,
and a whole lotta lovin' goes down. Then they make for the kitchen."
The wisened speaker is quick to assert an interjection to his own words.
Couldn't reveal soft heart when a hard front stood before him. A chain link fence of 'em.
"Now, I ain't saying that's a woman's place.
Though I best tell you my ma made the best chicken you'll ever be lucky enough to get your grubby fingers on, though
Pa had the pleasure of being chief pancake maker.
I'm talking every Saturday
we woke the same time we needed to be up for school to get us some of them cakes."

"Naw, naw. Stop slapping them paws.
You lot gots it wrong again.
Mama *was* the breadwinner.
She was something fierce.
Intimidated all the boys before Pa.
Had them looks and all the smarts.
Studied law. Got him straight. Raised us brood right."
The old man savored the silence a beat before speaking on.

"So, right, what I *am* saying is food; *that* shows love.
I know y'all heard that talk about the way to a man's heart and how it be through his stomach.
'Course that saying came from something,
but what I meant to be telling you lot of was
the second half of that whole ordeal youngin' me

212

went through
when yearning to prove my worth.
Worth it to, man, to get that rep.
Didn't no one mess with me lightly.
They knew what I was up for, and what I was
down with—
I got me a name that preceded me.
I went forth unabashed. Only bashed if I needed to do
so, mind you."
Silence reigned at the end of that bit. The boys were
ready to listen.
They knew him to be more than a tool,
more like an enforcer.

"So then I had to set someone straight about kicking
people when they're down.
And way down that giant went.
Made quite a splash.
I again turned the tables; who knew thumb wars were
such a big deal to some people.
Oh, and finally I evened the score on someone who
always tried to fit people to size.
We ain't made to live in anyone's boxes, brothers.
For real though.
Then shit got serious."
He took it in as they all leaned forward, giving him the
rapt attention a storyteller savored.

"To kill the child of a Queen should be punishable
by death.
But some say sleeping with an animal would merit
the same.

Mine? Oh, Tar!

Me, I attended the Queen shows on the regular and I've been known to be a party animal myself. I don't judge, for one never knows when someone accused of being a beast is in truth a god.
Bro code, yo.
Truth be told, though
arguably the most powerful of them powers-that-be sent the creature that the 'lady' bedded."
The old man digressed again,
only half aware he was reminiscing as much as he was telling a tale.

"So, no, I didn't mess with peeps who were just looking for a good time.
Nothing to see here; move along.
'Cuz, ya know, you can't take back wrongs,
at least according to the drawn out words of the All American Rejects.
And don't we all aspire to be All-American, to be on the A-Team. And not to be rejected—man." Sounds of accord punctuated his last proclamation.

"Y'all feel me on that, eh?
Yeah, yeah.
Serious tho,
too many teams haven't wanted me on 'em.
I didn't quite check all them boxes,
stacked so high they be.
Sometimes I swear they gonna just topple down and bury them shippers.

"So, anyway,
I liked me dames, drama queens, dime pieces,

and I digress again.
But,
I gotta tell you about this one broad.
Mind your manners, now, young men.
There ain't no putting a woman in a bag.
And ain't no putting bags over their eyes.
Ohh, man.
You youths should have seen this bombshell.
Get to the details already?
Okay. But you asked for it."
He winked before spinning on with the stories of his prime time.

"There once was this empress,
like she *was* the powerhouse, men came to *her* for sugar.
She never had much use for them. But she took a shine to me,
said I'd sire her a good, strong son.
So, cool, cool, I can help with *that* prerequisite activity.
I got you.
Especially if I don't gotta be much more than a sperm donor."
The old man reflected, then tacked on an addendum.
"Being a dad would have been Greek to me back then."
Grumblings about responsibilities and demands rose
to meet him.

He shushed the lot of 'em.
"Now, listen here,
I know a thing or two about stepping up to be the man.
About the different types of women.
I'm a quick learner.
And a good study.

Mine? Oh, Tar!

So shut it.
Y'all know why God gave you one mouth hole
and two ear holes, right? Good."
The old man shook his head.
Not to clear any cobwebs,
but to get back into the headspace he'd been in
before discontent threatened to drown him out.

"So, I was on my Cali tour, you see.
I spent some time acting as an inspirational speaker,
'cuz I knew how it was…
been down some roads before,
made it to some mountain tops.
Wild places, man.
Anyhoo, I met this queen of scheming.
She assisted me with regaining my rep.
That thing is just too easy to lose, I tell ya.
One night we were sitting in a hotel bar
and she turns to me
and says, 'Be my alcohol hero?' I hooked her up with another,
loved her one last time, and made my getaway."
One of the listening lads cued a song.
Got a gruff bark of laughter from the old man
before he spoke on.

"Ain't no need for all that hooting and hollering.
You're drowning out the point here.
It's not about scoring.
It's not about losses.
True, true, it *is* about the game.
But sometimes you gotta play it off.
Sometimes you gotta stop keeping score.

Estelle Parcoeur

T'aint about winners and losers."
He paused.
Good, they were listening again
and weren't going to interrupt him—again.

"We all have embarrassments we cover.
For the king of letting heads roll it was
the living evidence of his queen's dalliance.
He offed people's heads to pay for that one.
Musta took his cue from that Wonderland Queen
of Hearts.
Maybe the snakelike way Medusa could be.
That's why he needed me to step up and in.
His head just wasn't in the game."
He laughed along with his audience at the play of
his words.
Then turned half serious.

"So, 'course, I got my game into the situation.
Just like we tell women; if you got it, flaunt it."
He waited for the punchline to hit before he spoke on.
His tone deadpan, then light.
"His daughter now hates me for it.
Not so much the flaunting, but the situation.
Well, one of the two daughters he had;
we'll get to the other one…
I always gotta be putting out fires.
It's my curse, I tell you.
It ain't no hero's life for me."
He expected sympathy for his woe,
but didn't get much laude from the lads.
He amped up the bravado.

Mine? Oh, Tar!

"But, seriously,
I'm happy to save the day.
Just helping where I can,
and helping myself.
Gotta make the most of a situation, after all.
I've made plenty of lemonade.
Cools one down when they get hot.
And I was raised in the South, don't you forget,
so I know a thing or two about heat.
Let that be a lesson to you fools looking to lasso a hot date for a night.
Be sure you can handle what you put your hands on, boys."
The old man got another reaction he didn't appreciate.

"Yes, another lesson from grandpa.
You gotta make use of lessons—
don't want to leave any opportunity behind.
Gotta settle them scores too.
Keep that playing field level.
Why you think footballs shaped like lemons?"
He paused to gauge his audience.
They were again considering his ideas, so he spoke on.

"So, back to this particular tale I'm trying to tell you.
After one son was lost, the ol' king let his wife's bastard deal with his enemies.
One could say this provided purpose to something that was providence.
Annually seven sacrifices atoned.
After three years of hearing tell of this scenario,
I decided chitlins no longer needed to sacrifice for the sins of their father."

Resounding resonance surprised the old man.
He didn't think his old fashioned values kept with their times and lifestyle.
He rolled with it,
would think more on it later—the echoes of what remained burning in hearts.

"You know it, Mama raised me right.
And there are some things I just don't abide by.
So by-the-by, I went down to see this guy, and this monster problem he had."
Don't wink, the aged speaker told himself, *don't wink, or they'll think it overplayed.*
He paused for effect instead.

"I needled my way into his daughter's heart and she provided a thread."
He rushed the connections of his next words,
"Not golden like those three crones who croon about their control over fate.
My fierce femme took matters into her own hands.
I loved her for that. I did.
Sadly, love is just as fickle as it is a
many-splendored thing.
And I was but a babe, splashing around in it.
Wasn't trying to take nothing too serious then.
Again, I digress."
He was telling them too much and yet not enough,
he chided himself.

"A web woven by false love too quickly unravels to reveal a ball and chain."
He was quick to incorporate their reactions.

Mine? Oh, Tar!

"That's right; time to look grim.
Time to speak up about it.
When the chain was pulled up and the anchor loosed,
the fair maiden who refused to play fair was no longer
there at my side."
He let his words linger.
Saw on their faces he didn't need to elaborate.
Each had their own monsters to sate.

"Fair turn around, I'd say.
I mean, I did leave her after that last time,
but she'd given up on me first.
Decided I was a playboy; lover material,
not a long term investment.
You want all your dividends to be in that account?"
He cocked an eyebrow for effect.

"Oh, we be whooping it up again?
Well, let me tell you about the storm my choices whipped
up around me.
Trying to return to something left behind. Whoee."
After a quick pause to make sure he'd reeled the boys
back in, the old man spoke on.
"Uhh, that don't go over so well, sons.
Don't often play out that it do.
And damn, communication twists be what cause that
turbulence."
He carried on with the lesson application,
looking at each listener in turn.

"You say one thing, then do another?
There gonna be consequences.
I tell you.

Some gonna shift blame to you and call it con sequences.
Like the space between is all to be shouldered by you."

The speaker sighed and carried on.
"True, true, that though.
We leave a lot in our wake when we live large.
Make them gaps in our own stories.
Now I don't want to talk about it,
but I had a bad break with my dad."
He decided to keep it real brief, real shallow,
this segment of his life story.

"The waters where the evidence of my mistake lies deep
are the grave of my father and birthplace of his legacy.
Ya know, that refuge of international waters,
where I make my runs south of the border."
He allowed the audience to shape the reaction.

 "OK, I'll crack a smile for that one."
He spit out an old school ditty for them
then settled back into his porch rocker and story time,
tapping his feet and swaying to begin a slow movement
which calmed him but also created a mood for his tale
of triumph.

"Everything is all good there, on them open waters.
No domains.
Excepting that Panama canal;
too many skirmishes there.
Always makes me nervous when I'm in
contended waters.
I don't like to be told I'm somewhere I'm not welcome.
Some hero's embrace, eh?"

Mine? Oh, Tar!

He boomed a laugh, then a warning.
"Don't you go getting ready to set sail just yet.
Those landlocked gonna take aim at you.
And others inhabiting the waters gonna call out to you,
try to waylay and crash you.
People always want a piece of the action."
He enjoyed the echoes of 'true, true.'

"For a while I went gaga about all the promises,
promises that everyone wanted to extract from me.
Aghh, just loose me already. Can't a man be free, sail to
the places he wants to go?
And who said Helen didn't want to join us?
She enjoyed a few fine adventures of her own, caused
some conflicts herself.
Maybe we were just trying to save her from all that,
ever think of that?"
He ignored their inquiries about Helen.
Went with another life lesson application,
opposed to a history lesson.

"Now listen here,
women have every right to tell their side of a story.
Truth be told, they probably being more honest 'bout it
than you lot.
The way you carry on about your escapades."
He gave them time to let it out.
Then continued with his account.

"Now, now, just to set the record straight,
the only child a woo-man knows I claim as mine

just so happens to be that one I seeded in the sister of the
cling-on I had to shake.
Oh, and that wild woman, remember how I told you she
hunted me out as good stock?
Well, she bore a child the sister-wife fell for—hard.
So, guess in a way you could say it's been kept
in the family.
Weave our own webs, don't we?"
He only paused to take a breath
wouldn't let himself get caught up again in it all.

"Anyhoo,
them babes were part of my past life,
part of my journey to who I became."

He paused to let it sink in again
then it became his hook
for the next lines.

"Love and truth hurt, eh?
Not as much as denial.
Makes a man blue.
But we don't press the issue."

The old man had to lead with an eye-roll
at the evolution and spin of words and their meaning.
"Stop your sniggering. I'm warning you.
I see them smirks. Yeah, you know it's true—
that base track your mind is stuck skipping on.
Still, I think y'all know what we're getting at, deep down.
Learn to control your urges, man.
Real men have feelings.
Real men don't need to take; it's given to them.

Mine? Oh, Tar!

People ain't gonna give you the time of day?
Shake the dirt off and walk away.
Gotta rise up and ready yourself for them real feelings.
Voice that weighing heavy.
Respect and establish boundaries.
Even if it means some 'lone time.
Trust me, livin' like that is better than any loaner."
What they had to say about that life flooded and overpowered his voice,
but quickly petered out.

The old man resumed his story with a wry jab.
 "Not that I stayed that way for long.
You know the life, apparently.
Taking cars off the lots and giving them a spin.
Was always dusting myself off and trying again.
Lured by siren call.
Gotta work. Gotta have papers.
I was legit though.
Them cars I just spoke of—
all metaphorical in the veins of our test-driving relationships conversation.
No home felt like it when I was only playing house."
The sounds of protest and the raised words surprised the old man.

"Naw, c'mon now,
I mean that with all respect for the beautiful ladies.
They ain't to be tested.
Nor driven.
But you young 'uns,
you hear what I say about what makes a house a home?"
He leveled a wise look and spoke on.

"True, true,
I might notta heeded all their words,
but that doesn't mean I don't hear them out.
I learned from the lessons of another as he rowed
that the sweet song of a lovely woman can lead a man
to his grave.
And I'm not a fan of grave situations,
despite what my meddling track record
would have you believe
I find myself drawn to—
recall, I never quartered there long during them early
legs of my journey.
I understand well what it means to be a man
on the move.
Making my way in this world, that's all.
Won't let nothing cut me down to size.
I live large. I go big 'cause I don't want to go home."
He let the words linger and create the punctuation
of his point.
They felt him on that.

The echo in his mind came out his mouth this time.
"Home. Such a foreign and lofty word.
An ambitious endeavor.
A trap, if it only tethers a person to one place."
He spoke to himself and the boys now.
"Time and time again I've shown I must live free.
I live beyond the circumstances that produced me.
Live far beyond those who raised me, or would raze me.
I've supported others in that journey."
Time to punctuate his point again.
"That's why I'm sitting here schooling y'all on

freeing your minds.
Freedom in speaking one's mind, there is, ahhhh.
It's about time I get to let my record drop about each beat of my story.
My deeds have echoed long enough.
I'm ready to resound.
So, let's break it down."
He jigged his antsy legs,
Still didn't like to sit too long
Still let his mind lead him along.
Saw now how he was strung by song.
That first boy to approach him kept pulling up songs that resonated too.
But the rest of them—
Groans?
He'd not expected groans
after all they'd already been through together—

He responded with his defenses up.
"What, I'm not allowed to reminisce?
As I recall, you wanted to know the how,
and that leads to the why.
And at times the who and the what.
Where and when can be factors too.
You know how I speak true of context.
Allow me some recollection.
I'm giving you a treasure trove here.
I'll tell it how I see fit."
He waited and got the silence he'd wanted, he'd craved, and now found uncomfortable and something he needed to reframe.

"Ready for some more stories now?

Some more lessons?
Gonna give grandpa here the time of day?
Good. Glad to hear it, gentlemen."

"Some of those 'monsters' I battled
were misunderstood too.
Always trying to get people to take sides
creates that dichotomy.
And so often only one side of the story sees the light.
Now, I'll agree two wrongs don't make a right.
But all the righting, doesn't that make up for a wrong?
That's why I'm writing now,
in this place and time, within this embodiment.
This here notebook,"
he said with vim in his voice,
which quaked and cracked.

The old man paused,
held up his diary, and shook it.
Held it in his lap and caressed journal cover,
speaking on in a soft, reverent tone.
"This here spine
holds the tales and truths
I'm telling you: my legacy."
he blinked back a tear before continuing on.

"I'm meant to embolden bodies that have been
too long at rest.
Have settled with a piece and called it peace.
Let me serve that pie up to you.
I've charted territories few men can lay claim upon.
I've happened upon situations where I've needed to
step up.

Mine? Oh, Tar!

But others' accounts of my life, naw, they ain't the
real thing.
Sometimes those storytellers just a dog with a bone.
I'm glad to con the tensions.
Why not play to one's advantage?
We all grew up on these advantageous adages.
Hear me out now.
Place me between two rocks and you'll find me in a…"

He awaited their filling in the ideas he'd led them before.
Then he spoke of an outcropping
a vista—
a safe place
where hard knocks could harbor more than life had
in store
see above and beyond the fray.

"Right. Climb every mountain. Rock on.
Each age though, they got a wrong
these generations have gaps
in what they see and grasp.
What gets filled in leaves some gasping.
But there's value in each iteration, each interaction.
I don't mean to go getting all phileo-sapphical
in my old age here.
Though my brothers in arms, I'll pound my chest
for them
until the day the old ticker inside my ribcage
don't beat no more."
The old man paused to regroup his thoughts
and gear them back to the beginning
and his intended ending.

"Lads, listen.
You asked for this.
You wanted to know my secret.
You want to know my ways with the ladies,
then you gotta understand all my ways.
All the forms of love.
For a man's character is composed of many compartments.
The trick is just to keep them compartmentalized
at times.
And so we here today gotta conceptualize a few things
for you to be getting your education."
More shifting of his words ensued.
The old man again shook his head.
Tried to quickly sift through them,
as to set course aright.

"An edumuckation, you say?
Well, we called it the muddle in the middle.
Your ma probably dubs it a midlife crisis.
But crisis brings us to the point of change!
You ready to hear of the aftermath of all my
adventures?"
He was ready to marshal and lead the charge.

"Changing my tune?
Changing my own story?
What you mean to say I haven't claimed all I've
contributed to yet?
I've recounted my track record for you all.
I've told you of my greatest hits with women.
Of my ambitions.
Of my feats.

Mine? Oh, Tar!

The locals and milestones of my notable journeys."

The first lad to approach him spoke up now.
A brave one he must be to take over and finish my story.

"But, she—she didn't tell me the child was mine.
That's why you were curious about my past with women?
Well, er, son."
The old man was at a loss for words.
Realized too late what he claimed with
a simple, meaningless, turn of phrase.

Oh, tar!
Another sticky situation.
"Leave an old man to sit in peace on his porch, won't ya?
Shoo now, all of you boys.
A man needs time to think.
You, lad, who led this whole conversation.
You may stay. Sit with me.
Let's recount."

* * *

The boy settled himself on the stoop.
The old man lowered himself down beside.
Butts on porch, feet on bottom step,
The next leg of their journey began.

"It's time to talk on
of what we birth
and what we hold at bay.
I mean to speak of inspiration

of innovation and invention—
What you trying to make of yourself, boy?"
The old man prompted, tried not to prod.

The lad listened and took in that spoken
but his words languished.

"Ah, that is
in truth
what you do not yet know."
The old man spoke to
the heart of matters
which beat within both of them.

He slowly leaned forward,
placed a hand on the youngster's shoulder,
and used it to stand.
"Come, we need a walk or a drive for this talk."

As they strode, side by side
the father began to speak to the son.
"It runs in our family
that seeking quest—
my father before me
journeyed to see
if I would be as foreseen
and I journeyed back to his side
hoping to secure his pride.
You've sought me out—
what are you about?"

Contemplative silence was all the old man got in return.
He offered more words, hoping to inspire a response.

Mine? Oh, Tar!

"What bricks have you laid?
As for myself I've said oh no
to lions, club men, and tree-benders
But it runs in our blood
to say oh my
when it comes to women.
They'd woo us, chastise us
and cling close to our house.
My own mother acted as meek as a mouse
What appalls you about me?
What awls do you see?"

Only silence greeted the aged man
so he wielded his own wizened words.
A ready answer at hand
let loose out his pressed lips.
"If things come too easy
we don't value their role."
And too late see the toll.

He thought back on the giant,
who'd likened him to a bean pole.
Of the neck that turned so quick
upon seeing a missed mark.
And the boulder removed
that proved a dart
to his own heart.

"We all play a part
as we seek.
Add venture
and it all unfurls."
He mind wound around

all he'd invested in,
the journeys he'd made through towns.

He looked around now
and saw many come to a stand still.
Not used to seeing him off his porch.
He reflected on them
looking outside of himself a moment.
They stop and stare
without a care.
Inside he grew ill
thinking of how foolhardy he'd been.
Too eager to show his skill.
To ready to make the kill.

A voice shrill
interjected itself.
Overlaid upon ideas
he'd placed upon a sill.
There were lessons still to instill…

He'd eaten up the valor.
He'd trashed those who blathered.
Now, he wondered what it all mattered.
His strength was a weakness.
His weakness had taken over his strength.
When one must prove, they are always on the move.
He continued to muse.
Think back on all the dark hues.

He'd only heeded that he thought fate.
He'd returned too late.
No white picket fence gate.

Mine? Oh, Tar!

All because he had to sate
anything that dared negate
the reputation he sought to elevate.

This boy of his
seemed to savor silence
when as a youth
all he'd done was boast and
strive for that toast.

"Cheer up my young fellow,"
He now bellowed
with more gusto
than the breezes of Calypso.
Her voice too had trapped
another hero attempting to make his way back.

"Back to allegory?"
He offered up another story.
This one fully intended
for further illuminating
the price of glory.

"So much ages us.
Just ask Aegeus.
Or Pegasus.
Perhaps Artemis.
We're always hunting
always gathering
always falling prey
to another's storyline—
hooked, and then a sinker."

Estelle Parcoeur

He let his words settle once again,
realizing these ears were not so deaf.
Not so full of cotton as his had been.

*How to bring his conclusions
to an apt end?*
The old man mused on.
He'd been so confused when he'd gone on
his first scouting expedition.
To think of that frame now
that his son sought him
as he'd sought his father.
Why are heroes always questing?

His wondering
led to even more pondering
He hoped not more panhandling
Matters were getting hot—
though thankfully the evening winds
were finally cool. Almost calming.
Practically balming, as if he were beached
with a tide that moved the sands of time.

He realized with a start
it was not his words his son was after.
The old man walked on with the boy
in companionable silence.

The words had been for him.
He stopped, turned aside,
used finger to prop up the boy's chin.

Mine? Oh, Tar!

With an exchanged smile
this moment too became a milestone.
"What would you like to tell me of home?"

Minutes After Midnight
Gregory Coley

Percival's slippered footsteps echoed down the domed corridor, his reflections on the black walls making it look like there were three of him. Movement to his left made him turn. Sipping his steaming coffee, he stepped closer to the curved wall. Heart racing, he leaned closer. At these depths, it could be anything in the black. The darkness swirled and moved like ink. Frost coated the surface, with his nose nearly touching it. The frigid air seeped through the glass like a morning fog. A gray mass skimmed the other side of the wall, a sizable horn tapping it.

Percival raised his coffee mug in salute. "Good morning, narwhal." As he turned and walked down the corridor, the narwhal swam along with him on the other side of the glass. "H.O.P.E., why don't you play whatever the kids like to listen to these days?" he called out.

Without voicing a response, the computer system that ran the complex, Helios' Omniscient Programmed Eminence, whirred to life and searched the internet for what was popular.

H.O.P.E.'s light soprano voice echoed through the complex. "Song found. Playing: 'Lego House' by Ed Sheeran."

The bluesy, folksy sound of acoustic guitar echoed through the facility. Percival nodded his head appreciatively. Better than the boy bands of the previous decade.

As an immortal in charge of recording all human history, including pop culture, Percival had seen some wondrous and horrible things: bell bottoms, records, leg warmers, grunge, tomography ... Furby. The worst was the internet. Trolls living under virtual bridges, thinking they're invisible like cats with their heads under the bed. Cat videos, though. That was a trend Percival enjoyed.

Pushing open the rickety wooden door at the end of the corridor, he stepped into the heart of the complex. Stone floors and walls with large, glass covered windows filled the space. It was a strange mix of prehistory and futuristic that Percival wasn't a fan of. The gods built the complex long ago before sinking it to the bottom of the frigid Antarctic ocean. He kept record of all of humanity. Inventions, histories, diseases, wars, death ... all of it. For millennia, he received visions and wrote them upon scrolls. As time went by, books joined his collection, as well as newspapers, music, and movies. Foods would appear. Computers, smart phones. He didn't know how these items appeared as they became important to humans, and he didn't ask questions. The gods gave him this job, and so he did it.

Stepping over a pile of newspapers, he weaved through the maze of items. It had stopped being stored decades ago, and now it just piled up like he was a hoarder. Knocking over a Tickle Me Elmo, he sat down at the central computer system.

Scratching as his salt and pepper beard, he brushed hair from his eyes, the glow of the dozens of screens lighting the stone walls. Taking off his robe and green crocs (wonderful invention), he straightened his gray sweatpants and white undershirt before drinking heavily from his coffee.

"H.O.P.E., bring up recent headlines from the largest human settlements please."

The screens before him changed like a morphing mosaic of the timelines. War. Anger. Puppy saved from a well. Rockets into space. Spreading disease versus stringent hygiene. Arson. Social media. Conspiracy theories and con artists. Disagreement about what was real. The steady advance of science. Hell, he wasn't sure if he was recording fiction or nonfiction anymore.

Percival shook his head and sipped his coffee. "How are these humans alive? Hell, they're barely functioning."

"Netflix alert: New season of 'Stranger Things' now available," said H.O.P.E.

"Play on screen four."

Percival grabbed a bag of Cheetos. Half watching his show, he scanned screen two to check the other sub functions of the facility.

H.A.T.E. (Holistic Archive Thoth Enterprise) was the ever-growing recording of human history. Now that all records were recorded automatically in real time, he didn't miss when he used to have to do it by hand. It was in working condition, recording every shameful, laughable headline. Percival skimmed the most recent lines. JFK coming back to life. Flat earth? Didn't humans prove that was bogus centuries ago? This thing was full of plot twists.

E.N.V.I. (Environmental Nemesis Variable Index) were the environmental systems. They regulated the facility as well as keeping track of major meteorological events across the globe. Temperatures were approaching one hundred degrees Fahrenheit in the Antarctic and multiple 'once in a century' storms raged across the planet. Everything seemed normal.

Percival sighed heavily, rubbing his face. "This is fine. Simply fine."

G.R.E.E.D. (Generic Revenue Encrypted Executive Directive) was the record of human currencies, stocks, companies, power structures, and everything in between. The money of the Slavs and goths were in the tank. A brewing war.

Closing the window, Percival brought up D.I.S.E.A.S.E. (Detrimental Infections Systems Epidemics and Subordinate Exports), where the record of all human diseases were kept. This season, D.I.S.E.A.S.E. had grown rapidly. Percival had to expand the section of the complex where samples were kept.

Moving to another screen, he zoned in on P.O.V.E.R.T.Y. (Preemptive Objectionable Vejovis-Eir Registry Telehealth Yield). It was the record of all human medications and scientific breakthroughs. This too was growing exponentially. Despite the discoveries, D.I.S.E.A.S.E. was growing much faster—to the point the medicines were at a standstill. Though, humans were close to the cure for a decades-old disease.

"Good for them!"

Careful not to hit D.E.A.T.H. (Demeter Extinction Action Thanatos Hotfix), which would have activated the self-destruct of the facility, he moved away from humanity and checked on the facility itself. Percival skimmed P.A.I.N. (Preventative Attack Ingrained Network), which was the self-defense of the facility in the unlikely event of an outside attack. All was quiet. W.A.R. (Web Applications Reinforcement)—the cyber defense system—was also quiet.

Convinced everything was in working order, he turned his attention back to his entertainment. Putting his feet on the desk, he began mindlessly snacking. One episode turned into two, which turned into four and five. At some point between the fifth and sixth episode, drowsiness pulled him into sleep.

When he awoke, the screen was staring back at him, asking if he was still there. How much time had passed? He couldn't say. Wiping his Cheeto-stained fingers on his shirt, he lowered his feet off the desk. The pain as blood rushed back into his feet was excruciating. Still, he stood, stumbling toward the door. Over piles of nostalgia, he made his way to the corridor that led to his quarters.

Pushing the door open, he stepped into the semi-darkness. The sleeping quarters were one of the four structures added later, which meant the walls were translucent material, along with the kitchen, bathroom, and gym. The gods that placed him here didn't think about things that would pass the centuries, clearly. As for the other rooms in the complex, they held all the storage space for the sub functions.

Stepping onto the platform on the far side of the room, he sat on the bed. Things were getting old. How long had he been in this box? Last time he wasn't at the bottom of the arctic ocean, humanity was still worshiping the Ogdoad. The group of Egyptian gods consisting of Amun, Amunet, Nu, Naunet, Heh, Hauhet, Kuk, and Kauket hadn't been worshipped since Ra took over in Egypt's golden age.

Now the year was ... what? He counted in his head. It had been centuries. Barely able to talk or think clearly after so long in isolation, he doubted he could do the math anyway. Laying back on the bed and intertwining his fingers behind his head, he dozed, dreaming of the warm desert sand of his youth prickling his face and the light of the sun—Ra's love on display for all to see.

He shivered, waking himself up. It was dark, and cold. Always cold. Something scraped across the glass like nails on a chalkboard.

"That's enough, Narwhal! I'm trying to sleep in here!"

The sound came again.

Sitting up, he called out to H.O.P.E. "What is that sound?"

A small light on the wall began to flash red. On and off. A heartbeat of something that should never live.

"WARNING. BREACH DETECTED."

In the glaring red light, Percival leapt to his feet and bolted out the door. Over piles of books that dotted the room and corridor, he ran like he was playing a game of hopscotch, until he slammed into the door of H.O.P.E.'s mainframe. The room was bathed in red light like it was engulfed in blood. Every screen was red. Black text scrolled by too fast to read. His head spun.

"H.O.P.E., what is going on? Report!"

"NOSOI virus detected. Breech imminent. Attention required. East wing of the facility."

"NOSOI? Breech? What the … east wing!"

Exiting a different door than he had entered, he made a beeline for the east wing where G.R.E.E.D. was kept. He tore down the corridor towards the door labeled Generic Revenue Encrypted Executive Directive. It rattled against its locks like a caged animal was attempting to escape.

Sliding to a stop, he investigated the glass porthole in the door. Inside, it looked like a dragon's hoard from a fairytale. Coins, paper money, credit cards, and gold figurines towered to the ceiling like a maze of opulence. Within the stacks, sparks flew. A green figure knocked over stacks of gold and hammered at the outer wall. *Is it trying to escape? How did it manifest? Does it have its own intelligence?*

The thoughts barely had time to run their course through his head when the whole facility shook. A section of wall crumbled into the G.R.E.E.D. dome. Percival watched helplessly through the porthole as water rushed in, pulling centuries of monetary history into the abyss. As for the personification, it swam away unhindered.

Percival ran back down the corridor. "H.O.P.E. lock down the west corridor!"

Hydraulic doors slammed shut behind him, one after another crashing down, separating the corridor into sections. As he slid into the internal chamber of H.O.P.E., the last door clamped down.

Percival was safe. At least he felt safe. The flooded section was gone, but he was unscathed. As for the G.R.E.E.D. subroutine escaping ... That could do considerable damage to humanity.

"ALERT. NOSOI virus detected."

Percival struggled to catch his breath. "Where now?!"

"Southwest wing of facility."

Percival set off down the southwest corridor, his crocs squeaking on the cold stone floor. This door housed P.O.V.E.R.T.Y. The room beyond the porthole was white and spotless, containing tables of science equipment, medicines, and surgical equipment, along with every medicine ever invented. From herbs to vaccines, this was the most valuable wing.

Within, a figure in a white coat smashed a rolling stool into a glass porthole on the other side of the room.

"Stop!" yelled Percival, banging on the door. "H.O.P.E. stop it! Restrain P.O.V.E.R.T.Y.! You control the entire facility!"

"I'm sorry. Unable to find anything with the name P.O.V.E.R.T.Y."

The glass broke. Medicines washed into the ocean, useless and soon to be forgotten. As for the personification, it fled into the water.

"H.O.P.E. lock down southwest corridor!"

Percival hurried back to the central hub. This time, he made it long before the last door shut behind him. The virus was working its way through the facility. How could he stop it?

"H.O.P.E. activate W.A.R. subroutine. That should wipe out any internal threat."

Percival stood in the ominous glow of the red screens surrounding him. The groan and creak of bending metal drew his attention toward the southeast corridor. His heart jumped at the sound of rushing water.

"H.O.P.E. lockdown southeast corridor!"

Distant doors slammed. Percival chanced a peek through the open doorway. His eyes widened as a wall of water rushed towards him like a stampeding beast. Before he could react, it slammed into him like Poseidon's fist, knocking him to the floor. The last emergency door shut, leaving him lying in a puddle of frigid seawater.

H.O.P.E.'s monotone voiced echoed around the room. "I'm sorry. Nothing named W.A.R. found."

"Damn it! H.O.P.E., where is the virus now?" asked Percival, climbing to his feet.

"Scans show it is working its way westward through the conduits. Approaching the Preventative Attack Ingrained Network."

Taking off down the southwest corridor, he called over his shoulder. "Shut down H.A.T.E.! It cannot get the archives of humanity's history!"

Halfway down the corridor, bullets tore through the piles of hoarded memorabilia. Percival dove behind a stack of books. As he looked over his shoulder, more bullets rang out. P.A.I.N. was armed to the teeth against physical attacks on the base. That was fine. At least until the armory saw him as the intruder.

Percival ran for cover behind a nearby stack of board games closer to the doors of P.A.I.N. before sliding to a stop. More bullets pierced the clear dome of the wall. Ocean water trickled next to Percival. Distracted, he wasn't looking when a bullet struck him in the shoulder. He growled in pain and fell, blood running through his hand in rivulets as he grabbed the wound.

He gritted his teeth. "H.O.P.E.—"

Cracks spread across the wall like spiderwebs, closer to P.A.I.N. and racing toward H.O.P.E. as water began to spray through the cracks. Percival abandoned his hiding place as the water rose around his legs. In momentary shock from the temperature, he shivered, standing still. The tunnel quaked and began to tilt downward on one end. The water ran away from his feet toward P.A.I.N., filling the compartment, and much of the tunnel, with ocean. It silenced the defense guns. That was something.

Piles of games, books, clothing, weapons, and a plethora of memorabilia slid into the frigid water filling the corridor bottom to top like a soda bottle. The complex shook again, the P.A.I.N. compartment impacting the sea floor.

Below him, the water rose quickly, and above him the emergency protocols began to shut metal doors to protect H.O.P.E. from the incoming water. He had to hurry. Once those doors were closed, there would be no opening them.

Climbing up the tilted floor, he slid back down into the quickly rising water. The cracks gave way and water rushed into the tunnel in a deluge. It rose over his head toward H.O.P.E.'s door.

Overcome by the water, he ignored the cold in a rush of adrenaline and swam. Onward and upward he shot. Grabbing a book that drifted lazily by, he reached the surface less than a foot from the rapidly closing doors. Searching the surface of the water, he found a bar. With the book, he used the two to hold open the door. They would only hold a moment.

Reaching through the half-closed doors, he clawed at the dry floors of H.O.P.E.'s chamber. Finding purchase and kicking wildly, he heaved himself out into the cool dry air. Pivoting, he kicked the bar and book down into the water. The doors slammed closed, airtight.

He lay on his back in the flashing red lights of the chamber. Coughing and gasping, he stumbled to his feet. "H.O.P.E. Status on H.A.T.E.?"

Percival waited. Moments crawled along like hours until the hollow, electronic voice replied. "Nothing named 'H.A.T.E.' found."

"What? Come on! Holistic Archive Thoth Enterprise! It's the whole of human history!"

"Calculating … Negative. Name not found."

Percival unceremoniously shoved a stack of books to the ground. "Then why am I even here? I've failed!"

Centuries. Centuries Percival had sat here. Twiddling his thumbs, absorbing all mankind had discovered, enjoyed, and suffered. Now, because of some virus, all the worst things history had to offer were being released on humanity. All because of him and his failures.

Pacing the room, he stopped. Typing away on the back-lit keyboard, nothing changed. The same red screen and black script taunted him. It was all gibberish.

"H.O.P.E. is there any way to stop this? To contain it?"

"Negative. Virus beyond point of containment."

He sighed heavily. "Damn it! At least shut down the drives in D.I.S.E.A.S.E. Save as many lives as we can."

"Searching for subroutine: D.I.S.E.A.S.E … Detrimental Infections Systems Epidemics and Subordinate Exports…"

"Tell me the diseases haven't been released. It's two thousand and nineteen. We've had a great run."

"…No file by that name found."

Percival sank to the ground. The facility shook, groaning like a giant awakening from a long slumber. He watched out the round windows that broke up the timeless stone at regular intervals. Bubbles rose into the darkness. A shape moved by quick as a serpent. Seemingly made of white data code, it was gone before the breath could catch in Percival's throat.

"What was that shape?" he asked, creasing his brows.

"D.I.S.E.A.S.E. breaking containment."

Tears ran down his cheeks, getting lost in the drops of ocean that clung to his skin. He wiped them away.

"Activate D.E.A.T.H ... code Perseus8913."

"Acknowledged."

Nothing changed. No countdown, or shifting, or alerts. Then, the lights flickered before going dark. The only light came from the flashing screens.

"H.O.P.E ... did you activate self-destruct like I asked?"

"No such command found."

Percival stood and threw his chair across the room. Running his fingers through his hair, he yelled into the void, spittle landing on a nearby screen. Seeing spots, head swimming, he stumbled forward before falling to one knee.

"It's hard to breathe ... H.O.P.E ... Status on E.N.V.I.," he asked, gasping for air.

"NOSOI damaged the Environmental Nemesis Variable Index. Environmental program f—f—f-failing."

Percival fell to the ground. The lights flashed again without returning on. He rolled over to his back, eyes fixed on the red, flashing screens. The incessant beeping and warnings hammered on his brain like mallets. His vision swam.

He mumbled, his words slurring. "All the systems are gone, aren't they?"

"Only H.O.P.E.," the mechanical voice echoed. "H.O.P.E. will always be here."

Seething from Missed Passes
Estelle Parcoeur

"Hey, Seth. How's it hanging?"

In response Seth gave Eddie the oddest look ever.

"Don't look at me like you don't know me. Eddie. Friends since, like, forever?"

"Eternal brotherhood, you say?" Seth had a sly smile now.

Ruffling Seth's hair, Eddie continued to tease his best friend. "I know, I know. It's been since yesterday we seen each other. You forget who I am, old man?"

Seth was almost seething. More likely because Eddie had messed with the coif than due to the age slight. That was a running joke since their birthdays were about a month apart.

Eddie backed off when he again got the stare down that suggested Seth was not at all entertained. He threw up his hands in mock surrender. "OK, man, sorry. No need to charge me. Save it for the field."

"Tonight a vengeance will be secured," Seth vowed solemnly with a nod of his head.

"Whoa. C'mon. Practice was brutal yesterday. I thought Mondays were supposed to be recovery days. And you *did* take that hit to the head Sunday. So stop playing. We cool, right?"

Silence as he marched forward was Seth's only response.

Seething from Missed Passes

"Look, dude, I know you don't like to be touched, and your hair has to be just so. But can you lighten up?" Eddie was getting irritated.

Seth sounded back, full blown pissed.

As he listened, Eddie wondered if Seth had drunk off the pain again last night. Messed up Monday was almost something that yesterday had him considering himself. He tried not to think about the loss of his dog. Didn't need to emanate that mood too.

After rambling on for a bit, Seth summoned an accusation. "You confound and muddle the subject. Why, pray thee, do you not speak the literal? Do you not know me as I have become? Do you not recall the assignment you were given?"

"Whoa, duuude. You're taking that English project a bit too seriously and far too lit-er-ally. Have yourself a little something something to take the edge off, and go a bit deep in the bottle?"

Seth honed in on how Eddie punctuated the syllables. "Lit?" he inquired.

"Like the gods of fire or that Bacchus guy got things started," Eddie quipped.

"You provoke me. No good, sire." Seth again gave Eddie a mercurial look.

"Look, Seth, I know we were both pretty into that Shakespeare remake of the Abbott and Costello routine. But I'm not sure I can or want to keep this up."

"What's that I hear about you struggling to keep things up?" One of their teammates, Jack, came through the locker room and smacked them each on the backside with a towel.

"Shut it, ya arse," another voice bellowed after him. Flynn from the sound of it. At least that's what Eddie figured, for though his teammate's speech was accented heavier than usual, he was the only one to call the others arses. Maybe they all needed to sleep something off.

"Stop dicking around." Jack jabbed a finger into Eddie's side, giving him jumper cables.

"Drink up, suit up, and I'll see you on the field," Seth ordered Eddie. Which he took in stride since Seth *was* the team captain. He didn't dare question if his friend was alright to play. He'd watch him though, knowing how bad those minor head injuries could turn out to be.

That day in football practice it was Eddie's turn to miss a pass and take one to the head. Seemed to him an intentional throw on Seth's part.

"Welcome to the team," Seth said, offering him a hand up. "It's all chaos all the time."

"I'll have none of your hounding," Eddie slurred back in a bit of a stupor, remaining on the ground. He watched a dog run off with a football. Found himself fascinated by the dog. The patch of wildflowers it sniffed then rolled around in. The way the breeze brought such peace.

"How cunning you are," Seth and Eddie spoke at the same time. Eddie was talking of the dog. He couldn't quite place why Seth would be directing those words at him, though he appreciated the attribute.

"Swift now," Seth said and again offered a hand up.

"No, no. Let me be. Say, have you seen that dog before?" Nodding his head to indicate brought on a wave of dizziness and dazzling colors. Eddie would have shaken his head to clear it, but figured that might reproduce the effect.

Seething from Missed Passes

"Why you gotta be doggin', man?" Jake yelled from where he stood watching while Flynn came over and grasped Eddie's other arm. Together he and Seth hoisted him up. Far too easily. And it seemed to Eddie more like Seth's hand had simply still been clasping his, then Flynn hauled him up as if he were a toddler.

Eddie's eyes darted between his two teammates. They shared a knowing look. "Something going on you guys figure you should clue me in on?" Eddie asked. He felt a bit more like himself. Then the waves of nausea kicked in.

"Please, don't sick up on these shoes," Flynn requested.

"OK, fly man. I'll be sure to aim my spew. Cuz it's like I can control—" a retch came out in the place of any more words, but Eddie did manage to only get the grass between his own two feet. *Was he wearing sandals? And a leather skirt?*

He hadn't smoked since the weekend party. Surely no token effects lingered. Eddie felt defeated, like he'd set up a powerplay and something had stolen away what he offered. Maybe he should take to the sidelines for a bit. Likely had the wind knocked out of him. Needed to rest up if he was to maintain his starting lineup position. They had a Wednesday away game. He *had* already participated in today's practice.

"We storm the field again, men." Seth gave Eddie a charge he knew he couldn't refuse. Captain's orders and all.

"Flynn, dude, wh-what?" Eddie couldn't settle on words for the wondering.

"Give it a rest, man. Come morning you'll be walking out the ways of a man come before you. The legacy meant for you. T'was that way for me yesterday."

"You tryin' to tell me to man up?" Eddie was getting heated and it had nothing to do with the sweltering Southern conditions. Dust Bowl fishbowl this town was—

A small fish. A larger pond. A reflecting pool. *Where the hell were his thoughts going, or more accurately where did they come from?* He hadn't been some literati before. That was brood boy territory. Eddie glared at Flynn.

"Just give it time. You'll tap that stored up treasured knowledge in your spine," Flynn advised him.

Poetic pep talk. Eddie smirked. Was he talking kinesthetics, muscle memory? Flynn *was* built—maybe Eddie could learn a thing or two from his overnight change in weight class.

"Are we preparing to battle or are we preparing to lose?" Seth shouted a summons, already back in position on the field.

"Why you gotta be riding me when my head's riddled with pain?" Eddie was not amused. *What had gotten into his teammates?*

Eddie stood still for what seemed an eternity. He didn't feel steady on his feet. Didn't feel at home in his own body. He moved his arms like he was a puppet. He'd have to cave and take a bath tonight, maybe even ask Ma for some of her soaking salts or he'd sure enough be one sore and stiff unit tomorrow.

"Storm's coming in, boys. Time to ride out." Seth changed his mind about continuing practice though the skies showed no warning.

Coach consulted his phone, nodded, and added, "It's forecasted to be a doozie. Make haste for home, men."

"To the chariots," Eddie joked back.

Flynn helped him to his car, then displayed the same suddenly stormy face Seth had. "On second thought, you best be coming with me." His words were the only indication that Eddie was to be manhandled into his teammate's truck. He was too tired and strung out to argue. Maybe he should partake upon his return home. Might help him join whatever trip his teammates were clearly taking.

* * *

The first bell of Wednesday brought stabbing pain to his head and too much to think about into Eddie's mind.

"Praise the Lairds that we only have to make it through this school day, eh, before we're back on the field, back to our roots?" Flynn was suddenly at Eddie's side.

"Didymos, that warning—it brings us forth to where we'll learn to wield what gifts we've been given. Means it's step time." Seth slapped him on the back. Held firm to Eddie's shoulder as he steered him into English, the first period class a good chunk of the football team starters attended.

Flynn again cajoled him. "Eddie, what mythic figure you choose to present, lad?"

Since when had Flynn acted so Irish? "Uh, Didymos." Eddie turned to Seth. "You wisecracker." It had taken him a bit of time to process the play in his friend's greeting.

"He may be wise, but he's no cracker," Jack jumped in, slinging an arm around Seth. "There are codes to brotherhood."

"Like not ghosting?" chimed in Nat. She'd been like one of the guys until the team captain had dropped her. She narrowed her eyes at Seth then turned to Eddie, offering a big smile. "I know how you loved your dog. Did you know in Egypt dogs were revered after death? Don't worry—he's got it good now."

Eddie wondered how long she'd been working on that line of rubbage. They only talked when they saw each other in this one class they shared. Not that Seth had forbidden anyone to talk to her, that's just how it was between them.

"Natalie," Eddie nudged Seth. "Dogs were sacrificed to be ferried into the afterlife." Eddie really wished Seth would speak up for him. He should know how much the loss of the family dog meant. That it had marked Monday as Maunday.

Being in the classroom reminded Eddie of another looming. They'd joked last Friday when given the English assignment about what Thorsday's due date would bring. Their teacher required presentations to be submitted electronically the day before presenting. She said it forced preparation, opposed to last minute ad libbing. Tuesday—a scheduled day off—should have been a saving grace. Not that he'd been any good for anything yesterday, even before fumbling his way through practice. Not after that last vet visit. Eddie felt himself choking up.

Needed to buck up in front of his teammates. School or not, they took to the field, especially the day before a big game. Ugh. He sure as hell wouldn't get anything done with the away game tonight. Study hall tomorrow couldn't be social hour. He hadn't done any preparations for the presentation.

Eddie's attention drifted out the window where the scent of fresh cut grass lulled him. He took several deep breaths, then started to sneeze. Clearly still had the allergies. *Stupid, stupid.* He wanted to hit himself in the head for the inhalations. A shudder ran through Eddie. He didn't like their regressive play acting anymore.

"Like a rite of passage." The solemn voice and nod were odd on his once jovial friend. Eddie was feeling less and less like Seth had his back, more and more like a nomad.

"My dudes, they were the gatekeepers," Jack interjected. "Now shoo fly," he waved Nat off.

"No beating a dead horse, now," Nat retorted, but she did turn her back on the boys.

"By Jove," Seth started, but a glare from Jack stoppered him.

"Hitting too close to home?" Nat called over her shoulder.

"This means war," Flynn muttered.

"Ever-ready to defend a maiden's honor, are we?" Jack challenged.

"Men, let it go. Let her go. I've got another lined up." Seth was dismissive with them too, Eddie noticed. Not that everyone on the team was tight. Most of the starting line up were seniors being scouted for scholarships and big things. Maybe this was the drift apart Ma had warned him about. She'd said it was inevitable things would change this season.

Wild thoughts bloomed again. *Who were his friends? What was becoming of them?*

Jack and Flynn continued to jockey for the team captain's favor. None of them were really sure what was going on between Seth and Nat. It was a complicated relationship. Most guys at their school would have moved earth and sky to be with her, but for Seth the mom thing was a sticking point. His dad had remarried and everyone knew who came along in that package deal.

Seth had a rep for trying it all when it came to the ladies. Half the girls at their school were drawn like moths to flame, holding lofty ambitions of landing the football star while the other half vibed secretly on the brooding first string player. Flynn, their Quiet Man.

Seth had flirted unabashed with Nat until their parents got together. Flynn had always spoken soft and sweet of her. Eddie could see where it was headed: the Bermuda Triangle of lost love.

The dog motif stuck in Eddie's head; something significant there. He tended to only half listen, but he was becoming a bit pastoral as the assignment and practice merged in his mind. Something shifted within him. His mind churned.

Rack it as he might, the only dog symbolism that stuck in his mind was the modern slang. Seth had a rep for being a dog, yet the ladies at this school were still doggedly about him. "Chasing tail," he muttered.

"The past is always chasing us, always with us," Seth said suddenly. The guys all took it as his cue to end the conversation. Seth continued to give Eddie a hard look.

Then the real education began.

"Class, today we shift to focus on the mythos of Africa. Please take your seats." If the teacher they were all hot for had been a man they'd have called her a tall glass of water. Little Miss's wavy hair reminded Eddie of Mermaids. The blue-green dye job added to the fantasy.

In walked a new girl while they loitered by the door. A gorgeous new girl. Skin kissed by the gods. Hair done up to perfection. Nails more like preened claws. Eddie's heart beat ferociously. He glanced at the other guys lined up looking.

"Rawr," Jack gave sound to what Eddie considered. He'd better not pounce—Eddie planned to call dibs.

"Oh hello, Anansi," Golden Girl growled back.

"I like this girl," Seth proclaimed her place of popularity.

A guy walked in behind her. "Yo, sis, you sure they put us in the same class?"

"My brother, Ogun," Miss Spice supplied. "He's got a bit of a stubborn streak."

"More like an iron will," he shot back. "She tell you she's Oshun yet?" His words were directed at Eddie because Oshun smiled at him.

"Nah, man, but now I know."

"Oh, what do you know?" Ogun asked, raising an eyebrow and a challenge. "She can roll right over you and your crew." He dismissed every all star with a dark look.

The jersey suddenly felt itchy against Eddie's skin.

"Meet our sisters," Oshun shifted the conversation to introduce Ala and Oya as they breezed in.

"Fresh meat, and looking tasty," Jack crooned.

"Can it," Eddie cautioned him.

Ala smiled at Eddie and created a warm atmosphere.

Oya wrapped an arm around Oshun. "She has more depth than you can fathom, boys."

Jack hooted at that.

"Your neck will get you in trouble, the way you swivel it so," Oshun calmly informed him. Though her eyes looked like bedroom ones as she spoke sultry.

"I like spicy and salty," Jack shot back with a wink.

"Jack, ahem, ass." Eddie covered his words with a fake cough for the teacher's benefit.

Oshun placed fingertips on Eddie's forearm. "You'll do." Her smile sent waves through him.

"Now children." The teacher's words worked to calm the boys down. Though all she could do was present class, not demand it.

"Sit," Oshun said and directed Eddie to a desk next to the one she took. Her brother sat in front of her and her sisters took seats behind her to the left and right while Seth claimed the one directly behind her.

Eddie noticed Flynn quietly sat down next to Nat a few rows over. Jack grumbled and worked his way to a seat in the back, his usual preference. A place he said he could get into the most trouble without actually getting caught.

***

As they flowed out of the classroom, Oshun asked Eddie what his next class was and where she could find the art room.

"I'll walk you there," Eddie offered.

"Oh, I know my way to where I'm going. Ala has art class. She paints like Matisse."

"A la bright impressions and suggestive forms?" Eddie shot out before slapping a hand over his mouth and center of his face. "Ugh, I probably shouldn't have played with her name that way."

"She gets that a lot, with varying ideas about Matisse's work and her presentation. Almost as much as our old friend Sarah gets asked upon introduction if her middle name is Jessica."

"Hey, I'm Shane." The fastest runner on the team, also the leanest and strongest, propped himself against the wall as he casually introduced himself to Oshun.

"And I'm in the middle of a conversation," she replied.

Shane smoothed his braids back, not that they weren't picture perfect. "Care to supply your name? It *is* the nice thing to do."

Shane didn't give up easily. Of course, he didn't usually have to work for the ladies, often second choice to Seth for those who liked the spotlight type.

"Who said I'm a nice girl?" Oshun spoke for herself. Eddie was really getting a hankering for her.

Shocked to near silence, Shane muttered "Whatever," and moped away.

"Tell him, girl," Ala affirmed before asking if Oshun figured out where she should go for class.

"Eddie's going to walk you," she informed her.

"Uh, yeah, sure thing." He smiled at Ala but looked wistfully after Oshun as she walked away.

***

Eddie spotted Oshun again at lunch, like the crowded cafeteria parted for her.

"Did ya miss me?" he offered hopefully and playfully as his greeting.

"Ah, Didymos. Yes, but of course. You have beautiful designs." She winked.

Eddie faltered. "Uh, I wouldn't say I have designs, more like intentions. And they're good ones." He rushed to add the last phrase.

"I'd turn you away if they weren't," she informed him before walking away. Thank all that's good she turned back and beckoned him to follow her. She picked a table by the window overlooking the courtyard garden.

"Beautiful design, isn't it?" she pointed out the window.

Eddie studied it a bit, then surprised himself with what he spoke. "I'd change the arrangement a little. That shrub can be transplanted into two and form an entry way. Then the tree becomes a focal destination. It could be ringed with additional tall flowers to create an alcove. And a sitting rock would be ideal. It'd likely get a lot more visitors then." He shut his mouth quickly.

"Uh, I'm no landscaper." He tried to shift into something that would make him seem all manly. He puffed out his chest and announced, "I'm a starting player for the football team."

"Ah, a player. Are you also then a manscaper?"

Eddie choked on his milk. Found it didn't taste right anyway, and he was craving the team's hydration drink almost as much, if not more than, this woman before him. She was no child and she was not playing around—right to business.

"A, uh, what?" He didn't want to let on he knew where her mind traveled. Her words were below the belt. His suddenly felt a bit too tight.

She winked. "Oh, you know. Or maybe you should look it up." She slid him her phone after unlocking it. "While you're in there, why don't you add your number. Might be handy to have."

Good thing he had an excuse, two tasks actually, as reasons not to talk, for he was at a loss for words. She floored him, confounded him. *Wait—Seth had used that word.* Eddie's thoughts floated away from this precious moment to previous preoccupations. He simply held Oshun's phone as thoughts rolled through his mind.

Why had Seth been quick to welcome the new crew? He knew he ruled the school and incited others to follow. Why did Seth and Flynn insist on calling him by the name of the mythological figure Eddie researched? And why did he use that name as a pun to introduce himself?

"It's taking you a bit longer than anticipated." Oshun pointed to her phone. "You just want me to explain it to you and make you blush? I do like it when a guy gets a blush on for me." She dazzled him with a smile that made those words sweet instead of shocking.

He gave her a goofy grin back. *I must look a fool,* Eddie thought. *Play it cool.*

Oshun's phone started ringing and Eddie recognized the lyrics as the bridge and title from that Tal Bachman song. It had dropped years ago, but he swore all the girls dropped their panties if a guy suggested he felt the words about her. He hated how the singer reminded him of Flynn. Figured that was part of his charm for the lasses he lassoed these days.

"Uh, I should take this." Oshun's words were the most unsure he'd heard from her.

"Uh, okay. I'll be here."

She didn't return to the lunch table before the next bell bid him on his way.

***

"Damn it, man." Seth was in a foul mood again, Eddie noted as he walked into the locker room to ready. They'd do a light warm up before boarding the bus to the game. It was routine to make the different turf feel like an extension of home.

Jack began hopping about, rapping as if he were Pitbull. Their quarterback still amped himself up to the song that came out when they were freshmen.

"You ever want to throw down lyrics and lines, you let me know." Shane was chill, but got competitive when it came to spitting words and laying them down on the ladies.

"Nope, I'm just dope," Jack shot back as he sniffed and rubbed his nose then bounced over to his locker.

Their running back turned the words around. "You sure you ain't telling on yourself about what's got you hyped up?"

"Watch yourselves and hold your tongues," Seth said with a pointed look to both of them. Then he turned to Eddie. "How you feeling? Any different?"

"I've been a bit off, but acting more like myself than I can say for many here."

"Oh really?" Jack got out before Seth shot him another shut up look. The energy radiating off him

Seething from Missed Passes

made it seem Jack could just fly away, but he awaited orders from the team captain.

Seth spoke a directive to Eddie instead. "How about you and I throw some passes before these others take to the field? We've got some stuff to talk about."

"Sure, Captain," Eddie found himself saying. *He wasn't usually so formal. Pulling rank had never been a thing between him and Seth before.*

Eddie had his own agenda he wanted to talk through. He took charge of the conversation. "When did all this shifting begin?" He demanded an account from his best friend, now someone he didn't recognize.

"Oh, so you've noticed a change to positions now?" Seth inquired before explaining how Coach had approached him, and asked Seth to taste a new Gatorade flavor. "'A special home brew. Nectar of the Gods, I tell you,' coach said."

"And you do know Coach is dating our English teacher, right?" Jack jumped in, supplying hook up information as he darted around them in circles.

"And he erred when he thought literally making an assignment come to life would impress said teacher. I hear she's pretty pissed," chimed in Flynn announcing his arrival.

"Hey, McCoolio," Jack gave him five. "You right. English teacher ain't sparing no lovin' for Coach. He put himself on the hook."

Eddie shook his head, and felt the lingering effects of the hit yesterday. He must have looked sick too.

"You ain't been shot, Cupid ain't practicing on no team targets," Jack stated as if reassurance.

"Uh," Eddie got out before his fellow players continued to take him play by play through the changes they were all going through.

"Think of it as you're just on a little trip down memory lane. They say we contain the memories of our people before us," Flynn began.

"That why you've been embracing your Irishness?" Eddie asked.

"By Jove," Flynn started.

Jake stopped him. "Let me answer that one for him with an I-wish."

"It's not wishes we lift up, but strength." Flynn was quick with his reply.

Jack puffed up his chest. "You want to see strength, *lad?*" he sneered.

"Oh Jupiter, Jewel has you on lock, crooning the need for a little heart to be still," Flynn bit back.

"Perhaps you should swallow your tongue," threatened Jake.

"Love always did bring you trouble," Seth remarked dryly. He then held out an arm, running interference between Jake and Flynn before they could come to blows. "I haven't called for chaos. I'd like us to lead Eddie here to victory over his confusion before Coach shows up."

"Why's it taking him so long?" Flynn asked Seth.

"Maybe he's a mutt," Jack chimed in.

"What a row, man." Flynn slapped back.

"Hey now, you know I'm supremely about the Romans. None of that word-smithery at my people's expense." Jack's face and demeanor darkened.

Seething from Missed Passes

"If anyone is brewing a storming, it's me." Seth silenced the warring words.

"Now, now, boys." Oshun appeared, a very welcome sight to Eddie. Especially in the tight tank and short skirt. Their school colors looked good on her.

"Come to supervise?" sneered Jake.

"Apparently you lot need it," Nat added, walking up to stand beside Oshun. Both crossed their arms, tilting heads and raising eyebrows. They stood with pompoms limp on hips. Apparently Oshun already made the squad. Nat *was* cheer captain, and Seth *had* anointed her welcome.

"Great, Nat is here," Jake muttered.

"Someone going to get hit too hard today?" Seth asked Nat with a strain in his voice.

"You know we aren't all here in official capacity," Nat calmed him with her words. "We can't help the change in form, but we don't have to operate as others anticipate."

Oshun too offered comfort. "Don't mind Jake; he's clearly a bit vain and easily jealous."

"Takes one to know one," Jake bantered back.

"Oh, childish games now, eh? Someone really has been into their Jewel," Oshun quipped.

"More like jewels, gems, and trinkets," Flynn muttered. "Manwh—"

"What are you muttering, mere mortal gifted with strength and knowledge, bound by a book he loves?" Jake's passions were rising in the form of unrestrained anger.

"Rain, reign, let's be careful what we let precipitate now. We've already had one practice ruled out by weather this week. I think we can all appreciate the changing conditions. Let's rally now, men." Seth again attempted to marshal his teammates.

"Would you like me to get Oya?" Oshun offered.

"Oh, please *do* bring her here," Jack joyfully said, his leer clear across his face.

"Perhaps you require Ala instead. She'll know how to deal with you," Oshun retorted.

Coach approached them. "Games and the bleachers are for spectators. It's time for my boys to take up the ball. Enough of this bantering. Do I need to inform your English teacher of the lost love manifesting here?"

"What's she going to do about it?" Jack challenged.

"Oh, you should know, Jack." Coach said the name in a tell-tale way. "She's made you a tool many a time in your trades."

"What have you lot traded?" Eddie spoke up, now demanding. "In all earnestness, I beseech you to make clear that my eyes do not see."

"Oh, the way you be talking, you'll be seeing crystal clear soon enough," Jack said with a masochistic smile as he slicked his hair back before putting on his helmet. "Let the practice begin," he decreed. "Y'all know how I love the games." He ran onto the field.

"Later, if need be, you'll get more of an explanation," Seth promised Eddie. At least he sounded more like the Seth Eddie knew and not someone attempting to parrot some era lost to the sands of time.

Eddie's mind cued up a Steve Miller band song. Damn Jake and his jump-off on songs.

As he jumped to catch another slightly off pass, Eddie rammed into Shane. After they both rose from the tumble, Shane slapped his helmet hard. "Ever look to see

Seething from Missed Passes

what's going on around you?" he demanded before ripping off his helmet and jogging to the sideline to guzzle from the team cooler.

The gatorade! Like sipping kool aid. The nectar of the gods. Thoughts laced together in Eddie's mind finally made connections. There was a link between the drink and the head hit.

Shane shook his head. Wiped across his eyes. Glanced at the other first string players and shook his head again. Threw down the cup and crushed it underfoot. Jogged back over to Eddie. "Um, hey man. Can we talk? I've got some questions."

"Well … I think you better talk to the Captain." Eddie settled on words that seemed apt. Only after did the logic behind the idea present itself.

Again Eddie calculated the changes. Drinking the juice plus taking a hit to the head. It's like they were all raging. But how would drugging explain the jump to taking on a persona one was researching? Eddie felt a split within himself. He had his own thoughts, but he was beginning to understand the positions of the other players, that playing out. A part of his history became his present. They had a future to secure. Tonight's game was a titleship one. Would earn them a legacy. Put everyone's arms around them. Coach usually got his victory hug from their English teacher … that rush of love … Eddie saw clearly now. Knew who the teacher really was, what Coach hoped to snatch away. How history was always bound to repeat itself. He wondered if the transformation was permanent. Wondered if he shouldn't take another sip of that cool drink calling out to him.

* * * * * *

2010 Team Roster

Seth (Set)—Egyptian God. Trickster. Power over storms, chaos, and warfare. Worshiped for protecting the dead. Associated with necessary creative force and destruction. Team Captain and Left Tackle.

Eddie/Didymos—Roman soldier who followed after the dog that stole his sacrifice and became enraptured by nature, team Safety.

Jack (Jove/Jupiter/Zeus)—"Top god", team Quarterback.

Flynn/Finn M(a)cCool—Irish Legend. Seer and poet known for strength. A magic thumb of wisdom. Team Center.

Shane—team Running Back.

Lead Characters

Natalie/Nat (Nephthys)—Egyptian Goddess Nebtho, daughter of Nut, paired with sister Isis as protector of Osiris and sister-wife of Set.

Ogun—African God associated with exile, rum; god of iron.

Oshun—West African Supreme Being; river deity; goddess of divinity, femininity, love and beauty, destiny and divination.

Ala (Odinala)—SE Nigerian deity of earth, morality, and creativity; rules over underworld; spouse to sky deity.

Oya—Santeria Cuban Orisha. Force of change and nature.

Coach—Chaos.

Faculty Advisor/English teacher—Aphrodite.

Cy Pearce Deserved to Die
Ark Horton

Cy Pearce deserved to die. After a decade of working in homicide, that wasn't a conclusion Detective Cassandra Troias reached lightly, but it was far from the first time she had. The more she learned about this victim, the more she knew he'd had it coming.

Despite that, she had a job to do. Solving murders kept her employed, and killers must face consequences for the good of society. She had a rule about never letting off a perp, and Cass didn't make an exception for any of her rules—even if the courts were quick to dismiss her statements time and time again. *Hopefully, I'm done with this Pearce case for good.*

Cass opened the filing cabinet and inserted Cy Pearce's folder into the Case Closed drawer. She would have a few more hours that day to get acquainted with a new case and maybe get a full night's rest for once.

"Shouldn't steal from the few friends you've got," she said to Cy's ghost, still shimmering in her scrying mirror. As always, his mouth hung open in terror. *Why hasn't he left yet?* Hanging on the wall beside her desk, the black oval of a mirror housed the spirit of the victim she currently investigated until she solved their murder. "You can go now." His shimmer's crimson hue deepened. He pulled at his skin, a scream shaking his body but making no noise.

Cass raked her dyed red hair back as she groaned. On occasion, the spirits lingered in her scrying mirror, and she had to go back to square one. *Goddamn it! I guess I haven't really solved this yet.* She opened the cabinet and pulled Cy's file out. She sat at her desk and rifled through the file's contents, including photos of Cy's slain body. They'd found him lying in a pool of blood, the result of several deep and disturbing lacerations. *Never piss off a satyr, especially if he's your dealer.*

Cass winced at her own bigotry against satyrs. However, the only ones she'd ever met were violent criminals and it was hard to get over that. Atlantis PD suspected this one, Thad, of murdering countless innocents in drive-bys. Yet even Thad had more redeeming qualities than a misogynistic troll who spent his days harassing women online and his nights consuming more potions than any addict she'd ever come across.

When she turned the last photo over and reached the printed transcripts of Cy's late-night conversations with his dealer, Cass had to take a moment to rub the weariness from her dark brown eyes and the even darker circles around them. She had pored over these words for hours and hours before connecting the dots and making an arrest. *All for nothing.*

Cass glared at Cy's ghost. "For a recluse, you sure screwed over a lotta people. I'm getting a little tired of your company." She read through the texts again, trying to see past the lines she'd highlighted before. Her eyes stopped at a section that always made her laugh.

Thad: Slow down, Cy. I got other customers. Don't need to be dry.

Cy: Don't call me that anymore. I'm Pygmalion.

Thad: Pyg-what? You're already high, aren't you?

Cy: High on love!

Thad: That's the funniest shit I've read all day. I'll be over in twenty.

Those words from the same troll who claimed all women were ugly sluts and not worth his time, while he still had the nerve to beg for nude photos from them. *But what if he really was in love?* Cass chuckled at the thought. He'd have an impossible time finding a woman to give him a chance.

Her eyes scanned the text again. *Pygmalion is an odd choice for a new name.* He'd taken it on in the last week of his life as if he wanted to start all over again. His presence online came to a halt. He'd even deleted his accounts on social media.

The only evidence they'd found of how he'd spent his last days was the marble chunks and dust littering his apartment floor. He had carved something big, but his murderer had taken whatever it was with them. *I'd thought to cover his overdue debt to Thad, but...*

Her mind turned in a new direction, and Cass typed the list of various potions he had purchased from his dealer into the Atlas search engine. A bunch of alchemy sites popped up as results. One, in particular, caught her interest right away. "Get love like magic with the right ingredients!" *Love. Is that what this is really about?*

Cass opened the site. A dazzling photo of a smiling and winking goddess took up most of the home page. "Losing at love? Can't find your other half? Then make one!" Cass scrolled down and saw a spell for how to make your lover. It included a list of ingredients, most of which Cy had purchased from his dealer. One, however, could only be purchased from this website, and only if you had a spare one hundred thousand drachmae.

Cass's breath stopped, and her heart pounded when she saw what it was. *Marble stone, blessed by Aphrodite herself.* She looked up at the specter who glinted in her scrying mirror. "What did you do with that marble?" she asked.

He said nothing. He couldn't. He could only continue his silent scream.

She pulled out her cell phone and dialed Myke, her favorite forensic alchemist at the station—and not just because he was handsome. "Hey, Myke," she said after he answered in his usual charming manner. "Can you tell me if any of these potions are present in that marble dust the Evidence Department collected?" She gave Myke the list from Aphrodite's alchemy site, hoping for the right answer.

* * *

In the morning, with a clearer head and fresh caffeine perking her up, Cass returned to the scene of the crime. She ducked under the police tape, which still blocked the entrance to Cy Pearce's loft. No longer distracted by the hubbub of crime scene investigators taking photos and measurements, Cass found it easier to soak in the setting. She took advantage of that for a good half hour.

Cy had clearly thought of himself as a misunderstood artist. At some point, he must have watched a movie or read a book that showed them living in lofts bare of comfort but replete with aesthetic mess. Splatters of paint and hills of marble dust were both a blessing and a curse for evidence. On the one hand, there were fingerprints and footprints everywhere. On the other, no one could touch any of it, which proved almost impossible.

Cass approached the area where Cy's body had lain. Her eyes scanned the chalk outline and markers left by the forensics team. *The landlord will need to re-floor this room.* She squatted, her eyes lingering on the blood-soaked drop cloth covered in marble dust and chiseled pieces which Cass suspected came from Aphrodite's blessed marble.

"Statues don't just walk away," Cass muttered to herself. "But with a goddess involved..."

As Cass straightened into a standing position, her cell vibrated in the back pocket of her black slacks. She set it on the only clean surface nearby and put the phone on speaker. "Cassandra Troias speaking."

"Troias, how's it going?" Myke's familiar voice brought a smile to Cass's face. The forensic alchemist had helped her out of her abusive marriage, even testifying in court on her behalf. There was no one at the station she trusted more. "I have the results of that alchemical lab you ordered yesterday. The dust had all of them. Every single one."

Another hunch proved true. Not that the courts care about any of that. "Anything else?" she asked.

In the corner, past the drop cloth and leaning against the baseboard, something pale, blood-splattered, and almost cylindrical caught Cass's attention. She squinted to see it better.

"Well, you didn't order this, but..." Myke said. The playful tone in his words made Cass giggle.

"You couldn't help yourself?" she asked, tiptoeing around the piles of mess and evidence everywhere. "As usual?"

Closer to the cylinder, she could tell its true shape. *A finger?* She pulled a vinyl glove and a baggie from her other back pocket.

"I got permission from the necromancer to get a skin and hair sample from Pearce for another lab," Myke said, while Cass placed the marble finger in the baggie.

"What did you find?"

"The guy didn't just stink because he had been dead a couple of days." Myke paused to laugh at his own dark joke. "He was saturated with one of the strongest love potions on the market. And by market, I mean the black market."

Aphrodite's approval wasn't enough for this guy? He needed a love potion too? "Thanks." Cass eyed the marble finger in the baggie. "I'll have something else for an alchemical lab in about an hour. Maybe we can grab a sandwich?"

"Sounds great."

When Cass hung up her phone, she realized she'd been twisting a lock of her hair around her finger. *Flirting in a murder scene? Classy, Cassandra Troias.* Her smile fell and her face took on the appropriate concern a detective at work should have. She reexamined the marble finger. Cy had even chiseled in the trace of a delicate fingerprint. *What a waste of talent on that troll.*

***

After a pleasant lunch with Myke, she asked him to run another lab, this one on the finger. She wanted to know if it had the same results as the marble dust. As usual, Myke was quick to accept the task. She knew he had other lab requests and was only prioritizing hers because of their friendliness, but it didn't stop her from loving that he chose her every time.

That afternoon, back at her desk, she returned to Aphrodite's alchemy website and scrolled to the bottom to find contact information. Cass groaned at the expected generic help desk email and the customer service hotline. The physical address was here in Atlantis instead of Olympus, though, and hanging around a factory or call center until she got information might prove fruitful.

Yet, the moment she arrived at the location, her stomach sank. She checked and double-checked the address on the website. She also checked her Atlas app. *This is the place ... Somehow.*

Cass exited her car and approached the boarded-up door. The wood had rotted there for years, just as it had on the windows. Either the company had posted false information about its location online or it closed without notifying anyone. Cass thought back to that lifelike marble finger. *It can't be closed.*

Taking a step back from the blocked entrance, Cass looked up and down the empty street. This was the bad side of the industry sector. Aphrodite wouldn't build anything worth keeping here. She had the money to operate her business anywhere she wanted to. *But then why run a skeezy business like this at all?*

Something glinted at the periphery of her vision. Cass turned to see light bouncing off the metallic frame of a security camera. It pivoted in her direction. *She may not run a business here, but she certainly wants to know who shows up to find out.* Cass flashed her badge at the camera, long enough for whoever was watching to know who she was. Then she hopped back into her car and headed to the station.

* * *

Cass lumbered to her office the next day, clasping her travel mug of coffee as if dropping it would kill her. Try as she might, her mind hadn't settled until almost dawn, and then she'd had nothing but nightmares. It didn't surprise Cass. What she'd assumed had been a drug deal gone wrong had become a murder case involving one of the most powerful gods in Olympus. *Of course I'm gonna be rattled.*

To make matters worse, her ex was at the station that morning. He eyed her from the Chief's entrance as she passed by. *So much for that restraining order. Guess it doesn't matter when you're one of the boys in blue.*

"Morning, Cass," he called out to her.

Morning, asshole. Cass didn't even look at him and kept a polished mask on her face to hide the roiling in her guts.

Once safe in her office with the door shut, she dry-heaved into the small trash bin beside her desk. She startled at the soft knock at her door. For a half-second, she feared her ex had followed her, but remembered he didn't knock on doors—he barged through them. Still, she turned the doorknob with hesitation. To her relief, Myke's face greeted her on the other side.

"Hey, did you know Ajax is here today?" he asked with hushed words. When Cass nodded, he stroked her arm, sending delightful shivers through her. "I can't believe the Chief hasn't booted him out. What a crock of…" Myke shook his head and sighed. "Anyway, I didn't come here for that. I came here for this."

Cass looked down at the hand he extended to her and saw a piece of paper. She took it from him and unfolded it to find a lab report. "Thanks," she said. "Can't wait to see if this matches up with the rest of the marble we tested."

"No, you don't understand," Myke said. He took a quick glance at the hallway and then ducked into her office, closing the door behind him. "This isn't just a list of potions found present. There's … DNA. Like a woman's DNA."

"So a woman handled the statue?" Cass asked.

"No." Myke pulled his fingers through his hair, letting the strands fall in a cascade of glossy brown. "It has its own DNA. It may look and feel like marble, but this is a real finger."

Cass's chin dropped, but she didn't have a moment to respond further to that shocking revelation, because her desk phone rang. The only people who ever called her on that phone were the Chief and important civilians that barged past the station's receptionists. In either case, she knew she had to answer it.

Keeping her wide eyes locked on Myke's, she moved the phone's receiver to her ear and answered, "This is Detective Troias."

A husky man's voice greeted her on the other end. "Detective, I understand you are looking into the murder of a man named Pygmalion."

Cass's heart leapt to her throat. *He said Pygmalion, not Cy.* "May I ask who is speaking?"

The man let out a pleasant chuckle. "Oh, my apologies, I'm…" the man paused for a beat. "Archer Lovegood."

"How can I help you, Mr. Lovegood?" *Besides ignore your obviously fake name.*

"I wanted to help you with your investigation," he answered. "I think I may have some information that you'll find helpful."

Typically, Cass would have doubted a claim given in such an unorthodox way, but he had called Cy by his alter ego and nothing had been straightforward about this case. She looked up at her scrying mirror. Cy's spirit had paused his screaming. His eyes focused on the phone. Cass waved, but it didn't disrupt his attention.

Cass picked up a pen and notepad. "I'm listening."

"Not over the phone. I need you to meet me."

Alarm bells rang in her head. *Is this guy gonna kill me?* "I'm afraid I can't do that. Not unless you want to come to the station."

"What if I said we could meet in Olympus?"

Cass gulped. "Oh."

"Be at the gate within the hour," he said, ending their call.

Cy's gaze lifted from the phone to Cass. For a heartbeat, he seemed calm, though his eyes glimmered with sorrow. Just as his stillness lulled her, he snapped, slamming his fists against the glass of the scrying mirror and continuing his silent scream.

"What was that?" Myke asked.

"A summons to Olympus," Cass answered.

***

Olympus Gate had more visitors than any train station or airport that Cass had ever visited. Yet, its efficiency moved the crowds through the correct channels quickly. While dozens of others stood in front of Cass when she arrived, she found herself face to face with a gatekeeper within minutes.

"Name and reason for visit," asked the woman on the other side of the scratched and yellowed plexiglass, with words flattened from constant use. Her eyes stayed glued to the computer screen and her fingers hovered over her keyboard to type the response.

"Cassandra Troias," Cass said and the woman's fingers rattled along her keys. "I was summoned."

The gatekeeper's fingers froze, and she looked up at Cassandra. "Going to need a birthday for that."

They're really serious about this. "November 3rd, 1989."

The gatekeeper entered all the required information for the request to process. A moment later, she clicked a button, and a ticket appeared. Cass reached to grab it, but the gatekeeper snatched it back. "Not that easy," she said. "Don't want the wrong person taking this from you."

"Then what—"

The gatekeeper snatched Cass's arm and slapped the ticket onto it. A thousand sunburns tore into Cass's flesh. She screamed, but the gatekeeper must have known that would happen because a silencing bubble surrounded her head at once. *Is this what Cy's ghost feels like in that scrying mirror?*

The gatekeeper ripped the ticket off her arm, and the pain ebbed away. Cass yanked back her injured limb. As she rubbed it, she saw the ticket had imprinted like a tattoo onto her skin.

"That will last for the duration of your summons," the gatekeeper said. "Once the god says it's over, that goes away. Then you'll be back at the gate with whatever we confiscate."

Confiscate?

Cass might have asked the gatekeeper for more information, but at that moment, something pulled her up through a hole in the roof with such force that it took everything in her not to vomit. She came to a sudden stop in a metal tube of a room where her sidearm and taser flew to the walls and disappeared from view.

An exit slid open in front of her, and she squeezed out at once. For a moment, she bent over with her hands on her knees, taking deep, desperate breaths of the refreshing air around her.

Footsteps behind her reminded Cass where she was, and she stood up while trying to slow her breaths.

"Thank you for your expediency, Detective Troias."

Cass turned in the direction of the man's familiar voice. His face matched it—golden, poised, and confident. If she had met him at a party, she'd have swooned. Under these circumstances, his warmth and flawless features came across as artificial.

With a nod, she said, "I'm not one to sit on a summons, Mr. Lovegood."

"Detective, please," he said, one flirtatious corner of his mouth lifting. "We're not on a recorded line now. You can call me by my real name."

Cass cocked an eyebrow. "Which is?"

"Eros, of course!" he replied, showcasing his body with a waving hand. "Could you not tell by looking at me?"

Aphrodite's son. I must be on to something. "I try to never assume."

"Very wise. That's why you make such a great detective."

Cass shrugged. "I don't know if I'd say I was a *great* detective, but I do okay."

"Detective Troias, hush." Eros offered his elbow for her to hold, like some gentleman from a bygone era. They walked down a marble corridor, with baseboards and crown molding of gold and gemstones, toward a gigantic iridescent door. "I read about the work you did on the Paris case. Brilliant."

He researched me. Is that how much trouble I'm in? "I wouldn't call that my shining moment. The killer got off on a technicality."

"People don't often believe you. Do they, Detective Troias?"

Cass opened her mouth, but paused, not knowing what to say because he was right—and she hated it. The massive door swung open, drawing Eros's attention to it, and Cass sighed with relief. That sigh sharpened to a gasp when she took in more details about the door. It was unlike any she had ever seen, made of Mother of Pearl and dusted with gold.

A splash pulled Cass's attention from the door to the room's contents. A clam-shaped pool, wide enough for dozens of swimmers and deep enough for a diving board, took up most of the space within. Cass could taste the sea salt thickening the air, which made sense when she saw Aphrodite sitting on her pearly throne at the center of it all. She had long, bronzed limbs, and her sun-bleached hair cascaded around her in sopping wet ringlets. Her ocean eyes spoke of the deep and powerful love Cass had longed for all her life.

"So," Aphrodite said, directing her gaze at Cass. "You flashed your badge. You got my attention. Let's make a deal."

Eros guided Cass to a seat. All the while, her heart thundered, feeling Aphrodite's eyes burn through her. Cass darted a glance at the goddess's swimsuit of golden shells and almost laughed. *A goddess that both wears shells and has a shell business.*

Cass sat on the tufted velvet chair next to Eros. Finding her courage, she said, "Cops don't really make deals. It's illegal. We can put in a good word, though."

"You're a homicide detective," Aphrodite said. "I haven't killed anyone … Well, not in a few centuries, at least. So, why can't we negotiate?"

Cass fought back the urge to groan. It wouldn't be professional, and she had no desire to anger a god. "I have to report illegal activity, whether or not it falls under my responsibilities."

Aphrodite gasped and clutched the actual pearls dripping across her décolletage. "I'm not asking for you to turn a blind eye to anything illegal, Detective Troias!"

Yeah, right. Cass's face must have betrayed her because Aphrodite frowned and Eros laughed.

"She's telling the truth," Eros said. "Yes, her listed address online isn't the headquarters of her operation, but she's famous. Do you really expect her to make it so easy for weirdos to find her?"

"I see your point," Cass admitted, "but why do you want to make a deal with me if not for that?"

Eros shrugged. "Like I said before, you're a great detective. It's only a matter of time before you solve this case."

Cass bristled. "And I still intend to."

"I'm glad," Aphrodite said, leaving her throne and swimming to the edge of her pool. Attendants rushed to her with plush towels and a silk robe. She lifted herself to the floor from the pool and let her servants fawn over her. "I want you to catch and convict the killer. I can even tell you who it is, but I need you to do one important thing."

"What's that?" Cass asked.

Aphrodite waved her servants away and strode over to Cass. Once she got close, she peered down her long, elegant nose at the mortal. "Don't let any of this make it to the public. I can't have anyone knowing about this travesty. That marble is how I grow my worshiper base."

"I can do that," Cass agreed. "You said you know who the killer is?"

"Her name is Galatea. She was Pygmalion's wife."

* * *

The information Aphrodite gave Cass led her back to Cy's block several days later, where she spent an entire morning interviewing the residents of Cy Pearce's neighborhood to find out what she could about Galatea. Many had seen glimpses of the woman—covered in a film of chalk, her movements stiff and jerking.

"She looked like a dolly," a little girl said while peeking at Cass from behind her mother's skirt.

Cass bent to get eye level with the child. "How so?"

"She was so beautiful, but her arms and legs didn't move like ours do," the girl answered. "They moved like this." Coming out of her hiding spot, she marched robotically.

The girl's mother smoothed the hair on the child's head and pulled her close. "When we saw her, she was entering that building they're getting ready to demolish. Is she all right?"

Cass squinted. "All right? I don't know."

"Then why are you looking for her?" the woman asked. "Family searching for her?"

"She's wanted for questioning," Cass answered.

"She seemed so sweet," the woman muttered. "Confused but sweet."

Sweet? So they did more than see her in passing. "How so?"

The woman bit her lip and her face flushed red. *Ah, so you were trying to hide this.* "Well, she said she needed to get away from a bad man."

"And she gave me this flower!" The girl, squealing with excitement, shoved her prize in Cass's face. The child's palm had crushed an anemone's red petals, but the marble petals remained perfectly delicate.

"Beautiful," Cass said, even though it terrified her. She returned to the mother. "Where's this building you were talking about?"

Cass followed the directions the woman gave her. When she got there, she could understand why someone wanted to demolish it. It wasn't just a blight to the neighborhood. It likely harbored vermin and hosted drug deals. To be safe, Cass took her sidearm from its holster before entering.

Fortunately, this building had once boasted large bay windows, and plenty of afternoon light streamed in. So, when her steps echoed around the haunting interior of the building, she didn't jump at her own shadows.

She walked up a flight of stairs and scanned the second floor. A scuffling noise above caught her attention. She looked up and the soft shuffle turned into a labored thumping rhythm. *She's trying to make a run for it.* Cass sprinted up the stairs, but when she made it to the third floor, she saw there hadn't been a need to rush.

A scantily clad woman, trembling and disheveled, wept as she swung a heavy, half-marble leg forward. A painful whimper slipped from her lips.

"Galatea?" Cass asked. "I'm Detective Cassandra Troias with Atlantis PD. I need to talk to you about the murder of Cy Pearce."

Galatea looked at Cass with wide, terrified eyes. Dark circles rimmed them, and Cass could tell she had more than the police to fear.

"Help me!" Galatea screamed. Her arms reached for Cass, and the purpose of the homicide detective's pursuit flipped from capture to rescue. The closer she came to the frightened woman, however, the clearer it became that Galatea wasn't reaching her arms out. They were stuck in that position—an everlasting appeal for an embrace. Cass grabbed her and let the tired woman rest on her shoulder.

"Help..." Galatea's hoarse voice cracked as she repeated the word over and over.

Cass examined the woman in her arms. At first glance, it looked as if someone had plastered parts of her. Then Cass noticed the fleshy fingers that moved with difficulty from her marble hands. Her human calves struggled to support stone-hard thighs. Her face seemed completely human, much to Cass's relief, but she couldn't feel a breath or a heartbeat beneath her rock-solid chest. *How did she even make it here?*

"My arms are so sore. I can't put them down."

"It's okay. It's okay." Cass offered a soothing shush as she held onto the woman's arms. *Maybe Myke can fix this.* "What happened?"

"Pygmalion, he made me like this. He, he…" The woman screamed through another sob.

Cass tried to smooth Galatea's hair to calm her, but her fingers snagged on hard lumps of marble between the strands. "Did he hurt you?"

"He brought me to *life!*" Galatea may have been carved from marble, but her eyes shone bright with rage. "I have no home, no family, no history. I don't even know who I am. Is there any greater injury than that?"

Cass struggled for a response. "He wanted someone to love…" *That's what Aphrodite told me, anyway.* "He didn't want you to hurt."

Galatea sneered and let out a bitter chuckle. "He didn't want someone to love. He wanted to force someone to love *him.*" Her eyes shifted toward a distant, painful memory. "And that's what he did. He forced me to join the living, and when I felt no affection for him, he tried to lure it out of me with stinking oils."

The woman trailed off into tears again. Cass looked down at the woman's hand—a thumb, three fingers, and one stony stump where a finger had been. *Let me be wrong this time.* "Galatea, did you kill him?"

"There comes a time when a bad man stops trying to coax," she said, "and starts to demand. That's why

I'm missing a finger. So, I took the knife from him. I kept him away. I didn't even know how bad I hurt him…" She winced, trying to move the fingers she had left. "Not until I got to this street and parts of me started turning back to marble. That must have been when he died." The woman motioned with her chin towards her outstretched arms. "It won't stop."

Cass had a rule about never letting off a perp. At that moment, however, she knew it was time to make an exception.

* * *

Cass sat in Myke's car several days later. It idled at the station parking lot to keep the heater going that cold morning. The radio played popular tunes, interrupted by traffic reports and local news.

"So, you think it's going well?" Cass asked Myke over the travel mug of coffee still cooling in her hands.

"Getting there," he answered. "May call in a few favors with some other alchemists to turn around the petrification. There's this satyr I knew in college who could figure out anything."

Cass grimaced. "A satyr? Really?"

"They're not all dealers and murderers, Cass. Stop being such a bigot." Myke rolled his eyes, but a playful smile told her she hadn't lost any points with him. Then his face grew serious. "I'm less concerned with our progress there than whether you're safe."

"I'm fine," Cass said. "Promise. I met up with Aphrodite and showed her the finger you tested. She bought that Galatea's dead. Thank goodness we never submitted it to evidence."

"What if she wants to see the rest of the body?"

Cass shrugged. "Then I'll send her a pile of the marble dust in Cy's apartment." Myke had asked a fair question, but Cass couldn't think about that too hard—not if she wanted to sleep at night. "Aphrodite got what she wanted. This whole potentially disastrous mess is behind her. No one will ever know how limited her ability to inspire love really is and every purchase of that blessed stone earns her a new worshiper."

"Yeah, but..." Myke fidgeted. "Do you feel okay pinning this on the wrong guy?"

"Do I feel bad about convicting someone who has never gone to jail for countless drive-by murders?" Cass shook her head. "No."

Myke squeezed her hand. "I believe you. I just … I care about you. A lot."

He drew so close to her that his breath tickled her lips. Their eyes stayed locked when he cupped her cheek. *Is this happening? Are we going to kiss?* Just then, the blaring horns of the radio station's special update startled them both.

"Yesterday, Atlantis PD closed a homicide case that led to the arrest of one of the most notorious drug dealers in the city," said the news reporter. "We here at WAPB were lucky enough to receive a few words about the arrest from Aphrodite herself."

Aphrodite's husky voice spoke over the crackle of the telephone recording. "It's just such a shame," she said, sounding for all the world as though she'd lost one of her dearest friends. "One of his victims came to me for help, you know. Unlucky in love, but a wonder of an artist. I sold him some of my blessed marble and he built himself the most beautiful wife."

Aphrodite paused to let out a heart-rending, yet delicate, sob. "They'd only been together for a week before that drug dealer murdered them both. What a tragedy. I'm so grateful to Atlantis PD for taking that monster off the streets."

"Well," Myke said with a raised eyebrow. "She's certainly turning what could have been a disaster into a PR boost. It's almost like she wanted this all along."

His words hit Cass like one of Zeus's bolts. Aphrodite had been much too eager to approach the public about how well her product worked when she'd made it clear to Cass she wanted it kept hush-hush. Cass didn't say anything, though. She wanted to chew and digest this thought before bringing it up.

Myke and Cass exited the car and headed to the station entrance. When they got to the doors, Ajax walked out. He smirked at Cass as they passed each other.

"Great job closing that murder case yesterday," Ajax called to her. Cass tried to ignore him. "Helped Vice out with that too, I suppose." Cass kept her eyes forward and her legs took her further from her ex. "The bigwigs in Olympus made the right choice with you!" he yelled.

Cass snapped her head in Ajax's direction. "What do you mean?"

"Oh, Chief didn't tell you?" Ajax said, a smile slicing across his face. "Olympus put a hold on that restraining order so I could make sure Chief assigned the Pearce case to you and that you closed it too."

"Olympus," Myke whispered and grabbed Cass's hand.

"I told them you solve a lot of cases, but the courts don't usually believe your statements." Ajax shrugged. "They didn't seem to mind that for some reason." Cass's face flushed with anger and embarrassment. Ajax chuckled in response. "Anyway, I've been summoned. But uh … Don't be surprised if you see me again *real* soon." Ajax waved and walked away.

"Time to hit the salt mines," she told Myke with a sigh, and they entered the station.

Once inside, she returned to her office and her eyes flickered over to her scrying mirror, where Cy Pearce pounded his fists against the glass in futility. Cass knew, if he could reach through, he would strangle her last breath out of her. Ghostly flames burst from his crimson eyes. Tusks emerged from his twisted, frothing, and silently growling mouth. He resembled a furious boar. *More like a pig than a man. Perhaps Pygmalion does suit him.*

Cy reminded her of nights when Ajax would come home ready to throttle her. Cass already missed the days she felt a little safer from his abuse before the bigwigs in charge had put Ajax's restraining order on hold and he'd returned to the station.

All so Olympus could make sure Chief assigned this case to me, and that I closed it myself. Cass thought back to her conversation with Eros and his interest in her past as a detective.

"People don't often believe you," he had said. *"Do they, Detective Troias?"*

And if I hadn't promised to keep it all a secret, they knew no one would believe me, anyway. She took a sip of her coffee and it harmonized with her own bitterness. *Never mind. Justice is served, and all that.*

Cass set her travel mug on her desk and pulled a black, velvety square of cloth from her purse. She stood in front of the mirror, unfolding the fabric. "Looks like we're going to share an office for a while, Pyggy," she said and smiled at the spirit trapped under glass who riled against his new nickname. She covered the mirror with the velvet. "But sometimes, I like a little privacy."

There was one thing Cass knew for certain—Cy Pearce deserved to die.

The Beowulf Files:
A Detective Double Feature
Emily Ansell

Case 1: The Hotel Heorot

In a business like mine, you don't go looking for trouble. Trouble tends to find you on its own. 'Course you got to recognize the trouble when it comes, and that's usually how they get you.

It was a quiet morning, nondescript, when a couple of guys show up at my door.

"You Beowulf?" the one mook asks, pointing to the name etched into the glass.

"You see anyone else in here, buddy?"

"The mayor wants to talk to you."

"Business or pleasure?"

"Both. Now, come on."

The car ride was a quiet one. The mooks weren't real friendly and I wasn't sure I trusted them. But, we pulled up to a swanky restaurant instead of an abandoned warehouse, so I didn't mind so much—less likely to get my knees broke in a place like this. Or, so I figured.

We filed into the restaurant and they led me to a table near the back. The mayor was there with a bunch of his councilors. I knew then something was up. The question was, what? It musta been something, they were all avoiding looking at me. Except the mayor of course, but he was family.

"Beowulf, my boy! So good to see you! How's business?" Mayor Hygelac stood and kissed me on each cheek. Family or not, I suddenly felt like I'd been marked.

"Business is good, Uncle. So, what can I do for you fellas?"

He laughed, slapping me on the back, and motioned toward the table. "You're so suspicious! Come and sit, my boy! Have a drink, something to eat. It's on the city. Tell me, how is your mother? I've been so busy I haven't had time to see her."

As soon as I sat down there was a waitress at my elbow, smiling brightly.

"What can I get for you?" A professional voice. Too bright and bouncy to be anything else.

"Irish coffee to start. After that, whiskey. Neat."

"Bring him a breakfast special, my dear." The mayor looked at me and winked.

Once the coffee was in my hand and I'd had a shot of it, I looked around the table. "Alright, what's going on here? We both know this ain't no social visit. What d'you really want?"

Hygelac sighed. "Business then. Alright. You've heard of Hrothgar, my boy?"

"Some kinda big-shot tycoon. They call him King of Scylding City or somethin' like that."

"Well, it's Mayor of the City now. He and I go back a ways. He did me a favor once. I'd like to reciprocate."

"That's where I come in?" I asked as the waitress put whiskey and food in front of me. I tucked in as Hygelac spread his hands on the table and began to explain.

The Beowulf Files

"Yes. Hrothgar's got trouble. I can't send my guys, they got no jurisdiction. You're independent, you can run under the wire."

"Hrothgar ain't got his own cops to take care of trouble?"

Another sigh. I was gonna need more whiskey if that was all I was gonna get. But the mayor continued. "They're scared. They can't handle it. It's too dangerous. Or they're on the take, but Hrothgar doesn't think they are."

"And you think I can do it? Even with a few of my boys, you think I can do better than the whole Scylding City force?"

"You get shit done, Beowulf. And you don't have regs to deal with."

"All right. Don't keep me in suspense. What's the job?"

"Hrothgar built himself a hotel. The Hotel Heorot he calls it. Not just a hotel, mind you. There's a casino, dancin' girls, and every kind of live entertainment you could want. Hrothgar and his missus even got a penthouse there. A real swingin' joint. Or it was. Then trouble started with the mob. They call themselves the Grendel Gang, and they don't like this hotel on their turf. Their leader, Grendel? He's a big, mean son of a bitch. He's whacked a bunch of Hrothgar's guys already. Doesn't mind getting his mitts in there, either. Messy stuff. The place has been losin' money hand over fist for years 'cause everyone's afraid."

"So you want me to take care of this Grendel character? You better have one hell of a sell, sir."

"It'll be worth your time. Not just in pay, either. Word gets around you took out the leader of the Grendel gang? It'll do wonders for your reputation and gettin' work. Now listen, I got a private boat you can take across the bay. You and your boys would be noticeable on the ferry. The quieter you get in there, the better."

"Alright. I'll make some calls."

The mayor handed me a card. I recognized the address, a warehouse down by the docks. He nodded.

"Whenever you're ready, this is where the boat'll be."

"I'll take care of it, Uncle. Thanks for breakfast." I stood as I put my napkin down on my plate. Not to waste what was actually good stuff, I finished off my whiskey in one go and straightened my jacket.

The mayor nodded. "Take care, my boy."

* * *

The Coast Guard wasn't too happy when me and my boys pulled into the harbor at Scylding City. They stayed pretty frosty even when I explained we were here to see the mayor on business. But at least we ended up with a police escort to the Heorot, though they sure looked like they were hankerin' to take us straight to the Big House. But my boys were good ones, and they knew when to behave themselves.

The Hotel Heorot was every bit as grand as Hygelac said it would be. Or at least it would've been, if it weren't all but deserted. Even during the day this place should've been swinging. But no one was headed in or out of those big glass doors until we walked in.

"Good afternoon gentlemen, what can I do for you?" The maître d', in a bowtie and tails, looked over at us from behind his counter.

"Name's Beowulf, private dick. These are my boys. We're here on assignment from Geatland. I need to talk to Mayor Hrothgar about the case."

"What kind of assignment?"

"From Mayor Hygelac himself. A bit of personal business. Repaying a favor from a long time ago, you could say."

"One moment, then."

He picked up the phone on his desk and dialed, turning away as the call began. I could hear the voice on the other end, but none of what he said. On our end, the maître d' explained we were here, but too quiet for me to catch much of it.

Eventually, he put the phone down and adjusted his collar. "The mayor will see you. The private elevator is at the end of the hall. The lad there will see you up to the penthouse."

The 'lad' was a hulking fellow who squinted as he looked us over. But, he let us on the elevator. We rode in silence, watching the dial above us tick past each floor's number.

At the top stood a couple of guys in front of a big double door. They opened them in unison and waved us in.

The mayor was waiting for us, sitting around a table with his lieutenants. With a smile, he shook my hand and laughed. "Beowulf, my boy! I haven't seen you since you were a youngster! Come in, sit down, and tell me what brings you to Scylding City! I hear you're a detective now! Do tell me how you are."

"Thank you, sir. I had a meeting with Mayor Hygelac. He told me you were having some trouble, asked me to look into it. And yeah, I'm not on the force. Self-employed. My uncle thought that would make it easier for me to come by and see about this Grendel business."

"And a bad business it is. I'm sure you saw for yourself how quiet things are down there. It doesn't get much better later on, either. That thug's run off most of my clients, and bumped off more than his share of my lads trying to shake this place down. He doesn't go after the guests directly, at least. But it's enough that word gets around." He sighed, shoulders drooping. "I can't ask my boys to put themselves in the way of that monster. That Grendel, he enjoys causing hurt, killing. It almost ain't human. But after everything I've put into this place? I can't abandon it and let him have it, either."

"Well, we're here to see that things change." I gestured behind me. "Me and my boys, we're gonna do something about it. We've had some difficult assignments before, taken on our share of tough guys and hardcases. But we get the job done. That's why we're here, Mr. Mayor."

"Oh, really?" one fella sneered at me like he knew something. "The same Beowulf that ran up against Breca and got showed up? Rumor has it you were told to stay off that case in the first place." A young guy, sitting this close to the mayor? He musta thought he was hot stuff.

"You gonna close your yap now? Cause if you keep giving the bum steer, I might have to close it for you," I warned. "You got a name, or you just fulla talk?"

"Name's Unferth. You gotta problem?"

"Nah. I'm not gonna start a fight in front of the mayor. You heard about that case but you ain't got your facts straight. There was no showing up. Breca and I started out at the same time. Only difference is I got ambushed by a posse of Sea Snakes. Nasty cats, hang out down by the docks in Geatland. Besides, if you were half as good at your job as you were jawing, there'd be no problem in this here hotel and me and my boys wouldn't have come."

Unferth started to stand up from his chair, but the mayor put a hand on his arm. The kid sat down again. Smartest thing he'd done by far this whole conversation.

"So what do you need from us, Beowulf, my boy?" Hrothgar asked.

I smiled. "Open the doors. Get this joint movin'. Make this like Grand Openin' Night all over again, really shoot the works. When Grendel and his gang show up, then I go to work. We're takin' care of this problem tonight, Mr. Mayor."

* * *

The mayor was good as his word. It wasn't just word-of-mouth, either. Announcements on the radio, signs in neon out front; by nightfall the place was packed. Shows ran on the hour in the amphitheater while on the casino floor a steady din of shouts, laughter, the rattle of dice, and the slap of cards. There was even a wall of those fancy bell machines that let you pull a lever to spin them for a nickel each time.

And Mayor Hrothgar sat in the center of it all like a king. The conversation around him was loud and boisterous, and he had a smile and a hearty word for everyone he saw. Though he saved his best smile for his missus. All eyes turned to her as she made her entrance; dressed in a silvery silk affair that brushed the floor, makin' her look like she was floating when she walked. Her hair fell in elegant waves that glowed like gold under the casino's lights.

She sat down at the table beside the mayor and gave me a smile. "Let me get you a drink, Beowulf?"

"Why thank you, ma'am."

A waiter appeared behind her, and she passed a whiskey from his tray to my hand. As she did, she laughed. "Now, now, my boy. You don't need to be so formal. Call me Wealhtheow."

"Uh, of course, ma'am," I stammered.

She laughed again. But I could see she was watching the place, the movement of my boys, and Hrothgar's men with a keen eye. Despite the gaiety in the air, we all knew the stakes here. This big of an invitation wasn't going to go unnoticed. Eventually, Grendel would show up to claim his turf. But this time things were going to be different. I was going to see to that.

***

Eventually, the mayor and his missus announced they were retiring for the night. It was late and things were starting to slow down. If the pattern held, soon Grendel and his boys would be coming around looking for trouble and the night's winnings. The mayor and I shook hands again.

The Beowulf Files

"Good luck, my boy. I hope you teach that Grendel a thing or two tonight."

"I'll do everything I can, Mr. Mayor."

We took a couple of tables closest to the entrance of the casino and waited. The shakedown would happen anytime now; he'd know we'd had a good night and the coffers were flush. I'm sure he'd see it as easy pickings like before. What he hadn't planned on, was me and my guys waiting. A few of them were already outside, scouting for any sign of trouble, and we were ready to back them up.

We started throwing our own cards, passing the time. But it wasn't long before we heard gunfire and a crash. We stood, and hustled out to the foyer.

Any lingering customers had lit out as we stepped through the broken glass and outside. Grendel was there, the big lug. He had one of my boys already, Handscio, who'd been keeping watch outside. The poor kid was already dead, and we came out just in time to see Grendel put a foot in his back and tear his head clean off.

"The mayor was right. This one's a monster," muttered Halsten beside me.

I handed him my hat and coat, not saying anything. I stepped out, pushing up my shirtsleeves. If this was how Grendel wanted to dance, then we were gonna dance.

The brute was laughing, and threw Handscio's head down on top of his body. The scars that criss-crossed his ugly mug pulled his face in all kinds of strange ways as he grinned.

"You up next for a big sleep?" he growled in a thick voice.

"Just try it."

One fat paw took hold of my arm, and he yanked. But he couldn't pull me like he expected. I tossed his arm off, throwing a fist of my own at his face. As he stumbled back I saw his whole expression change. Surprise and fear lit across his face. He thought he'd found an easy mark, but he'd got a surprise instead. It was the look of a man who'd never fought someone who could equal him in a fight before, and now realized he could lose.

He pulled away, and made like he was gonna run. But this time *I* grabbed *his* arm. He pulled away, but couldn't break my grip. He pulled harder, and I had to dig in my fingers. But I held on. After everything Grendel'd done, I wasn't letting him slink off that easy. Not when I already had him scared. He owed me for Handscio, and I intended to make him pay.

We grappled. As we did I could see Grendel still wanted to light out of here, but now the fight was coming back in his eyes. He started swinging with his free hand, but randomly and with no real skill. He was just looking to catch me off guard and loosen my grip. But I was ready for his tricks, and I held on. He was shrieking now, hollerin' and making a scene. We'd started swinging each other around; Grendel still tryin' to throw me off while I was tryin' to take him to the ground. For a minute, it looked like neither of us was getting the upper hand.

We were still doin' our little dance when Grendel suddenly stopped short and with a clang. He'd come up against one of the parked cars. The valets must've taken off when these boys showed up and left this one out in the street. He lunged at me, but I threw him back against the car again, leavin' a sizable dent in the back quarter panel.

Grendel grabbed the edge of the door, sitting partly ajar. He flung it out at me as he sagged back on his heels. He was starting to get winded, and I wondered if he'd ever gone toe-to-toe like this before. I caught it, and flung it back as hard as I could. Grendel had no time to get out of the way, and the door slammed with his arm fully in it, makin' an awful wet, crunching sound.

He gave one hell of a shriek then, and tore himself away from the car. His arm didn't follow, and blood came out of his shoulder like a fountain. He was startin' to waver and look mighty pale already. He fell to his knees and I thought that was it, when a car screeched up beside us and a couple of his boys pulled him into the backseat, then away.

I had half a mind to follow them, but the fight was coming out of me now, too. I pulled a smoke from my deck of Luckies and considered the situation as I took the first drag. There was no way Grendel was coming through that unless they had a doc right there and then. He'd nearly bled out already; he'd be dead before they got themselves any kind of help.

I opened the car door, and pulled the arm out. It was a hefty one; that Grendel had been one big fella. Now that the fight was done, I was feelin' the strain of holding onto his weight while we'd thrown down. I flicked my spent butt on the ground and stubbed it out. Now all I wanted was a drink and a place to sleep.

Swinging Grendel's arm over my shoulder, I picked my way through the blood and broken glass back into the hotel. I threw it down on the maître d's counter and headed straight for the bar. There was no one behind it at this time of night, so I rounded the counter and selected myself a bottle. Throwing some ice into a glass, I poured myself a good, stiff hooker of the Hotel Heorot's finest whiskey. And she sure did go down neat, too. The boys gathered around, and we all took a hearty victory drink.

"This one's on the house!" I announced as I poured one out for each of them before returning to my own glass.

Once we'd finished we set up a perimeter and a guard rotation. Grendel was done for, I was pretty sure, but what if his gang came back? I wasn't going to take any chances. Those of us who weren't going out first hunkered down on the couches in the foyer for some sleep while the rest fanned out. In a few hours, we'd switch. Until we knew no one was coming back for trouble.

* * *

I was having a smoke and watching the street through one of the unbroken windows when the elevator dinged. The night had rolled over into morning and people were starting to head out to start their day. Wouldn't be long before someone called the fuzz about the mess out front, or maybe they'd seen it like this so many times now that they wouldn't bother. At least *this* would be the last time.

Mayor Hrothgar and his missus stepped out as the elevator opened. I watched them coming down the hallway, only to stop when they saw the big arm thrown on the counter. It was then I wondered if the thing had been leaking blood all night on that fancy countertop.

I stubbed my cig and turned away from the window just as the mayor started to laugh. Once I was close enough he pulled me into a bear hug. The dried blood on my shirt crunched.

"Beowulf, my lad, you've done me a miracle! I was starting to think this place was cursed, but you've changed everything! I'll see this glass is cleaned up and replaced and we can really open the hotel properly again! I can't thank you enough!"

Wealhtheow smiled, putting a hand on my arm. "And we will see that you and your men are more than well compensated for this." She nodded to Hrothgar then quoted me a number that nearly made my jaw fall on the floor.

"That's awfully generous, ma'am," I sputtered. "I mean, I'm more'n grateful for the thought, don't get me wrong. But that's a lot to pay for an arm. For that I shoulda made sure the whole body was here." I was thrown off, and lit another smoke to cover it.

"Nonsense, my boy! We'll be celebrating your accomplishment tonight! No one has been able to do what you've done! Now then, you and your men go get cleaned up and get some proper rest. I'll deal with all of this; the mess, the police, and your pay. I've got the best rooms in the hotel waiting for you."

How could I say no? We followed a bellboy up the elevator and to a series of suites that looked about fit for royalty. Then room service came up, and boy did they deliver. We ate, showered, and soon were sitting around the room with drinks in hand. But it wasn't long before the lot of us all found a bed and dropped off to sleep. After the night we'd had, we'd earned it.

***

The shindig that evening put the previous night to shame. Things started with a supper spread at the penthouse with the mayor and his missus. Unferth was there again, but singing a different tune now and fawning over us. They'd arranged our pay, with bonuses, during the day and now we were all wildly richer than when we'd set foot in Scylding City. The boys were already talking about what they were going to do with their windfalls. We even had a share for Handscio's family, with extra for the burial.

After that feast, we rolled down into the hotel proper. This time we spread out; tonight we were celebrating, taking it easy, not working. It was good to see them let loose a little. My guys knew to keep out of trouble, but they deserved a good time before we headed back to Geatland.

When we finally stumbled back to our rooms hours later, it was back to bed.

In the morning we got ready to head down again one last time. Just had to say goodbye to the mayor, and then we were heading to our boat and back to Geatland. It'd be good to go home again. I wasn't used to this kind of decadence. I was ready to go back to my apartment, and back to work. A place like this was too rich for my blood for more than a day or two.

Stepping out of the elevator we could see some ruckus up ahead. Déjà vu hit me like a truck. Broken glass and blood littered the floor. There were coppers here, too, scurrying around the taped-off front of the hotel. One was talking to the mayor as I marched up.

"Mr. Mayor, what the hell happened?" I demanded, suddenly realizing we *weren't* going home just yet.

Hrothgar excused himself from the cop, pulling me to the side. "Another problem, I'm afraid."

"Grendel's boys come back?"

"No, far worse."

"Worse?"

"It was Ma Grendel. The brute's mother. She ran the gang for years until she retired and let him take over. A vicious dame, brutal and bloodthirsty. But she doted on her boy. He was 'bout the only thing she ever loved, too. I didn't know she was still alive, she ain't been seen for years. Kept a hell of a low profile, it seems."

"You're telling me there's another one now? Shit. How bad did she hit us?"

"It was a drive by. Shot out all the windows again, took back her son's arm. A few injuries, one death." He faltered then, his face makin' as if to cry.

"Who was it?"

"Ashhere. You didn't know him, but he was one of my closest business partners. We were friends forever, started out together and everything. He was my brother in all but blood, y'see."

"I'm sorry for that, Mr. Mayor. We're going to track this broad and her gang back to where they're hiding and we're gonna take 'em in. Or take 'em down. Any idea where to find them?"

The mayor shook his head. "I wish. Rumor is they hole up down by the docks, but that place is a labyrinth. We need better than that."

"Right then. I'll go get a few things from my room. I've got some ideas."

***

Three hours later I'd shaken down a handful of street punks and got myself a better idea of where to find Ma Grendel and her gang. And now that I had the location, I was back at the hotel, fillin' in the mayor.

"I found 'em. And I'm goin' in, sir. But I've gotta ask you: if I don't come outta this, send word back to my uncle with my boys. And forward my pay to my Ma."

"I will."

"Thank you, sir."

***

The hideout was down at the old part of the docks, and looked rundown and halfways to in the water itself. No different than the rest of these old, abandoned buildings left to rot and collapse in on themselves. But that was the trick to keep people from nosing around. A perfect hideout.

I moved in the shadows and made my way toward the shack. The street was quiet, and I didn't see another soul till the doorway of the hideout. There were two goons there, smoking and keeping an eye out. There wasn't going to be any going around these two, either. The streetlight overhead shone a wide circle that I couldn't avoid.

"I'm here to see Ma Grendel." The goons' heads whipped up as I stepped out. Both dropped their hands, but couldn't clear leather fast enough. Each took a bullet, then a second one to make it stick.

And now Ma Grendel knew I was here.

I put my shoulder through the door and burst into a surprisingly ordinary kitchen. She was waiting, piece in hand. She was a tall, spare dame with a cruel glint in her eye. We both moved, firing as we did. Most went wide, but two of hers got me in the vest. I was glad then I'd thought to wear it.

Now we were empty. Not wanting to waste time reloading, I charged at her. Grabbing her shoulders, I tried to swing her about and down. But she was a wiry one, and turned it back on me. I hit the floor hard, narrowly missing the table, and saw the gleam of a blade as it came down.

I twisted, the knife cutting into the vest instead of my skin. It was hard doing, but I threw Ma off and staggered to my feet. I was up against a set of cupboards now and I scanned it looking for anything to use as a weapon. There was a knife block, and I took hold of the biggest handle there.

It was going to have to do, because Ma was back on me again. She was cussin' me out now, for being here and for killin' her boy. It was all I could do to keep her at bay. So when she swung and left an opening, I moved.

Her momentum carried her right onto the knife as I lifted it. There was no more cussin' now; the knife had gone fair and clean through her throat. She pulled it out as she collapsed, but not much after that.

I waited for a good long time just to be sure, but she didn't move. I fell into a chair, trying to catch my breath. Eventually, my heart stopped racing and I did a check of the rest of the house. Grendel was there, lying in a bed. The blood loss had got him in the end, by the look of it.

I stumbled back out of the hideout. My own boys were waiting for me. I asked them to stick around and keep an eye on the place, while a couple came back with me to the Hotel Heorot. The car ride was quiet, the boys not asking about why I was covered in blood for the second time. They were canny enough to figure it out themselves.

The mayor and his missus were waiting when we got back. I nodded.

"It's taken care of. My boys are there. I don't know if you want to send the fuzz or you've got your own men to deal with it. But they're both there, Ma and the son. You can see for yourself if you have a hankering. But I think you'll be able to rest easy now, Mr. Mayor. Your hotel is safe again."

"Beowulf, my boy, I cannot thank you enough for what you've done here. You'll be well rewarded for this, as well. You're a good man, too good to be livin' this dangerously. You could do a lot of good if you settled down a bit. Ah, but listen to me! Let's get a drink to celebrate your success!"

***

The next day we stood at the docks, our boat was ready to go and so were we.

The mayor and I shook hands. "It's been good to see you, sir. But we should get back and tell Mayor Hygelac what's happened. I'm sure he'll want to know things are resolved."

"Yes, and give him my regards, and my thanks. You know, if your uncle ever decides to retire, you'd be a fine mayor yourself. Just something to think about." He clapped me on the back.

"Why, thank you, sir. I don't know about that, but I appreciate you thinkin' so."

"And, if you've ever a mind to come visit Scylding City again, the Hotel Heorot would be honored to have you."

Once we got our goodbyes out of the way, my boys and I headed onto the boat. When we got back to Geatland we'd meet with my uncle, but I was more looking forward to my own bed and the bottle of whiskey I kept beside it. It was no Hotel Heorot, but it was home and right now that sounded just about perfect.

Case 2: The Dragon's Den

"Sir, could you state your name for the court records, please?"

"Wiglaf, ma'am."

"And your association to Mayor Beowulf?"

"I was his assistant, ma'am. And distant cousin, by our family reckoning. But he was more like an uncle to me."

"And can you tell us what happened on the day in question and why the mayor was there?"

"Yes, ma'am. It started with all the arson. He took that pretty personally."

"Please tell the court everything that you saw."

***

"Another one?" the mayor demanded, slamming his hand down on the table. "Is the chief of police here, yet?"

"Yes, sir, he is," I said. "I'll bring him in."

The chief looked none too happy as I escorted him into the office. He lit a cigarette as he sat down across from the mayor.

"Mayor Beowulf…" he began.

"Cut that formal shit. We've both been at these jobs too long for that. Give it to me straight, what are we looking at? Who's burning down half my city?"

The chief handed over a file folder. "They call him The Dragon. Underworld, rolling in the dough. Guy's got more bread than he knows what to do with. Before now he was mainly white-collar crime, nothing like this."

"So what happened?"

"Near as we can figure, and we shook down a few mooks for this much, is he hired on a new guy. Not sure what happened, but the kid nicked something off him. No one's sure what, whether it was money or somethin' sentimental, but this kid took it to the mob and got himself made for it. You can see how The Dragon's reactin' to it."

"You said there was no connection between the places that've been hit." The mayor stabbed a finger at the chief.

"There ain't. Not really. Rumor is, The Dragon doesn't know where his man ended up. All the bosses are bragging they got some of The Dragon's stash, rightly or not. I think he's just gonna keep burning things down till he finds out who's got it."

"We can't have that. We need to find this Dragon and put him away."

"No arguments from me, boss. I got a few leads we're working right now. Once I've got The Dragon's hideout, we're flushin' him out. I'll send the whole department if I have to."

"All right. Keep me posted."

"Will do, sir."

The mayor scowled at the term 'sir', but the chief just gave him one of those smiles that said he knew right what he was doing. But that was just their banter. The two of them had been running the show since before I was born, they'd had plenty of time to make all kinds of inside jokes and the like. Hell, it was at the point where I'd learned it in school; how the mayor had took out the Grendel gang, and a bunch of other high-profile cases after. When Mayor Hygelac had died shortly after retiring, it wasn't long before Mayor Beowulf had run himself. And he'd been here ever since, getting re-elected over and over again.

I watched him as the chief nodded and made his way out. Once he was gone the mayor turned and got up from his desk. A cabinet sat against the wall behind him, and from it he pulled a decanter and two glasses. He set those down and poured some of the honey-colored liquid into both.

Handing me one, he sighed. "I don't like this, Wiglaf. If we can't find where this Dragon's holed up, this is only gonna get worse."

I took a sip. Whiskey, of course. The mayor seemed to drink nothing else. "We'll get him, Mr. Mayor."

"We will. I just hope we do before it's too late."

***

Hours later, those words came back to haunt us. At two a.m. I stood beside the mayor, watching City Hall burn. I'd raced over as soon as I'd gotten the call. The fire department was already there by the time I arrived, trying in vain to control the blaze.

The only thing worse than the fire was the mayor's expression. I'd never seen nothing like the grief on his face, nor seen it harden into anger like that before. The light from the fire put a glow in his eyes and a wash of color back into his hair. Right then I saw the Beowulf he must've been before he'd been mayor. The one who'd fought hand-to-hand against the big brute Grendel and won.

Then he looked at me, his voice suddenly real cold. "I'm going to find this Dragon and fill him fulla lead myself."

I looked out over the fire again. "I'm coming with you, Mr. Mayor."

"You think this old man can't handle himself?"

"No sir. That's not it!" I protested. "I just … I want in. I ain't sitting behind after this."

He gave me a peculiar look, but nodded. But before he could say anything, a cop car screamed up, lights and sirens all going. Pulling up alongside us, the chief jumped out.

"Beowulf!" The mayor turned that flint-hard stare to the chief, but the other man just smiled.

"We've found him. A squad of my guys are waiting for you there. We're gonna get this bastard."

***

An hour later we stood in front of what looked like a warehouse. The chief's boys were there, and as soon as we were ready they took a ram to the door. It flew inward, revealing not a warehouse inside but the grand entryway of the plushest pad I'd ever seen.

The cops fanned out, making a wide circle around the man who waited inside. The guy was tall, but lean. He looked quite the sight with slicked back blond hair and a partially-open silk shirt showing the head of a dragon tattooed on his chest. Raising his hands to wave at all the sudden company, I could see rings on every finger and not a care in the world. He was looking instead at the mayor, who'd come in behind and was now nearly nose-to-nose with him.

"Why, Mayor Beowulf, what a pleasure to have your company in my humble abode! Have you come to tell me where the miscreant who stole from me is hiding?"

"How about I take you in first? Whatever your beef with the mook who stole from you, you made it personal when you burned down half my city. Torchin' City Hall? That was your last mistake."

The Dragon sighed. "Fine. We can do this the hard way if you want. But I want that little punk, you hear me?"

"I don't care. You hear me?" the mayor snarled back.

Then, before I realized it, they were fighting. The fuzz were pulling their pieces while their lead man was shouting to stop before they hit the mayor. The two men trading fists back and forth didn't seem to notice any of this. I could see now why they called him The Dragon, and it wasn't for no tattoo. He moved fast, agile, and serpentine. This was a cat who knew how to fight. And he was more than a few years younger than the mayor. I didn't like it at all.

In the space of a second, The Dragon had pulled something from his pocket and thrown it. A bottle, or something. It broke against the mayor's arm, sending up a nasty smell of burning. Acid of some kind. The mayor swore, swinging a hard fist at The Dragon that stunned him, but he stayed up.

"Do something!" I shouted to the coppers, but they didn't move. Froze up, the lot of them.

As The Dragon got his wits back again, he saw I was standing with the mayor. My feet had done the thinking for me, but there was no way I could keep back any more. He threw another of his little acid bottles but we dodged this one. It sent up a hiss from the floor behind us.

He followed it up with a charge, pulling a knife from somewhere I didn't even see. It stabbed into the side of the mayor's neck, sending plenty of blood pouring out in its wake. I didn't think, I swung my fists at him, and in the fracas he dropped the knife.

Now, where the mayor kept a knife on himself, I don't know. All I know was it came from somewhere hidden just like The Dragon's had. And then it was repaying that stab, over and over. When The Dragon fell, he was full of holes.

The mayor sat down then, abruptly. He put a hand to his wound and absently looked at the blood. Then he looked up at me.

"Didn't fill him fulla lead, but that let plenty 'a daylight in."

"You ventilated him good, Mr. Mayor. We need to get you some help, call an ambulance…"

"Wiglaf, my boy, come here," he beckoned. I knelt down beside him, hoping the fuzz would finally do something and call the ambulance for us.

The mayor seemed pretty nonplussed about the whole thing. He instead gave me a smile, and a nod, lighting up a smoke. "You did good, Wiglaf. I've been mayor a long time, but you know I never had no kids, myself. If I had, I woulda wanted them to have your moxie. Nice to see that part of the family blood comes out in you. The city's gonna need folks like you to rebuild. It's gonna be a lot of work, but you can do it."

"Mr. Mayor, we'll get you to a hospital! We'll get you fixed up!"

"You're a good one, Wiglaf. But this stab here? It's bad. And I think there's some of that acid, or something in it. I can feel it burnin' in me. It's gonna have to be you. You'll do good. This is our city, and she needs a fella that can take care of her."

"I will. I promise."

***

"What happened next, Mr. Wiglaf?" This lawyer dame was a tough cookie, and she wasn't gonna stop until she got everything out of me.

I took a deep breath. It wasn't easy to talk about it so soon. "That's when the mayor ... well shit, that's when he died, ma'am. Those cops decided to grow their spines back and we lit out of there. But it was too late by then. The last week I've been standin' in as acting mayor while we try to sort this all out."

She grilled me for a little while longer before letting me go. And it was none too soon, either. Any later and I woulda left, lawyer glaring me down or not.

The chief of police was waiting for me when I got out.

"You ready to go, Wiglaf?"

"Yeah. I don't want to be late. Was hoping that deposition wouldn't take so long. They had to do it today, of all days."

"I know. Couldn't pick any other time, right?"

An hour later we were gathered in the church. I'd have rathered City Hall, but there wasn't enough of it left for a proper state funeral, so we were here. I listened to them talk about the mayor, even did a little talking myself. After that, we carried the coffin out to the hearse as the guns fired in salute. The procession that followed was a long one, and it took twice as long to get to the cemetery as the service itself had taken. But Beowulf had been mayor a long time, and the whole city'd come out to see him off.

Me and the chief ended standing together again at the cemetery. The graveside bit had been short and now everything was pretty much wrapped up. A few folks were still paying their respects, and we stood off to the side watching.

"So what happens now?" He looked over at me. For a fella with more than a few years on me, he looked a bit lost.

"I dunno. Mayor Beowulf kept things together. Kept this city runnin' and kept the scum under control. And did a damn good job. Now that he's gone, and with all the rebuilding we have to do, who knows? The rats are gonna sense the power vacuum, and it ain't gonna be pretty."

"But we've gotta try. That's what the mayor woulda wanted us to do."

"Yeah," I agreed. "And we're gonna. He might've been the best of us, but we can't do anything less."

We took one last walk around the grave, saying our goodbyes. Then we headed back to where the chief's car waited. There was a lotta work to do, and it wasn't gonna get done standing around.

The city needed us, and we were going to be there for her.

The Cyberpunk Tragedy of Orphy6 and Eury23
Mara Lynn Johnstone

Eury23 tossed fiber optic hair, laughing as she danced with the other dryads, their filmy skirts floating over metal-and-neon legs, glowing vents and exhaust ports. Everything shone teal and purple between the shadows of the room, as the floor light painted their dancing feet blue. Clear walkways wove above to lift dancers and partiers and skulking types. Bright drinks were indistinguishable from recharge packs.

When the song faded into another, Eury23 and her friends drifted out onto the street. That song had played at her wedding, fresh in her mind, and she hadn't been able to pass up the opportunity to dance to it again. Now she and the others danced over concrete and steel, with more than one song on the breeze, along with the ever-present symphony of electronic hums.

Holograms moved as they passed: some mindless advertisements and others free-floating people in their own right. Walls crawled with moving text and images of the cosmos. Nothing was still. Between distant skyscrapers, a holographic goddess gyrated, visible for all to worship.

Eury23 touched a treestack as she passed, not needing the access panel to connect her consciousness with the column of public data. A sleepy pseudo-mind greeted her and her friends, who all passed hands across the electronic trunk. Small green solar panel leaves rustled a hello. The dryads smiled and moved on.

Rubberized flooring encouraged pedestrians to slow as they reached a free market. Treestacks on every corner offered access to banking, and many voices called for attention. *Here is the best place to spend those funds. No, here. Nonsense; they only want to deceive you; my wares are the best.*

Eury23 and her friends skipped on by with polite smiles, avoiding eye contact. Some merchants tried harder than others.

One shepherd, standing at the edge of his green-lit pen, smiled widely with silver teeth and reached out a hand toward Eury23. "I have some lovely things to show you," he said. "Almost as lovely as you are."

Eury23 stepped aside. "No thank you."

"Don't be like that," he called after her. "I just want to talk."

With her friends close around her, Eury23 hurried away. A glance back showed other shepherds farther inside the pen, standing among the battery sheep. While the sheep's steel wool crackled with electrical charge, an undertone of ugly laughter circulated between the men. They leered at the dryads and urged him on.

The shepherd stepped through the force fence, its honeycomb pattern reflecting briefly on his clothes, and he made to follow her. Eury23 and the other dryads increased their pace.

Shouting entreaties, he followed. They broke into a run.

The dryads left the market for side roads, passing treestacks, buildings, and abstract light patterns. Steaming vents on the ground. Hovercars in the sky.

Walls covered in cubes, triangles, and light-filled cracks. A walkway lined in concentric rings of red and blue, hypnotizing at speed. The dryads ran until the shepherd could no longer be heard yelling after them.

Eury23 was in the lead, just starting to slow as she passed through a narrow alley with flickering lights, when she stepped too close to a snake.

It leapt into the physical world from a wall's access port, a glittering hologram of fangs and menace meant to distract from the infectious code that flashed by unseen. Eury23 dodged, servos whining, only to find the snake dissipated and a virus already burning through her system.

The dryads cried out and caught her as she fell. They were a flurry of concern, running disinfection programs and calling for medicbots, cursing both the snake and the shepherd, but there was nothing to be done.

She was already gone. Eury23, who had just been sprightly and full of joy, recently married and excited about the future, lay in an inert pile of metal limbs and slowly dimming lights. One by one her friends stopped trying to revive her, eyes iridescent with tears.

At a loss, they called her husband. None wanted to be the one to tell him. But he had to know.

Orphy6 arrived hard on the heels of the medicbot, leaping forward to embrace her cold form with no regard for anything around him. The medicbot made an affronted beep that he did not hear, performed a scan that he did not see, and stood aside with the ring of weeping dryads. All that Orphy6 saw was the sightless eyes of his new wife, staring past him in a dull gray that caused his core to shatter into uncountable pieces.

The Cyberpunk Tragedy of Orphy6 and Eury23

Orphy6 wept, keening a note of piercing agony just on the edge of hearing, stroking Eury23's dulled hair and searching for any sign of hope. When he found none, he wailed his lament in a way that only he could: in musical tones and infectious code. A wave of grief spread through the city like a shockwave. People found themselves suddenly bereft, with processors slowing and eyes leaking a variety of tears: glittering, glowing, burning with grief. The city ground to a halt.

The mournful soul at the epicenter didn't notice. Orphy6 held the body of his wife, thinking of nothing else as the seconds crawled by.

She had just been alive. How could this be? He had just seen her—just married her! It was too sudden to process. Surely something could be done. Something. Never mind every sign that said she was gone for good, her core wiped blank by a mindless back-alley virus. Something had to be done.

He moved sightless eyes across the alley, not registering the crying faces, unsure what he was looking for. The snake was long gone. The medicbot waited in useless silence. The alley was dark, lit by flickering lights and the glow of a treestack on the corner.

That caught Orphy6's attention. The trunk still pulsed with light—energy and information running deep underground to where its roots merged with the subterranean kingdom of data storage. Backups could be found there. For a price. Credit balances, encrypted files, and the recorded consciousnesses of compatible life forms.

Orphy6 didn't have to ask how recently the dryad he'd married had communed with a treestack. Her mind would be fresh among them.

It was just a matter of getting her back.

Orphy6 stood, shutting down the mournful song abruptly as he focused on a singular goal: confronting the overlords who held his wife's soul. It would be a difficult journey. An entrance wouldn't be hard to find, but passage to the depths wasn't granted to just anyone.

With a talent for musical code that had the entire city recovering from an intensely distraught moment, Orphy6 wasn't just anyone.

He stared at the treestack, eyes following its path to where it disappeared underground, and he planned. His wife lay dead at his feet, but he didn't look down. He would get her back. Nothing in Heaven, Earth, or elsewhere would stop him.

* * *

Another person might have paused at the entryway, taking a fortifying breath while the busy surface world still buzzed around them. Orphy6 did not. He barely spared a glance for the circuits that crawled across the arch, glowing a sickly green into the darkness. Visible code washed over him as he stepped through. He let it scan him. Let the lords of this realm know he was coming. They would grant him an audience, or he would see that they regretted it. Orphy6 strode across the obsidian floor, footsteps echoing with purpose and musical notes crackling off him like electricity.

The various doorways, code-barriers, and false walls among the staircases did little to slow him down. His explosion of grief earlier had caught the attention of several of the city's elite—some were impressed, while others simply never wanted to feel emotions that strong again. The blessing of their passcodes, along with his innate talents, let him breeze through the dark hallways with a melody of heartrending sorrow echoing off the walls.

He only changed his tune once, in a red-lit room on the lower levels where personal security barred his way in the form of a dauntingly large beast.

Cyberus had never been seen on the surface, but tales spread of his three mouths full of fangs that could rip a soul apart. He was quick, flashing from one side of the chamber to the other; he was impervious, made of hard light that could not be damaged; and he could deal alarming amounts of damage in return. He was the city's most terrifying guard.

But he was also just a dog, and a bored one at that. Orphy6 stood his ground in front of the red eyes and lightning-bright teeth, and he sang about simple joys. Running through a grassy field. Chasing a ball that bounced, a discus that flashed in the sunlight, a butterfly of many colors that was always just out of reach. Prancing through city streets, scenting out the food vendors. Rolling in interesting smells. Howling from the highest point around. Curling up for a nap after long hours of play.

Cyberus was enchanted. The great beast followed every word, every note, every subtle bit of code that suggested he take a real nap, all the better to dream about these visions in detail.

When the great black dog with the three heads had settled onto the shiny floor and closed every one of his eyes, Orphy6 ventured forward.

Cyberus dreamed of chasing battery sheep. One leg kicked in his slumber, and could have dealt a mortal blow, but the intruder was already gone.

Orphy6 passed through another doorway and a short hall, letting his dog-song fade in place of a new one. The lords would be expecting him in the throne room. He sang of grief and determination. Colors rippled over the dark walls around him, forming faces that shifted and wailed.

The door was golden and heavy. It opened on silent hinges. Orphy6 entered in a swirl of song, eyes forward with no regard for the vast chamber with false fire and holographic spirits roaming the walls. Only the two beings on the thrones held his attention. And judging by their stern expressions, he held theirs as well.

"Stop," commanded H4des, his hand flashing out in a cutting gesture.

Orphy6 let his song end abruptly. He halted while echoes trailed off, seeping into the corners where sadness lingered. He regarded the pair before him.

They had, he decided, both been crying. Though they did their level best to hide it. H4des glared, his posture stern and the blue flames of his hair snapping in anger. Perseph03 wouldn't meet his eyes. She tugged a spring-coil of her own hair as if she was an uncertain youth instead of a wielder of great power. But she seemed to come to a private decision, and shot her husband a look before sitting tall on her throne.

H4des continued to frown. "You dare much," he said to the small figure at the foot of his throne.

Orphy6 bowed, but didn't avert his eyes. "I do," he admitted. "Polite greetings. Thank you for hearing me. I have come for my wife."

With a snort, H4des sat back. "The entire city heard you. Possibly also the moon, and the depths of the sea." He tapped silver claws on the arm of the throne. "People die daily, however. Tell me why I should grant your request."

"My love is strong, my grief boundless, and the injustice overpowering," Orphy6 replied, standing tall. "We were just married. Our life together promised to be glorious and long, full of music and joy, then she was gone in an instant. A senseless accident that dimmed the world. I will sing about it if you permit me."

And possibly if you do not, he thought privately.

"No need for that," H4des said, just a hair too quickly. "We heard you the first time." He exchanged a look with his own wife, who intertwined her fingers and thoughts with his. He didn't look away from her eyes when he announced, "We are not heartless. But there are rules. We won't have half the city following in your wake, even if there are others as ... persuasive as you."

"What must I do?"

H4des turned eyes of blue fire down at Orphy6. "You must walk back to the surface the long way, with no singing to speed you. Your wife will be restored and sent to follow. *Do not look back at her.* Do you understand? You look, she dies."

Perseph03 added, "The code only resolves on the surface."

"I accept," Orphy6 hurried to say. "Which way shall I go?"

One claw flashed green as H4des traced an intricate pattern on the interface built into the arm of the throne. Circuits lit, and a spark of command sped from throne to wall, branching to frame a doorway that hadn't been there before. Ghostly faces writhed around it. Inside was a black void.

Orphy6 regarded the door. "How shall I keep from losing my way?"

"Just don't turn around," H4des said testily.

Perseph03 clarified, "There are no cross passages. Keep moving forward. Touching the walls is permitted."

"But no singing!" said H4des.

"I understand. And you promise she will be following after me?"

"We wouldn't lie about that!" H4des snapped, poise dissolving in his visible eagerness to be rid of this uninvited guest who could erupt in infectious code at any moment. "If you mess this up, it's on you, not us. Shoo." He waved both hands.

"Don't look back!" Perseph03 reminded him.

Orphy6 nodded. "Thank you." He took a deep breath that made them both flinch, but he didn't burst into song. Instead he strode forward with the same single-minded focus that had brought him here.

Blackness closed around him. He fought an impulse to turn immediately and see if the door had shut. Telling himself it didn't matter if it had, he stretched cautious hands toward the walls. Relief flooded him when he found smooth obsidian within easy reach.

He moved forward, feet tapping quietly on the floor and fingers trailing along the walls. His footsteps echoed. His fingertips squeaked. Loudest in his ears were the competing drums of his pulse and fans. The only dim lights that reached his eyes came from his own overheating electronics. He focused on that instead of the long dark ahead of him.

It was hard not to wonder when Eury23 would join him, and harder still not to doubt whether she really would. The lords were beings of their word, by and large. They wouldn't want to be known for letting misfortune befall him.

But who would know, if he never reached the surface? Who would accuse them of lying when they claimed no knowledge of his fate?

Orphy6 shook himself in a rattle of joints. Doubt was part of this trial. He would not submit. He walked quickly, tracing the walls as he went.

Then he worried that his eager speed would make it difficult for his love to catch up to him, and he slowed. He started to hum as a way to keep his spirits up, cutting it off immediately when he remembered the ban on singing.

Did humming count? Had he just broken a rule?

Was she actually there or not?

He walked, in a mounting state of terror and doubt, listening for footsteps over his fans, and hearing none. No crackle of electricity or hum of her own fans to echo his. No beloved voice to reassure him. Was she there? She must be. She *must*.

She couldn't be.

When would this end?

Orphy6 realized the floor was angling more sharply upward at the same time he saw the light. It was oh so faint, much like his hope, but it was there, far ahead.

Silence still followed him. Had she not caught up yet? Should he slow to wait for her? Was he only fooling himself? Surely she would have joined him by now if she was going to.

She wasn't there. He clenched his teeth and kept walking.

The light on the other side of the doorway was viciously bright after so long in darkness. Orphy6 squinted but didn't look away. The green of fiber optic grass spilled over the threshold; he could make out that much. This truly was a route to the surface.

He was almost there. He tried to step quietly. His fans were loud. No footsteps echoed his own. He lifted a hand from the wall to reach behind himself, going over the instructions for any reason why he shouldn't and finding none. His hand met empty air.

She wasn't there.

His eyes filmed over with tears, and his throat tightened with the urge to keen a mourning song. But he kept his mouth clamped shut. He was almost at the doorway.

She wasn't there.

She wasn't going to be.

He'd never see her again. All this was for nothing, a cruel example of why the lords who lived among the roots of the world never voluntarily released a soul. It had been foolish to think otherwise.

He took in a shuddering breath, mere steps from the opening, and blinked his eyes free of tears. He started to turn.

But as his vision cleared, he saw the ring of dryads waiting in the meadow, faces full of tearful joy. They were looking past him.

Orphy6 held his breath. He took the last three steps out onto the grass. Hands clenched, he stepped further until the dryads broke and ran forward in delight, their arms reaching.

He turned.

He saw her smile first.

The ghostly hologram turned to hard light, then flesh and metal, then she was embracing him as he held her with everything he had, and her friends wrapped arms around both of them.

Tears left iridescent trails. Fiber optic grass glowed under dancing feet. Fans and heartbeats sped while voices lifted in song, carried by the wind through the solar panel leaves of nearby treestacks and out into the city beyond.

The black door closed, and not one person noticed.

About the Authors

Emily Ansell writes from the great expanse of the Canadian prairies. Her work has appeared in anthologies: *Tales From the Year Between Vol. 2: Under New Suns; Welcome to Simmins, Detective Spencer; Nature Fights Back;* and *The Major Arcana*. Outside of writing, she is a voracious consumer of knowledge and a four-time recipient of the cat distribution system (with a 3:1 tux to tabby ratio).

Born in the great white north, **Darius Bearguard** works as a care aide for adults with disabilities and special needs, while he pursues his love of writing. His genres are as eclectic as his choices in music. He also loves Lego. He really wants you to know that he loves Lego.

R. A. Cheddi has been writing stories since he was seven years old. His first? A fanfiction about his life-long hero, Sonic the Hedgehog. Decades later, he's still writing fanfiction along with original content. Aside from writing, he can be found gaming, hanging with his equally nerdy wife and two kids, and at GamesWithCoffee.com. His magnum opus fanfiction project resides at MobiusVII.ca.

Gregory Coley was born in Dallas and ventured exactly an hour away before becoming a writer. The author of a dozen books, including a series, he lives in rural Texas with his cats, video games, and dialysis treatments. A love of reading and writing poetry led him to short stories and novel writing, most of which touch on his interest in the supernatural.

Mark Faraday graduated from a small university in California named Sonoma State University. The school had a strong Art History program which was his major. When he saw the movie *The Girl with a Pearl Earring*, it inspired him to take up short story writing.

Ark Horton is a small woman made of round shapes and long sighs. She's also a published speculative fiction author who writes a wide range of fantasy stories and the occasional science fiction tale. She has a thirst for history, mythology, folklore, and fairytales, which often serve as inspiration for her work. You can find out more about her and her published work at arkhorton.com.

Mara Lynn Johnstone grew up in a house on a hill, the top floor of which was built first. With a lifelong interest in fiction, she has published several books and many short stories. She can be found up trees, in bookstores, lost in thought, and at maralynnjohnstone.com.

Estelle Parcoeur is (one) pen name for a multigenre N(euro)D(iverse) writer. In a previous life she was a middle school and high school English teacher who left the public education system due to a TBI (Traumatic Brain Injury). Read more through that lens in *Nature Fights Back* edited by Nikki Mitchell or the MoveMePoetry Journal *We Are The Waves*. After a stint as a college composition adjunct, her current day job is being a direct support professional for individuals with disabilities. Find her sprouting ideas @isparkit.

Craig Rathbone hails from the north of England, where he lives in a small cottage in the middle of rural Cheshire. He likes to read books, write books and stare at books on his TBR list that he'll probably never get to read. He writes science fiction, fantasy, horror and will generally try his hand at anything if it gets him a pat on the head.

Katherine Shaw is a multi-genre writer and self-confessed nerd from Yorkshire in the United Kingdom, spending most of her time dreaming up new characters or playing D&D. She has a passion for telling stories of injustice and battles against oppression, often with a focus on female protagonists. She has published her debut novel *Gloria*, a contemporary domestic thriller, and has work appearing in multiple anthology collections. You can find out more at her website: katherineshawwrites.com.

Amanda Shortman is a queer, disabled, neurodiverse blogger and author. She writes about a wide range of topics, both fiction and non-fiction. She is married to Thea, and mum to Oscar. And she has more books than she'll ever manage to read, too many hobbies to count, and a head full of stories she hopes to tell one day. You can find her at aspiraldance.com.

David M. Simon is an ad agency creative director, writer, and illustrator in sunny Cleveland, Ohio. His first novel, a middle grade fantasy adventure titled *Trapped In Lunch Lady Land*, was published in 2014 by CBAY Books.

His writing and artwork have also appeared in numerous anthologies, and children's magazines including *Highlights*. His first novel for adults, *The Wild Hunt*, was published in 2022. You can find him online at davewritesanddraws.com, on Twitter/X @WritesDraws, and on Instagram and Threads @writesdraws.

A Filipino living in the UK, **Imelda Taylor** writes stories that are weird and wonderful, as well as heartfelt and cheerful. She gets inspiration from her two daughters' antics, disturbingly vivid dreams, and her love of food and culture. Although she is a multi genre author, her ultimate dream is to become a household name in children's books along with Julia Donaldson, Oliver Jeffers and Rachel Bright. A lover of fantasy, folklore and history, her work can be found in several anthologies.

About the Editor

Reality Collision Publishing is the professional hat Mara Lynn Johnstone wears when publishing books: everything from her own novels to writing prompts collections and multiple-participant anthologies, all of which are a joy. The one thing they all have in common is a distinct step to the side of our regular reality. You might find robots, aliens, shapeshifters, magicians, and more, possibly all at once. Exciting things tend to happen when realities collide. Learn more at maralynnjohnstone.com.